The Company She Kept

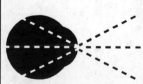

A JOE GUNTHER NOVEL

THE COMPANY SHE KEPT

ARCHER MAYOR

THORNDIKE PRESS
A part of Gale, Cengage Learning

GALE
CENGAGE Learning·

Farmington Hills, Mich • San Francisco • New York • Waterville, Maine
Meriden, Conn • Mason, Ohio • Chicago

Copyright © 2015 by Archer Mayor.
Thorndike Press, a part of Gale, Cengage Learning.

LIBRARY OF CONGRESS CATALOGING-IN-PUBLICATION DATA

Mayor, Archer.
  The company she kept : a Joe Gunther novel / Archer Mayor. — Large print edition.
    pages cm. — (A Joe Gunther novel) (Thorndike Press large print crime scene)
  ISBN 978-1-4104-8350-8 (hardback) — ISBN 1-4104-8350-9 (hardcover)
  1. Gunther, Joe (Fictitious character)—Fiction. 2. Police—Vermont—Fiction. 3. Murder—Investigation—Fiction. 4. Large type books. I. Title.
PS3563.A965C66 2015b
813'.54—dc23   2015030549

Published in 2015 by arrangement with St. Martin's Press, LLC

Printed in Mexico
2 3 4 5 6 7 19 18 17 16 15

To Margot

For what you contribute,
For what you take in stride,

What I feel for you
would go well over waffles.

ACKNOWLEDGMENTS

As always in the creation of these tall tales, I am indebted to many people. They give of their time, their knowledge, and their considerable talent to help me along. For my part, I try not to mess up their gifts. To all of you, my deepest thanks. You add joy and enlightenment to this process.

Margot Mayor
John Merrigan
Neda Ulaby
Sally Stott
Ed Miller
Jon Creighton
Julie Lavorgna
Paco Aumand
James Baker
Rick Holden
Will Hoyt
Ray Walker
Janet Ancel

Robin Brand
Rick Hopkins
Steve Shapiro
John Martin
Tom L'Esperance
Castle Freeman
Barbara Reinhold
Eric Buel

Also:

Vermont Dept. of Public Safety
Vermont Crime Information Center
Homeland Security Investigations
Vermont Office of the Chief Medical
   Examiner
Vermont Forensic Lab
Rutland City Police Dept.
Vermont State Police

CHAPTER ONE

"Pull over, Doug. I want to get a shot of this."

Uncomplaining, Doug Nielsen checked his mirrors, slowed down shy of the interstate crossover — marked EMERGENCY USE ONLY — and eased their rig across the empty northbound lane, to the scenic pull-off his wife had indicated. A cautious man, he was wary of any black ice that could launch them through the slender barricade and over the straight drop beyond it into Margie's planned panorama.

He didn't fault her artist's eye. The view from this ledge was vast, inspiring, and beautiful. The Connecticut River, far below, lined by glimmering fresh snow, sparkled in the late afternoon sun, which itself was the only object visible in a stark, freezing, ice blue sky. A few farms stretched out to both sides of the winding river, empty of crops or livestock, until their fields bumped up against the opposing Vermont and New Hampshire foothills. Several homes sported thin plumes of woodsmoke from their chimneys, making Doug think of feather quills protruding from toy-sized inkwells. He thought it might have been the sheer antiquity of everything before him that stirred up such an old-fashioned image, since — barring a barely visible utility line and a narrow paved road far in the distance — he guessed that little before him had changed much in over two hundred years.

He and Margie had been vacationing for the past week in the Green Mountain State, whose famous mantle had been deeply powdered by a recent spate of snowstorms. This had been good news for them, since they'd driven up from southern New Jersey to exercise the two snowmobiles they were now towing back home. There had been trips to New England in the past where the cover had been less than ideal for dedicated so-called sledders. But not this time. This visit had been perfect.

Doug rolled to a stop and they both got out, the cold air tingling their nostrils and biting the backs of their throats. The lot was deserted, which suited him fine, considering the combined length of his car and trailer. He'd been able to ignore the row of parking

10

spaces hashed into the cleared asphalt, and simply park alongside the barricade.

"Isn't this incredible?" his wife asked, pulling out her smartphone.

"Pretty nice," he answered briefly, no less impressed by the vista, but sensitive to the near-total stillness accompanying it. "Quiet, too," he added, encouraging his wife to take in more of what he was appreciating.

But there, she had her own style.

"I know," she said, ordering up the phone's photographic function. "Can you imagine how this would be next to the Jersey Pike? I'd have to hope the pictures wouldn't blur, for all the vibration from passing trucks."

He nodded and began walking the length of the extended pull-off, putting some distance between them.

"Don't go too far, Doug," she called out. "I want to take a selfie of us in front of the view."

Refusing to break his inner code of silence, Doug raised his gloved hand without turning and stuck a thumb up in acknowledgment. Margie went back to concentrating on her shot.

Doug had lived in New Jersey his entire life, in the city, amid people. He worked in a large building, at a desk in a room the size of a football field, under an endless stuttering of overhead fluorescent tubes and surrounded by an army corps of cubicles, all like his own. He and Margie had a good life. The house was almost paid for, and in good shape, compared to some on the street. They were all more or less of the same architectural model, which made any standouts that much more glaring. And Doug was happy. The kids had turned out okay, Margie and he were pretty healthy, retirement was looking feasible in another ten years or so — assuming the world didn't go to hell in a handbasket.

He stopped walking, Margie now much smaller in the background.

And last but not least, he had moments like this, when he could absorb the spectacular vestiges of prehistoric phenomena like glaciers, fluvial erosion, and the efforts of mankind to make a living off the land. It gave him a comforting sense of being in touch with what so many of his coworkers back home couldn't even imagine.

He turned from the view at the sound of a car speeding by on the interstate, attracted by how lonely it sounded, and how quickly the sound of it was swallowed by the surrounding immensity. It brought back Margie's comment about the Jersey Pike, which in turn made him think that he ought to get back to her to pose for that photograph.

He paused a moment longer, though, his eyes not on the hundred-foot rock wall across the pavement, looming as high above them as the cliff dropped off to his back. Instead, he found himself drawn to a sharp but distant twinkling of gold, perched on the edge of the roadway, bordering the southbound lane.

Intrigued, he went up to the edge of the parking area's barricade, and climbed atop one of the short wooden posts there to get a better angle on the distant object.

"I'll be damned," he said to himself, recognizing a large handbag, its clasp reflecting the sun's blaze.

"What're you looking at?" his wife asked from surprisingly nearby.

He wobbled briefly on his post, turning and laughing. "Whoa. Honey. You snuck up on me." He pointed across the double lanes. "That thing caught my eye. Probably fell out of a car."

She squinted in the direction he was indicating. "That purse? Why would it fall out of a car? We're miles from the exit. Stuff like that only happens when you're leaving — like when you forget your coffee cup on the roof or something."

Doug was scanning the road up and down, as much for an explanation as in preparation for a quick sprint over to retrieve the purse. Margie, however, had tilted her head back to take in the towering cliff above.

Several years earlier, the Department of Transportation had been delivered some bad news: As a by-product of the construction of Vermont's two interstates back in the sixties, rocks from the cliffs alongside the roads had begun breaking loose. Most of the overhangs had been expensively angled back with drills and blasting. A few, like the one facing the Nielsens now, had been deemed too daunting and had received the alternate treatment of a steel retaining mesh, dropped before the rock face like a chain-link curtain, to prevent any debris from bouncing onto the pavement.

"Oh, my Lord," Margie whimpered softly, her gaze halfway up.

The distress in her voice caught Doug's attention. "Holy Mother," he said.

Some forty feet up, hanging from a rope, was the body of a woman, dangling before the retaining screen like a talisman on display.

Margie, acting instinctively — her reflex

14

as modern as her surroundings were primordial — snapped a picture.

CHAPTER TWO

Joe Gunther was studying Gilbert's face from inches away, watching for any indicators of what might be going through his mind. But Gilbert was a cat, and fast asleep on Joe's chest at the moment, so the challenge was probably insurmountable, even for a veteran cop.

Joe had never been a pet owner, not since leaving the family farm as a young man, where his father had kept dogs. Gilbert had been thrust upon him. Actually, thrown at him by a woman trying to distract him as she drew a gun. That had worked, in the short-term, even though she'd then been bested by one of Joe's colleagues. In any case, Gilbert had ended up in permanent residence, no worse for the adventure.

Which Joe had found surprisingly to his liking. His young roommate had settled in without a ripple, greeting him when he came home, sleeping peacefully with him at night, and snuggling unobtrusively whenever he had a moment to sit and read late at night.

Gilbert Gumshoe — as Sammie Martens, Joe's sole female squad member, called him — had become a gentle grace note at this point along an eventful, sometimes tumultuous life.

Of course, as Willy Kunkle — another member of the team, and Sammie's "other half" — had put it in cruder terms, older people need pets as they get decrepit.

Joe smiled at the memory of the line. He did like his ragtag family of eccentrics. Just as he liked Gilbert.

The phone rang beside the couch, where Joe and the cat were stretched out. Gilbert half opened his eyes, assessed his chances of remaining undisturbed, and decamped for the floor in a graceful leap.

"Gunther," Joe answered.

"Susan's dead," a woman's distraught voice said.

"Gail?" Joe asked, recognizing his long-standing romantic partner of several years ago, now the governor of Vermont. Still a friend who called periodically — although usually not so dramatically — Gail Zigman had become an enigma to him, at times longing and sentimental, at others imperious and borderline ruthless. He had sadly found himself watching his choice of words with her — a caution he'd never practiced in the past.

"She was murdered."

"Susan *Raffner*?" he asked, sitting up, noticing at the same time that another call was coming in.

He ignored it for the time being. "Tell me what happened."

"I don't know. I just got a phone call. They found her dead near the interstate. I don't understand what that means, but they definitely said she'd been killed. They told me they called because she was my friend."

"Of course," he said soothingly, not adding that it was also because of Susan's being a state senator. The two women had begun in politics together, decades ago, when Susan had backed Gail for a place on the Brattleboro selectboard. She had been Gail's political adviser and trusted sidekick ever since.

"Did you get the name of the cop on the case?" he asked out of habit.

"I didn't talk to him," she said, sounding surprised. "They called the governor's office, not me directly. Rob told me." There was a sudden catch in her voice, and when she resumed, she was choked with emotion.

"What does it matter, Joe? Who cares?"

"You're right, you're right," he said, ignoring her flash of irritation. Rob Perkins was her chief of staff. "I'll get that later."

"You'll do this, Joe?" she pleaded. "You'll find out who did it?"

"I'll do my best," he promised.

"I already gave orders that VBI was to have the case, no questions asked, but I want you leading them. If you get any shit from anybody, you call me, okay?"

"Of course, Governor," he assured her. "I'll get on it now. I'll keep you informed. Promise."

His use of her title seemed to steady her, transcending their past intimacy to introduce a stabilizing formality.

Following a moment's hesitation, she said, "Thank you, Joe. I'll wait to hear from you."

"I am sorry, Gail," he told her.

He heard her sob as she hung up. He checked his phone to find out who'd called. It was Bill Allard, head of the VBI — the Vermont Bureau of Investigation — of which Joe had been the field force commander since its inception.

"You calling about the governor?" he asked as soon as Allard picked up.

"I'm calling about Senator Raffner," Bill replied, sounding nonplussed.

"I was on the phone with the governor. She called to say she'd asked us to look into this."

"Asked is hardly the word," Bill corrected him, not a fan of Gail. "But it does look like our kind of case."

"With me as lead?" Joe asked.

"Ah," Allard reacted. "She told you that, too, huh? Yeah. That's what she wants."

"I understand if you have to conflict me out," Joe told him. "Having the governor's old boyfriend running the investigation into her closest ally's death might get sticky."

"Not for me, it doesn't," Bill countered. "Raffner was a sitting state senator. I want my best team on it. We can't sacrifice quality to play politics — we don't have the manpower. Handpick whoever you want. We'll shift personnel around to cover, if need be."

The phone indicated a third incoming call. Joe said, "Roger that. Just thought I'd float the question. I'll call you back when I got something."

He hit a button on the phone. "Gunther."

"It's Sam," said his second-in-command, the weekend's on-call officer. "You hear yet? Hell of a way to start a sunny Sunday."

Her natural intensity reverberated over the line. She had a perpetual level of commitment — whether to him, the job, her baby daughter, or the acerbic Willy Kunkle — that radiated like a heat source.

"I just hung up on the governor and Allard," he told her. "Nobody's told me much beyond that Susan Raffner was found murdered."

"That's how it's looking," Sam said. "Unless she took herself out in the weirdest suicide I ever heard."

"What?"

"She was found hanging from one of those steel-mesh retaining nets they dropped across the cliffs lining the interstate. A couple of tourists called it in. It almost sounds like when a farmer hangs a dead fox from his fence, to warn other foxes. Totally crazy."

"But it's not a suicide?" he asked pointedly.

"VSP is guarding the scene," she reported, using the familiar initials of the Vermont State Police. "They're keeping everything as clean as possible for us, but it looks like a homicide, unless you know something I don't. For one thing, they're saying there's no car parked nearby. It could be a suicide combined with a car theft. Stranger things have happened."

Joe shook his head at the phone. "Okay.

It's not like Raffner and I hung out. I barely saw her over the years. But suicidal? I never got that — she was way too full of piss and vinegar, protesting every cause under the sun. You did hear we've been assigned to head this up?"

"Yup," she said, sounding happy. "I'm at the office right now, packing stuff up. Who do you want to come along?"

"The way the cages are being rattled," Joe said, "everybody, so we start on the same page."

He could almost hear her grinning. "Cool. I already got Willy calling the babysitter, and Lester said we could pick him up at the gas station off exit seven."

Which was one of the many reasons Joe had made her his Number Two. "I'm headin' out," he said gratefully. "See you in a few."

Joe had once imagined that if you took a sheet of paper, crumpled it up into a ball, and then flattened it out — creased lengthwise, like a small, rectangular tent — you would have the rough approximation of a 3-D map of Vermont. The mountains run down its middle, the right and left edges are calmed and flattened by water — the Connecticut River and Lake Champlain,

22

respectively — and the rest of the state's surface is as bumpy, irregular, and furrowed as the Ice Age relic that it is.

He loved every square foot of it. As he sat in the passenger seat of the unmarked car, with Sam at the wheel and Willy and Lester in the back, he watched the Connecticut River come into and out of view in the valley below them. The interstate this far north was never heavily traveled — certainly not by urban standards — and had been declared by various magazines as one of the country's most scenic byways.

And yet, he mused . . . There was always a flip side, as his long career attested: For all its sylvan beauty and apparent tranquility, despite its sparse population and square miles of emptiness, Vermont was also poorly financed, nonindustrialized, and far off the beaten path for everyone except tourists, and — more recently — drug dealers. None of that made it a crime magnet, but this very trip north was proof enough to Joe of humanity's chronic inability to live as peacefully as these calming environs suggested.

The VSP had sealed off an entire section of the road between two exits, rerouting the scant traffic to a parallel two-lane highway. Sam maneuvered their vehicle between the cones manned by a young trooper who

23

waved them through, and continued for four miles along a pavement now as empty of traffic as an abandoned movie set.

"Spooky," Lester commented from the back. "It's like some spaceship beamed up everybody but us."

"I doubt it beamed up the people we'd like to see gone," Willy said sourly, grabbing his withered left arm and shifting it so he could sit more comfortably. They were all dressed for the outdoors, in addition to carrying their standard tactical gear. "Be typical if only the good guys got zapped."

The other three smiled at the comment, typical of the speaker. Willy's arm — a reminder of a career-threatening encounter with a bullet on a case many years earlier — was a testament to both the one-liner and Willy's overall Eeyore outlook.

Any humor vanished, however, as the car rounded the next wide curve, and a cluster of vehicles came into view, most of them sparkling with various combinations of blue and white and red strobe lights against the craggy backdrop of a dark rock wall.

Lester hunched forward, craning to see up, which his great height and the car's low roof made all but impossible. "My God. That's awful."

No one argued with him, including Willy.

The sight of a single human body, hanging high and small and lonely halfway to the cliff's top, struck them all with its melancholy.

There was no need to pull off the road — trucks and cruisers were parked haphazardly, as if their drivers had subconsciously enjoyed not having to follow the rules.

"We're in the wrong place," Willy said as they got out, still staring at the mesmerizing vision overhead.

A state police sergeant proved him correct as he approached, saying, "They're waiting for you up top." He gestured with his thumb, continuing, "The next exit's a few miles north, but we cut a snowmobile path just past the cliff that connects to the road above. You could go that way if you don't mind one of my guys driving your car around the long way. We got sled operators standing by."

"Sounds good," Joe told him. "What about the people who called this in?"

"They're in their car." The sergeant pointed to the scenic pull-off and an SUV hitched to a trailer bearing two snowmobiles. "We got a video-recorded statement, but you're free to talk to 'em yourself, if you want."

25

Joe watched the man's bland, impassive face, looking for any signs that this was a dig. "Uniforms" versus "Suits" was a well-known rivalry within law enforcement, although less so in Vermont, given the small numbers involved. But VSP versus VBI was an additional factor, since the creation of the latter had seriously depleted the ranks of the former's Bureau of Criminal Investigation — and had eroded its influence.

The sergeant, however, appeared to be either totally lacking in such prejudice, or a skilled poker player.

In any case, Joe didn't care. "I'm good," he replied. "They tell you anything interesting?"

The man smiled and visibly relaxed. "Not really. They had the sense to keep their distance, but except for the obvious, they didn't see anything, didn't hear anything, and don't know anything. Our BCI guys called for the crime scene truck." He glanced upward. "They just arrived upstairs, so everything's looking pretty secure."

Joe shifted his gaze once more to the reason they were here. "This is going to sound a little screwy, but are we sure she's dead?"

The sergeant chuckled. "Not screwy to

me. First thing I asked when I got here. She's dead, all right." He indicated an athletic young trooper in the distance, talking with a couple of his colleagues. "The tall one there was first on scene. He called it in, checked her out with his binoculars — so far so good — and then the crazy bastard climbed the netting and checked for a pulse."

Joe starcd at him. "He climbed up?"

"Like a goddamned monkey. Wished I'd been here to see it. It's got to be forty feet. The female tourist took pictures. You should see 'em. I gave our boy a big thumbs-up, and then told him that if he ever did a thing like that again, I'd have him on desk duty for a month."

Joe shook his head, thinking that he would have pulled the same stunt a couple of decades ago. "I heard something about a purse," he asked.

"BCI took it. It was over there, looking no different than if you'd just put it down. The clasp was still closed, which is a miracle if it was dropped from that height."

Joe nodded without comment, and turned to face his team. "Okay. Let's go sledding."

They found five snowmobiles waiting by the side of the road, as the cliff tapered off to become a shallow, snow-packed gully that aimed back toward the hilltop. They divided up among four volunteer drivers and hitched rides to a two-lane dirt road above. Contrasting with the view they had been enjoying — and despite being higher up — here the road was screened by trees on both sides, with only glimpses between the evergreens of the Connecticut River valley.

They were met by a VSP van that took them to a second cluster of cars, including a large truck from the forensic laboratory. As usual at such scenes — which were blessedly few in this rural state — Joe was impressed by the number of people gathered. Besides the state police and the crime lab civilians, there were representatives from Fish and Wildlife, the local sheriff's office, EMS, a couple of local municipal cops, and even what appeared to be a town constable — most of them muttering and watching the very few people who were actually processing the scene.

He couldn't blame them. A cop in Vermont could go through most of a career without witnessing a homicide scene. A banner year in Vermont might produce twenty murders — fewer than he imagined New York City racked up in a month.

From inside the yellow tape enclosing a

generous semicircle, a plainclothes detective they knew from past encounters caught sight of them and invited them over. "Oh, boy, here come the big guns. Can we all go home now?" he cracked.

Joe identified himself to an officer with a clipboard before ducking under the cordon. "Rick," he said. "Long time. How've you been keeping?"

"Can't complain. I'm happy to be the lowly BCI guy on this one. This is gonna be a nightmare before it's done."

It was a custom-designed moment for Willy to say something insulting, but Joe knew his man. Kunkle was ignoring the chatter, his eyes darting around the scene as he submitted his ID in turn, instinctively cataloging every detail around him. A trained military sniper and a PTSD-plagued paranoid, he was someone who focused fast and hard.

Joe looked around as Sam and Lester took their turns at the checkpoint. The ice-hard dirt road was only twenty yards from the edge of the cliff, beyond the thin line of trees and the remnants of a dilapidated chain-link fence. Embedded in the otherwise pristine crust of snow, between the tarmac and the first tree trunk, were a set of tire tracks and some footprints. Joe saw a tied-off double loop of taut white rope around that first trunk, leading straight toward the cliff.

"You find any witnesses to anything?" Joe asked his BCI counterpart.

Rick frowned. "Not yet. I got guys pounding on doors, but it's pretty isolated up here. The road is rarely traveled, given both the interstate and the paved highway they're using for the detour."

Joe pressed his lips together before saying, "Makes you think. Whoever did this had to have been familiar with the area — the backwoods road, the broken fence, the proximity to the cliff . . . Even the trees being handy so the rope could be tied off."

He watched as the lab techs laid out a narrow sidewalk next to the tire tracks, giving them access while preserving the evidence. "We were having a conversation on the way up here about whether this could be a suicide."

"With no car?" Rick asked.

"It could've been stolen afterward," Sam contributed, crouched down with her small backpack and unloading her camera equipment.

Rick didn't laugh. "Great minds and all that," he said. "We thought the same thing, especially after we sent a unit to her house in Brattleboro and found her car missing. Problem is" — here he pointed at the tracks in the snow — "those belong to a pickup or an SUV. Raffner's registered to a Prius."

"Of course she is," Willy muttered, and moved away, shadowing the techs.

Rick and Joe ignored him. "You put out a BOL for the car?" Joe asked.

"Yup. Nothing yet."

"Curiouser and curiouser," Lester said, trailing behind Willy and now Sam, as they started coordinating with the crime lab team.

Because of the aging day's ebbing light, the protocols of how best to deconstruct a scene like this had to be altered, and provisions made to secure the area overnight. Fortunately, the weather was forecast to hold steady, making this an easy decision.

Less easy was choosing how to remove the body from its perch.

It couldn't be a simple matter of reeling her in by the rope from which she was dangling. Any tastelessness of doing so aside, the practical consideration remained of how the stressors of such a maneuver might play out. As Willy indelicately put it, "You don't want her head coming off."

As a result, after everything obvious had

been thoroughly documented and the evidence gathered, a high-angle extraction crew was summoned and dropped over the cliff and the remains placed inside first a body bag, and then a lightweight wire litter to be pulled to the top.

Nevertheless, for Joe, who'd known Susan for decades, the shock of seeing her dead after the bag had been partially unzipped — the rope still around her neck — hit harder than he'd expected.

Raffner had been Gail's friend, not his. He'd been open to some kind of relationship, given her importance in Gail's life, but he'd always felt that Susan didn't like him much. She'd respected him — both Gail and his own inner radar had told him as much — but he'd sensed that she'd viewed him as the loyal opposition.

That being said, he'd seen her laugh and cry and had shared meals and drinks with her for years — if always in the company of others. She'd been bright and smart and tough and good at getting things done — as well as devoted and dedicated to Gail. To see the source of such vitality so pale, stiff, and silent drove home what he knew Gail must be experiencing.

Her best friend — certainly her most steadfast one — had been reduced to a broken vessel, its vibrant contents emptied.

"You want to take a better look at her?" one of the climbers asked him, undoing the straps that held her pale corpse to the litter.

Shaking off his musings, Joe came alongside the device, asking, "How stiff is she?"

"Not rock solid. It's more than the usual rigor, 'cause of the cold, but she's not like some of 'em — straight out of the freezer."

Grateful to hear that, Joe slipped on a pair of latex gloves and crouched in the snow, a small crowd looking on. They'd all dealt with bodies that had truly frozen stiff. Not only couldn't you make them conform to anything, like a doorway or the inside of a hearse, but they took days to thaw prior to autopsy.

"Let's make sure," he announced generally, "that when she gets transported to Burlington, the hearse is heated to where the driver can barely stand it. We've got to do what we can to get her warm enough that they can open her up."

As Joe began helping with the straps and the bag's zipper, they all noticed how her underlying sweater, blouse, and bra had been sliced down the middle, exposing her bare chest.

"Damn," someone said.

Crudely cut into the flesh was the single word, "Dyke."

CHAPTER THREE

Joe escorted Susan's body to the medical examiner's office in Burlington by following the funeral home's featureless minivan for a couple of hours along I-89. This was Vermont's only other interstate, which cut a diagonal from White River Junction to the state's "Queen City," through the middle of the famed Green Mountains. It was arguably as pretty a road as I-91, and certainly one he rarely wearied of traveling. This was good news, given the number of times he had to do so, largely because Burlington was the state's largest metropolis by far, and thus where most people met to conduct business.

Weariness, however, was hardly a concern on this trip. Not only was Joe constantly on the new "hands-free" phone setup they'd mounted into his car, to conform to Vermont's new cell phone usage statute, but the vehicle ahead kept reminding him of the emotional cost of Susan Raffner's death, and its pending impact on the community at large. Joe had learned the hard way how this socially sensitive state could react when one of their own — a celebrity to boot — was cut down in her prime.

As if in confirmation, the cell phone came alive in between two of his own outgoing calls.

"Gunther."

"It's me," said Gail, sounding stronger and more resolute than before, which he knew from experience could be good or bad.

"Hey," he said, considering what to say and how to say it. "I'm escorting Susan to the medical examiner's office right now."

"What have you learned?"

"We're definitely treating it as a homicide, but we're a long way from reaching any conclusions yet."

"You sound like a press release," she said, confirming his fear that she'd balance her grief with an aggressive, take-charge attitude.

He decided, therefore, to get to the point. "You have to swear on a stack of Bibles not to let this out, no matter what the pressure."

"Joe," she began.

"It could be very important to solving this, Gail. As governor, we'll tell you what you need to know, but you more than most have seen how this works."

Her voice hardened. "What are you dancing around?"

He sighed to himself before answering, "I don't want anybody else telling you this: Someone, presumably the killer, cut a message on Susan's chest."

"*What?* What're you saying?"

"It's the word 'dyke,' Gail. I'm sorry."

She exploded on the phone. *"God*damn *it. Oh, fuck."*

He listened to her crying and pounding something hard repetitively on her desk, before he said, "I will do everything I can to find out what happened. And I will drive my people to do likewise. We will not rest."

He imagined her struggling to compose herself, especially given how superficial his own words had sounded to him — despite their sincerity. Joe had no idea of the shared history these two intimately connected women might have built between them, or of the true nature of Gail's pain right now.

"What are you going to do?" she finally asked in a subdued voice.

"The autopsy should give us some basic information — cause of death, maybe something about the sequence of events," he said matter-of-factly. "The crime lab is processing everything at the scene, and then we'll analyze whatever trace can be found on the body. We've also got people looking for her car, which seems to have gone missing. And Lester and Willy are going to her house right now to see what they can find there. It's basic, solid stuff, Gail, and it'll be done right. Additionally, I'll research any possible hate crime angles. It could be there'll be some buzz among the groups we track that'll be helpful. Do you know if Susan received any communications targeting lesbians or homosexuality?"

"Is that you diplomatically asking if Susan was queer?"

Joe kept his tone impassive, although he was startled that he hadn't actually asked the question with that in mind. "No. But was she?"

"Yes," came the answer, and the phone went dead.

"Thanks so much," he said softly to himself, feeling instantly guilty about his sense of relief that he and Gail were no longer romantically involved.

"I haven't asked," Lester said conversationally, "but how's fatherhood treating you, now that you've got a few miles under you?"

Willy took his eyes off the passing

countryside to stare at him. "You looking to hand off your own kids, or just being nosy? I'm surprised you're not a grandfather by now, the way you woodchucks breed up here."

Lester Spinney, as befit his easygoing personality, merely laughed. "*I'm* a woodchuck? How long you lived up here, speaking of which? You should almost qualify."

"Too long."

"You miss New York?"

"Like a canker sore."

"Emma sleeping well and enjoying day care and learning who's got the brains between her parents?"

That got a smile from her father.

Lester went back to negotiating the traffic lined up for exit two into Brattleboro. Willy was a hard case to crack. A transplanted New York cop, he'd been shot back when he and Joe and Sammie had worked together for the Bratt PD. The injury had almost cost him his job, along with the use of the arm. But that was one of the unique things about Vermont — there were few enough people making things happen that creative solutions often became the norm. In this case, that meant that despite Willy's injury and his almost toxic demeanor, Joe

Gunther had worn down some significant opposition to keep him employed. He'd pushed Kunkle's integrity and ability — and made some loaded references to the Americans with Disabilities Act — but he'd also taken full responsibility for him, which had eventually sealed the deal. The creation later on of the VBI had become the perfect opportunity to not only collect the best and brightest among the state's investigators — including Lester himself — but to build a protective niche for Willy Kunkle, as well.

And Les was happy for that, because Willy, for all his irritable ways, struck him as a hot, bright, eccentric source of insight whose absence from their ranks would have made the world a duller place — and resulted in a lower solve rate. The latter point wasn't a given, but Spinney's affection for his curmudgeon of a partner was willing to allow for the possibility. After all, Willy Kunkle was fun to watch.

Out of the blue, Willy asked, "How is your boy, anyhow? Flunked out of the police academy yet?"

"Nope," Lester answered cheerfully, "and my daughter's not pregnant, either, to your earlier point. Nor is my wife feeding a drug habit out of the hospital's supply cabinet. In fact, Dave'll be graduating in a couple of weeks, and then it's figuring out where to go next."

"He's a deputy sheriff now, isn't he?"

"Yup, but probably not for much longer. Time'll tell. He's done well, but it's not his first choice of places to work."

Willy didn't respond, back to staring out the window. He didn't actually care about what happened to David Spinney, or the rest of Lester's irritatingly wholesome family. It was his own daughter, barely learning to sit up, who had stimulated the question. Willy was an older parent who'd once sworn never to have children, and he'd been thrown by how much she filled his thoughts daily. It worried him. His past strength had been in cutting people out of his life, in part because he had such a low tolerance for most of them, but in part, too, because he wasn't convinced that he deserved their company. He saw himself as deeply flawed — even a bad man, if not for his persistent effort to avoid crossing the line. But the line remained. As a recovering alcoholic, he knew it in palpable terms; as a self-doubting father, mate, and colleague, he feared its proximity as he might have feared a trip wire attached to a land mine.

"Chestnut Hill?" Spinney asked, slowing down on Western Avenue as he approached the top of the hill heading into downtown Brattleboro.

"Take a left on Cedar and a right on Acorn Lane," Willy advised. "It's easier to see where you're going."

That was a matter of opinion, Lester thought as he followed directions. Susan Raffner lived in one of the town's more unusual neighborhoods, clustered around an ancient and no longer functional reservoir — access to which was challenging at the height of summer, and flat-out scary when banked by snow and covered with ice, as now. The challenges were compounded by the area being, as the name implied, on a hill, and fed only by a twisting series of narrow, steep, urban versions of poorly paved "goat paths." The sheer quirkiness of the locale seemed designed for an apparent character such as Raffner.

Lester crawled to the top — a loop road circling the reservoir and servicing a small number of homes — and was struck by how the romantic-sounding name contrasted with Chestnut Hill's mixed-bag reality. The reservoir was in fact a half-empty, crumbling, concrete-lined, weed-tangled frozen pond, primarily reliant on rainwater for its contents, and surrounded by a rusty chain-link fence. It was, put bluntly, ugly, if maybe not to the people living around it. And the surrounding architecture, as it often did in Brattleboro, added to the muddle by running the gamut from graceful and historical to forgettably recent and plain.

Susan had lived in a somber, two-story, shingle-clad example of the older category — a building at once historic and graceless. As the car rolled to a stop before it, both men observed how deserted the entire neighborhood seemed. This, they also knew from experience, would be short-lived.

They were only the vanguard of a specialized crowd that would invade as soon as the scene overlooking the interstate had been completely gone over. Crime techs, investigators, uniformed backup teams, and supervisors were all due shortly — and those were just the professionals, not the media and the gawkers sure to follow. But for the moment, it was Les and Willy on their own, which was just the way they liked it. They weren't even here to officially conduct a search and inventory — but merely to give the place a discreet and preliminary survey, albeit with a search warrant they'd secured along the way.

There was, however, one other person there already — a Brattleboro patrolman, sitting in his cruiser with his radio on. As he got out of the vehicle upon their arrival, they heard the soft wailing of country music leaking into the frozen air.

"I help you?" he asked.

Willy had been foraging around in the backseat of their car, hunting for his notebook. At the voice, he straightened and faced the man.

"Oh," the young officer said — taking in a local legend. "Agent Kunkle. I didn't know it was you."

Lester — by contrast tall, gangly, and disarming — chuckled at the touch of fear he detected. Willy didn't respond, making his way up the barely shoveled walkway to the front door instead.

"You been expecting us?" Lester asked.

"Somebody," the officer replied. He stuck out a hand. "Travis Newman."

"Lester Spinney. I work with Willy, upstairs from you. VBI. Why don't I know you?"

"Just started," Newman explained.

"Move it, Les," Willy called out from the door. "Need the key."

Lester raised his eyebrows, impressed that the young cop had already been warned about Kunkle — including a description. "Duty calls. We'll talk some other time.

Welcome aboard."

"Thanks," Newman said, heading back to the cruiser's warm cocoon.

Les pulled out the key they'd secured from Raffner's purse and dangled it before him as he approached his colleague. "Your wish is my command."

"That'll be the day," Willy grumbled.

Lester unlocked the front door before they both struggled into white Tyvek suits and booties. The entrance hall was dark, warm, and cluttered, thereby revealing to Spinney's eye the habits of a person as disheveled in private as she'd been polished and organized to the outside world.

Willy, whose own home was fastidiously tidy, let out a contemptuous puff of air. He'd never been fond of Raffner's politics or manner. "Typical," he muttered, pausing in the hallway.

"She live alone?" Spinney asked, standing beside him. He lived in Springfield, a forty-five-minute drive to the north. He'd heard of Susan Raffner, but didn't know the locals as Willy did.

"Far as I ever knew," Willy said, moving slowly into the room to their right, his head swinging from side to side as he took in everything. He adjusted his single latex glove by yanking on its cuff with his teeth in a well-practiced motion.

They entered a living room where most every flat surface was covered with books, documents, newspapers, and magazines, most of them apparently abandoned in mid-course — dog-eared, folded back, placed facedown at a certain article. It reflected a mind in a rush — impatient, driven, and curious.

After a few minutes of absorbing their surroundings, both men moved to the purported dining room across the hall. Purported because the table designed to hold meals no longer had room for a sandwich. It seemed that Raffner had seen any flat surface as fair game, and so had made every inch of this one the base of a small mountain of more paperwork, including box after box of stuffed manila folders, their contents peeking out like a multitude of breast-pocketed handkerchiefs.

"Wow," Lester said. "How did she keep track of anything?"

"Who said she did?" Willy countered.

The kitchen was next, toward the back of the house. Even here, there was a scattering of reading material, but the dominant clutter was at least in context. In no order that they could determine, there were jars, plastic bags, and boxes of powders, grains, cereals, and things they couldn't identify clustered along the counters and cabinet edges like small Disney characters jamming a set's balconies and sidewalks. The two cops mostly observed it all, sometimes reaching out to see past an obstruction, but otherwise content to simply interpret the nature of the woman who'd owned it all — and who'd attracted such a grisly death.

By the evidence available so far, the mind and spirit of that late resident had been committed to an impressively broad swath of social causes.

"And a vegetarian," Lester added softly.

"Golly," Willy replied. "What a shock."

Upstairs, they found an overstuffed, computer-equipped office, three bedrooms, and two bathrooms — one clearly intended for guests who took relative sanitation and the effects of mold in stride. Of the bedrooms, one had been moderately cleared for the occasional visitor, another had been sacrificed to the same purpose as most of the downstairs, and the last was an utterly surprising and totemic lair-within-a-lair, anchored by an enormous bed of rumpled and cast-about pillows, blankets, and even a few stuffed animals. At long last in this activist warehouse dedicated to intellectual passions, here was a clearly marked reserve for purely sensual delights.

From the Georgia O'Keeffe prints on the wall, to the lesbian literature near the head of the bed, the two cops felt the palpable heartbeat of a woman in love with the sexuality of other women.

"Okayyyy," Lester said after taking it in. "Is this a surprise?"

Willy was looking around like an art lover at an exhibition. For all his brusqueness and irritability, his primary targets were liars, hypocrites, and people coasting on the effort of others — or of society in general. He might not have agreed politically with Susan Raffner, but he'd never questioned her tenacity and zeal. All he saw here was the inner expression of someone who'd lived as she believed.

"A pleasant one," he answered sadly, thinking of his own continual struggle with an inner galaxy of emotional turmoil and guilt.

Lester cast him a covert glance. Though not a simple man, Spinney was not overly complex. He accepted life as it came, made adjustments if he could, and lived with what remained. That being said, he was no unquestioning observer, which helped explain why he found Willy an excellent source of human education.

He nodded silently, understanding his partner to be enjoying a kinship moment with someone for whom he'd only expressed contempt while she was alive.

Willy opened a nearby dresser drawer and extracted a vibrator, nestled among some silky underwear.

"Phew," Lester commented, absorbing it all. "I better take notes on what to buy Sue next Valentine's."

"Please," Willy groaned, as he circled the bed, toward the night table, and crouched to study a small plastic baggie lying on the floor. Without disturbing it beyond yawning it open to better see inside, he let out a small grunt.

"What?" Lester asked.

"The requisite Mary Jane," Willy said, straightening up. "I wondered — with all of this" — he gestured generally — "if she indulged in a little something to get mellow."

Les looked more closely from where he stood. "Well, this seems like it was the room for mellow — a love nest of Lesbos."

Willy glanced back at the bag. "Yeah," he said thoughtfully. "I'm actually surprised there's not more — maybe this is just a grab stash, fed off a mother lode somewhere else. Looks like pretty cruddy quality, too." He then smiled, his expression clearing as if moving on to other matters, and added, "The crime scene boys are gonna love this dump. We'll lose 'em for days in here."

CHAPTER FOUR

Most cops don't like dead bodies, which is hardly startling. Because TV has pushed the notion that they'll see ten corpses by the end of their first shift, people assume they don't mind keeping company with the recently departed. But in Joe's experience, a lot of cops could be quite squeamish.

That wasn't true for him. He'd been in combat as a young man, where he'd become familiar with death in quantity. Later, he'd come to see the dead less as sentimental bearers of memories and nostalgia, and more as conveyers of interesting and possibly important details. Their souls resided in the minds of those who'd known them, in his opinion. Their bodies were just that — the remains left behind.

As things had turned out, this was a good outlook, because the woman in his life — whom he'd trusted professionally for decades, but who'd just recently won his heart — was the state's medical examiner, Beverly Hillstrom.

Her office, called the OCME for short — the Office of the Chief Medical Examiner — was an impressively modern and pleasant, if small, facility located somewhere in the basement of the University of Vermont Medical Center in Burlington, which by contrast was a sprawling, oddly laid-out behemoth of a complex, parked on the edge of the university campus.

Joe escorted Susan Raffner's body through the underground passages to the door designated for such deliveries, and witnessed the handoff from the hearse driver to the OCME staffer who accepted her. Then, despite it being after hours, he continued into the small suite of administrative offices, following the glow of a light down the otherwise dim hallway.

Beverly Hillstrom, uncharacteristically dressed — if still stylish in his eyes — in blue jeans and a work shirt, turned around from a filing cabinet as he entered her small corner office, and draped her arms around his neck before giving him a welcoming kiss.

He ran his hands down her back and said, "Jeez, I should make late-night deliveries more often."

"You do just fine," she told him, and

kissed him again.

After which, true to form, they easily fell into their professional roles. Homicides were still rare enough to merit a special call-out by the ME, even late at night, and they both wanted to keep the momentum begun by the discovery of Susan Raffner.

"She was really a state senator?" Beverly asked, leading the way to the far side of the office suite and the locker room where they could both change into scrubs.

Joe wasn't taken aback by her ignorance. The chief medical examiner had to do her share of lobbying in Montpelier, but it still didn't amount to much, given Vermont's part-time citizen legislature. Most of the state's politicians were unknown outside the capitol building — even ones as outspoken and energetic as Susan.

"Yup," he told her as she preceded him. "And the governor's best buddy."

Beverly looked over her shoulder, familiar with Joe's history with Gail. "Really? They were friends? No wonder this was given such a high priority. I was impressed by the tone of the officer who called me."

She pushed open the door to the locker room and gestured to him to follow her. "Sharing this room after hours should rank up there with smoking in the bathroom. I do take it that you want to be present for this one."

"I do."

He knew the drill. They both switched from street clothes into scrubs, taking just a moment, while still in their underwear, to exchange another kiss, this one compellingly seductive.

"Something to think about for later," she suggested.

Back outside, Beverly continued leading the way, this time down the facility's main corridor, outside the admin suite, toward a broad door blocking the end of the hall. This was the entrance to the autopsy room.

On the way, he noticed that the gurney holding Raffner had vanished from where they'd left it, inside the receiving door. "You summon extra help?" he asked.

She didn't bother glancing back. "Todd. No fun doing one of these without a diener. And Mike — the new law enforcement liaison — he's here, too."

She pushed open the heavy door and held it for him, escorting him into a large, gleaming, L-shaped room with two autopsy bays. As advertised, Todd was there already, and had — as befit his job description — shifted the body, still in its sealed bag, from the gurney onto the autopsy table. Mike appeared as if on cue from another door.

The three men silently exchanged nods as Joe and Beverly assumed positions across from each other, and Beverly exposed Susan's pale, lifeless shape. She was still dressed as she'd been at the scene, rumpled and stained with mud and melted snow, in a pair of pants and the sliced-open sweater, blouse, and bra.

"Where was she found?" Beverly asked, reacting to the lack of a coat.

"Hanging by the neck, overlooking a scenic view on the interstate," he told her.

Beverly looked up at him. "Outside? Is she rock hard?"

"No, no. I had the funeral home guys crank up the heater on the way here. They weren't happy, but I'm hoping it did the trick. She should be just thawed enough for you to go ahead."

As Todd and Mike busied themselves taking photographs and removing layers of clothing — Mike bagging the evidence for later delivery to the crime lab — Beverly leaned over the crude carving just above the dead woman's breasts.

"Ouch."

Joe was startled. "Does that mean she was alive when that happened?"

Beverly straightened quickly and laid a

hand on his forearm. "No, no. I'm sorry. I was commenting generally. No, this was done postmortem — as if that wasn't bad enough."

Tempering her moment of spontaneity, she shifted to where the rope was still looped around Susan's neck. "I can tell you straight off," she said without hesitation, "that the hanging wasn't the cause of death. From past examples I've seen of such sequencing, she was dead for a while before this was done, as well."

Joe had thought as much. The way Susan was dressed suggested an indoor death, not to mention that the trace evidence at the scene had been consistent with a drag-and-drop scenario, versus something demanding more action on the killer's part — or any signs of resistance from the victim.

Of course, there were other possibilities, as his next question implied: "Does that rule out her being rendered unconscious and then killed by hanging?"

Beverly was keeping her eyes on her subject, moving her gloved hands about as Todd's efforts revealed more and more of the body to the bright overhead lights. "I wouldn't say that it rules out her having been rendered unconscious, as you so delicately put it." Here she cut him a quick look and an implied smile, which he couldn't appreciate through her mask. "But I can say that her cause of death wasn't this." She tapped the rope with a fingertip.

"So, she was assaulted elsewhere, given her clothing," he reiterated, "cut into and hanged after death, and presumably put on display, all to make a point."

Beverly resisted agreeing unequivocally, as suited her scientific approach. "Could be." She picked up Susan's arm and bent it slightly, adding, "And judging from what I'm seeing right now, your heater idea worked, if barely. She's still very cold, but I'm willing to give it a shot."

She then paused, Susan's hand still in the air. "Judging from the rest of her fingernails, I'd call this a clue."

He bent forward to scrutinize what she'd found. The fingernail of the body's right index was raggedly broken at the quick, leaving behind a smear of dried blood. "Damn. Painful."

"We'll be sure to scrape under the rest of them," she said, at which point Mike immediately set to work. "You never can tell when you might get lucky." She indicated several bruises across the ribs, previously hidden by clothing. "These, too, are telling, I would think."

Joe glanced at her. "Can you tell when they were administered?"

She touched his forearm with a gloved hand. "Exactly what caught my eye. They definitely predate death. They've been given time to get established. Not much time, mind you, but some."

"Maybe a struggle beforehand?" he suggested.

"They'd be consistent with that." She indicated more bruises around the body's upper arms. "Just as these would be with someone seizing her tightly, either holding or pushing her." She looked up at Todd. "Could you turn her over for a quick look?"

With an ease befitting his weight lifter's physique, the diener complied, revealing a horizontal bruise across Susan's lower back.

"Thank you, Todd."

Smiling in response to Beverly's trademark courtesy, Todd returned the body to its original supine position.

"Therefore possibly grabbed and pushed against something hard and horizontal," Joe said.

"Possibly," was her cautious reply.

They continued trading observations and information for a couple of hours, as Beverly examined what else Susan had to offer. Several times during the autopsy, she stepped away from the table to run warm water over her partially numbed fingertips.

There were essentially three distinct stages to a full-fledged postmortem examination, barring the final toxicology report: what the clothed body had to tell, what the naked version followed with, and finally, what the internal organs might reveal. To an old-fashioned person like Joe, only the middle stage stimulated a sense of inhibition, stemming back, no doubt, to a traditional upbringing involving modesty and discretion. For him to watch a woman he'd known for so long being slowly disrobed and then meticulously probed, scraped, and fingerprinted — every inch of her recorded by Todd's camera — made him feel like a voyeur, and brought home as nothing else had so far that Susan's vitality, like it or not, was never again going to be on display.

The third and last stage was by contrast a comfort zone for him. The autopsy seemed purely scientific, exposing a history that even the host body often hadn't known, such as a slightly damaged heart muscle. With Beverly as his guide, Joe learned about Susan's past as a smoker, her having once had an abortion, her sporting a sensual tattoo that only her most intimate companions had appreciated. He discovered that she might have benefitted from more exercise, less alcohol, and that she'd had a small but persistent argument with hemorrhoids. Most important, and late in the procedure, he also learned — once her face had been elastically peeled down and tucked under her chin, the top of her skull removed, and her brain exposed — that she'd suffered a stunning blow to the back of her head sometime prior to death and that she'd finally been done in as a result of a subsequent blow to her left temple, which had fractured the bone and caused, in Beverly's language, a "catastrophic" hemorrhage.

"You seen enough of this kind of wound to take a guess about what caused it?" Joe asked, fascinated by the amount of damage left behind.

He should have known better, of course. He and Beverly had been meeting over dead bodies for more years than either of them could recall. Never in that time had she ever speculated about any mechanism that wasn't blatantly obvious. She reported end results, supplying clarity and insight based purely on the evidence.

Nevertheless, she caught his eye upon hearing the question and suggested, "I doubt she was hit by a bird flying at high speed, if that helps."

He bowed slightly. "Point taken, Doctor."

Later that night, however, as they lay together in her home south of Burlington, alongside the dark immensity of Lake Champlain, she did allow herself more latitude.

"Seriously?" Joe asked. "A bird?"

"It just popped into my head. Maybe because you found her dangling halfway down a cliff. I can give you this much: It was something cylindrical at point of contact, perhaps an inch in diameter, and delivered at high velocity. Of course, that could cover anything from a chair leg to the butt of a pool cue to even the heel of a woman's shoe. Do you have any idea at all of what happened?"

He snaked his arm around her bare shoulder as she tucked in closer, loving how comfortable they were together. "Not yet," he said. "But we've barely begun."

Senior Trooper Tommy Redman radioed dispatch that he'd be out of the car on portable, before killing his engine and opening the door to the cold night air, at once reluctant to leave the cruiser's warmth and happy to be seeing his old friend Jack Muskett, ex-cop, current constable, always a good source of area gossip, and — last but most important right now to Redman — the unlikely brewer of the best cup of coffee in the county.

Muskett lived off a dirt road, in a trailer grown roots, with a retrofitted peaked roof, dilapidated attached porch, and cinder blocks skirting its base — hopefully but inadequately designed to keep the cold wind from sneaking in under the thin floor. It was as representative a residence for the rural northeast as were the surrounding maples and the sweet sap that dripped from them once a year.

Redman found Muskett burrowed into his beaten La-Z-Boy, one hand around a mug, the other clutching the remote, staring at a program featuring alligators, swamp boats, and men who looked like him.

"Hey," the trooper said, passing through the living room on his way to the kitchen.

"Hey, yourself," was the response.

Redman pulled a stained clean mug off the drying rack by the sink and poured himself some coffee from a percolator that had no reason to be functioning, before returning to the other room and carefully settling into an adjoining armchair, simultaneously balancing his mug and shifting his duty belt to allow him to sit comfortably. Between the Taser, radio, an extendable baton, his ammo pouches, two cuff cases, his gun, his OC spray can, cell phone, flashlight, and pager — this took some doing.

Muskett caught the body language. "Cuffs, a stick, and a gun," he said. "It's all we had. Don't know how you move around with all that crap."

"Why do you think I'm putting my feet up?"

Muskett raised an eyebrow. "For Christ sake. You just got out of a car. Cops don't walk anymore."

Tommy had heard it before. He actually agreed with much of it. Times had changed, and not always for the better. The onboard computers, the GPS units that told the shift sergeant where you were at all times, the audio-video equipment . . . It all was starting to make *RoboCop* look like a documentary instead of a sci-fi movie. Plus, most cops were a conservative bunch, and bitching about the sorry state of the world was an ongoing source of perverse comfort.

Tommy announced his reason for dropping by, as he did every week, keeping his eyes mindlessly glued to the two men on TV, who were poking into the water with oars, hoping for some angry reptilian reaction. "So what's new?"

It was their eight-year-old ritual, where Jack filled Tommy in on all the local skulduggery. In addition to currently being constable, Jack owned a one-truck towing company, drove a school bus every morning and afternoon, served on the three-man selectboard, and was a member of the fire department. He also inaugurated every day at the local filling station/coffee shop, opening the place up at five-thirty by being first in line. Amid all of these occupations, habits, and professions, Jack Muskett became privy to more information than might be jammed into a weekly soap opera. More times than he could recall, Tommy Redman's ongoing string of criminal investigations had been helped from just regularly tuning in, and sometimes asking a well-chosen question. Redman had four or five such dependable sources — men and women, both — scattered across the county.

They were about twenty minutes into their news update, as Jack referred to it, when he casually mentioned, "I had a complaint not twenty-four hours ago about activity in the middle of the night at Dana's junkyard. Pissed me off something royal, getting up outta bed for absolutely nuthin."

"You didn't find anything at all?"

"That is what nuthin means, Tommy. I drove up and down the rows, flashing my light around. No bodies, no party animals, no horny teenagers. Like I said, nuthin."

Dana's was the largest auto junkyard in a thirty-mile radius, recently defunct and increasingly a target of environmentalists and transplanted city dwellers who found the place unsightly. For pragmatists of Tommy's acquaintance, it remained a source of recycled auto parts, helping to keep a remarkable fleet of barely legal backwoods beaters on the road.

They wrapped things up shortly thereafter, Tommy knowing that his dispatcher would soon be wanting an update. But as he eased out of Jack's rutted and slippery dooryard, trying not to slide into any of the abandoned hulks lining the way, he set his course on Dana's, two miles away, responding to both instinct and curiosity. Jack, as Tommy well knew, might have been the best of gossip blotters, but he wasn't the most energetic of investigators. He hadn't seen anything suspicious at the junkyard — which also might have meant that he simply hadn't run it over in his car.

The place wasn't locked. It wasn't even fenced in, which was another complaint from the growing chorus against it. In the old tradition, places like this junkyard had simply evolved over time, born of falling crop prices, available farm acreage, and the instinct among hardscrabble people to make ends meet practically. What began as simply a way station for wrecked cars heading elsewhere had grown into a vast and loosely organized semipermanent resting place for hundreds of disintegrating vehicles, all of them roughly stacked in rows, with broad snow-packed paths between them. New additions to the rotting collection were both rare and probably against the law, given the legislature's ever-streaming current of regulations, so the towering piles on each side of Redman's cruiser hadn't changed much in recent years. But it was precisely the place's neglected reputation that had triggered Tommy's instinct to take a look. A party place or a lovers' lane it might have become, but its isolation and vastness were also magnets for things darker — and thus worth checking out.

The problem was that literal darkness was also what Tommy had to deal with. He had alley lights on the strobe unit atop his car roof, and a searchlight that he could manipulate as he crawled forward, but peering amid the inky gaps and jagged angles of one teetering stack of metal after another taxed one's concentration, and about fifteen minutes into this spontaneous and fruitless impulse, he began to rethink the wisdom of his action.

Until he saw the oddity.

That was often the case, after all. It wasn't so much with clarity that so many discoveries were made, but rather the small mental nudge that made one think that — just maybe — this one anomaly deserved further scrutiny.

As it did here. Just before his brain completely dulled to the slow, monotonous procession of piled, rusty, black and brown heaps, Tommy caught sight of the barest accent of something colorful. Not the fading paint job decorating a dented fender or door, but a small, distinct spot of bright green, reflecting in his searchlight like a beacon's flash.

He stopped the cruiser and backed up, looking for confirmation, and then emerged into the night with his flashlight in hand.

Lurking in a niche between two stacks that had slumped over onto each other like drunks on a subway car, was a Prius with a green license plate. It had been pulled into the gap as far as possible, and then not quite covered by a weatherworn tarp. The plate was just visible through a hole in the fabric, and only from one angle.

Under normal circumstances, a finding like this was followed by a request to dispatch to check the state's DMV data bank for the owner of record.

That wasn't necessary here. Tommy Redman simply returned to his front seat and consulted a scrap of paper that he'd taped to his dash earlier, listing the registration of Susan Raffner's missing car.

It was a match.

CHAPTER FIVE

Joe opened his front door cautiously and peered past his guest to see if anyone was standing in the driveway. Willy Kunkle stared at him, looking peeved.

"Really? No secret knock? There's nobody stalking where we actually work, boss. We don't have to sneak around like the KKK."

Joe stepped back to let him in. "You telling me the office parking lot had no camera trucks?" he asked. "And that our phone wasn't ringing nonstop?"

Willy didn't answer.

"Right," Joe said under his breath, and closed the door.

Lester and Sam were already there.

Joe waited for his last arrival to settle onto the edge of a sofa before he began. "This'll be super quick, and from now on we'll run the press gauntlet. I just wanted to compare notes among ourselves before more people join in and it gets harder to speak plainly and clearly."

"Things'll pipe down soon enough," Willy argued. "They always do."

"Normally, I'd agree," said Joe. "But I think we're in for something new this time. That's why I wanted to meet off the grid, if just this once."

"How's this different?" Sam asked. "I mean, aside from the body being a senator. It's not like it was the governor or something."

Joe rose and leaned against the counter that separated his small living room from his even smaller kitchen. Gilbert seized the opportunity to leap up next to him and butt Joe's shoulder with his head, before seating himself elegantly atop his master's paperwork.

"I may be wrong," Joe allowed. "But humor me for a couple of days until reality kicks in. Then we'll see. My instinct is that when it comes to gay rights and civil liberties and the rest of it, we Vermonters are living in a bubble."

"LGBTQ," Sam told him. "That's what they prefer — not individually, but as a group, like in a press release."

Joe stopped dead. "I realize that. I just can never get the order straight in my head."

"Lesbian, Gay, Bisexual, Transgender, and

Questioning," Sam recited. "LGBTQ. It's got a kind of cadence to it."

Willy snorted. "Spare me. Questioning? Why not H for Having a Bad Day?"

"You are such a caveman," she told him.

"We all set on this?" Joe asked, trying not to sound testy.

"Sorry," Sam said, looking down at the floor. As if sensing a soul in need, Gilbert abandoned Joe, leaped to the floor, made a semicircle around Willy, and jumped into Sammie's lap. She wrapped him in her arms.

Joe's irritation faded. "Sam," he said, "we'll make sure you're the one who speaks to the media when the time comes, okay? I'd just get the initials screwed up."

He cleared his throat to get back on track. "I'm just finding out how all this works, but I've heard through the grapevine that Susan Raffner was as involved with the BGL . . ."

"LGBT . . . Q."

"Thank you . . .

"That she was as keen for the cause as were the sixties radicals with their protests and sit-ins. The Internet is on fire with one group or another arguing its case, and Susan, no surprise, was very vocal, but *not,*" he emphasized, "to the extent you might think. She had so many other fish to fry that this one apparently qualified for a lower ranking among her enthusiasms."

"But she *was* a lesbian?" Lester asked. "That's solid?"

"Read the label on her chest, son," Willy said.

"*That* doesn't mean anything," Lester countered.

"It did this time," Willy continued. "It's just that no one gives a shit about it around here. That's what Joe meant by our living in a bubble." He pointed out the window. "Lester, you're a sweet, ignorant homie. Outside this white-bread, milquetoast state, people *hate* each other for no reason at all. Trust me on that. I fit right in out there in the real world."

Joe held up his hands. "Okay, okay. For what's it's worth, I spoke to the governor on the phone yesterday — she confirmed Raffner was gay. Let's kick around what we may be dealing with. I want to see what cards we can put faceup."

"Walks, talks, and looks like a duck," Willy predictably spoke first. "It's a hate crime by some fundamentalist right-wing wacko. Throw it to the feds and let them handle the publicity."

"I didn't know she was a lesbian," Sammie said. "And I doubt anyone else here did, either. So why target someone in a big

72

way that nobody knew was a target in the first place? No fed I know is gonna take this without compelling evidence."

"Joe said she was outspoken on the Internet," Lester reminded her. "This maybe has nothing to do with Vermont or her being a senator or close to the governor or anything else. Could've been someone from out-of-state who killed her."

"If that's true," Willy said stubbornly, "then it's the equivalent of a terrorist act, which means two things: Somebody's got to take credit for it or miss out on the headlines; and it again becomes a federal case, like I keep saying, which means we can get back to chasing psycho woodchucks and leave this crap to the big boys."

"You really don't want to get this guy?" Sam asked, genuinely surprised.

"Not if he's some Arkansas Bible thumper. I'm saying that if Lester's right, this belongs to the people with the deepest pockets and the most resources. I'm being practical, for once. Give me credit."

"We're getting ahead of ourselves," Joe cautioned them. "Let's work from the crime scene out, as usual, and see what's real. Is there any evidence that she didn't die in our fair state, regardless of where her killer came from?"

After a telling pause, Willy started over. "Single vehicle, probably a pickup, quick in-and-out, just long enough to string up the body and leave. That and Raffner's clothes imply a killing somewhere else, but nothing that says out-of-state. Plus, she lived here and was found here. Logic says she was killed here, too."

"What about the purse found at the bottom of the cliff?" Lester asked.

"Probably tossed there to attract attention," Willy replied. "Which is what it did, making them look up."

"The ME hasn't issued the autopsy results yet," Joe told them, "but cause of death seems to have been the second of two blows to the head. The rope was just for show — postmortem — as was the wording on her chest."

"She raped?" Willy asked bluntly.

"It doesn't appear so," Joe said. "She was manhandled some."

"Her house showed nothing unusual," Lester offered. "No signs of struggle, blood, or forced entry. The dog sitter she used said she dropped off the pooch like usual. Dog lived at the sitter's during the legislative session 'cause of Raffner's crazy schedule, so she hadn't seen Susan in a couple of weeks."

"She was a slob, though," Willy added.

"And had a little weed by the bed, no surprise."

"What about her car?" Joe asked. "Anyone get a copy of the report on that yet?"

"It was the state police who located it," Sam reported, "so it went straight to the crime lab. They also processed the junkyard where it was found, but so far, I haven't heard they found anything — sounds pretty much like the house."

"The legislature's still going strong," Joe continued. "So, she would've been in Montpelier, most likely, which explains the dog. A lot of the senators from far away either have apartments or condos locally, to cut down on the commuting, or they've got roommate setups with other politicos. Do we know about her?"

"She rented the top floor from an old lady who lives below," Willy said, causing everyone to look at him. "With the unlikely name of Regina Rockefeller."

"How do you know that?" Sam asked.

"I am the poh-leece," he replied. "And we got our guys from the headquarters unit going to check it out. I called the woman who's in charge of herding senators up there — some title with 'clerk' in it — and she gave me Raffner's particulars."

"Nice work," Joe said. "Along those lines,

have we started on a timeline for her? Last seen? Last contacted via electronic device? Last appointment met and missed?"

"I'm on that," Sam said. "I'm coordinating it with the crime lab folks. I figured we might as well use them as a conduit for now, since they're the catchall for everything else being collected from all quarters. So far, there's a cell phone, two home computers, a laptop, and a tablet. With any luck, we'll get an idea about her last movements from one of them."

Joe resisted reacting to anyone having or needing so many screen-equipped nuisances.

As if reading his mind, Sam added, "Along with those gizmos, she had dozens of filing cabinets filled with probably thousands of documents, any one of which might have something to do with how she ended up. She had hundreds of friends, allies, fellow protesters, and who knows what else that should be interviewed."

"And colleagues she worked with in the State House," Joe threw in. "They don't have personal secretaries or staffers under the dome. They share a clerical and legal pool of people. They should be questioned, too."

Sam addressed that, being the squad's

primary traffic manager. "Parker and Perry are on it already, that being in their backyard. We're gonna have to expand this conversation to include more bodies, if you want some of these answers. It's already gotten way beyond just us. The paper files alone are going to take an amazing amount of time to process, unless there's a break to help us out."

Parker Murray and Perry Craver were two ex–state police VBI investigators assigned to the central Waterbury unit, out of the headquarters building. There were five VBI squads, or units, across the state, located geographically for convenience. Murray and Craver didn't lead their squad, nor were they the only ones comprising it; it was the alliteration of their first names that always lumped them together, and gave the unit its identity within the VBI. It also didn't hurt that they usually teamed up on a case.

Joe spoke to Willy. "You mentioned fundamentalist right-wingers. Were you just being opinionated, or do you actually have a lead?"

Sammie let out a brief laugh. Willy cast her an amused look and asked generally, "What do you think?"

Joe ignored the humor. "So, who do we

know who hates lesbians enough to kill one?"

For once there was dead silence in the room, followed by Lester saying plaintively, "It's *Vermont,* boss. It's like a nonissue."

"That's what I was saying at the top," Joe reminded them. "We need to get our heads out of that cloud. If this killing was about Susan's sexual orientation, it wouldn't be the first instance of something happening in Vermont attracting a flatlander nutcase. We need to broaden our horizons."

Sammie had opened her laptop and was typing at high speed — another skill Joe didn't have.

"Southern Poverty Law Center," she said. "They collect so much information on these groups, they have their own intelligence unit. The fusion center in Williston put me onto them."

"Speaking of the fusion center," Lester suggested, "they'd be good to consult, too. If they don't get an immediate hit in-state, they can spread the word."

Joe nodded. It was a good idea. There were seventy-eight centers across the United States, many with staff experts on specific topics, who cross-communicated regularly.

"I'm sending an e-mail to someone I know up there right now," Sam said, her eyes locked on the screen.

Willy, who did his best to present as a troglodyte, was almost as comfortable with computers as Sam — although Lester had them both beat. Nevertheless, he routinely talked down his prowess, as he did indirectly now. "None of that typing's gonna nail the crazy bastard who did this."

"You know that for a fact?" Joe asked.

Willy tapped the side of his nose. "I smell it. We're not talking Timothy McVeigh and the Oklahoma City federal building. This is somebody who was pissed off — up close and personal."

"Maybe it's local politics after all?"

Willy canted his head to one side, considering his boss's question. "Maybe. Could also be sex-related."

"Fair enough," Joe agreed. "Another reason that we ask about any complaints, fights, disagreements — be they political or personal — when we start asking time, place, and last-seen questions."

"You're gonna have to talk to your old girlfriend, boss."

An awkward stillness caught the room. Sammie eyed Willy reproachfully. "Jesus. You are smooth."

Willy's eyes widened innocently. "I'm just sayin'."

Joe broke the tension. "He's right. I was probably the first person Gail called after she heard. She, Susan, and I go back. I doubt the governor had a closer friend, including me — even before we broke up. If Susan was having problems, Gail most likely would've heard about it."

"Speaking of which," Lester said, "what if this *is* connected to politics? Would that mean the governor's under threat, too?"

"What if it's connected to sex?" Willy offered, looking directly at Joe. "After you two went your separate ways, could Gail've found comfort in Susan's bed?"

Sammie, always the loyalist, slapped her computer closed. "You can be such an asshole."

"It's a fair question," Joe said calmly, adding with a tension-dissolving half smile, "if indelicately put. The answer is: I don't know. I'll ask."

"Better you than me," Willy admitted.

"You'd never get in the room with her," Lester said. "She *hates* you."

There was scattered laughter as everyone considered the long list of such people.

"You are an acquired taste," Joe told him.

Gilbert had returned to the countertop to be with Joe, who now reached out to scratch him behind the ears, changing subjects as he did so. "Okay. Unless somebody has something more to add, I think that wraps it up. Allard has given us a total green light — we can go anywhere, use anyone from the other VBI units, and we have access to discretionary funds to make it happen. That also means that if we screw anything up, it'll be our butts on the barn door, so we need to be careful, courteous, and thorough. We will be dealing with other agencies, entitled political types, hypersensitive true believers, and a growing number of reporters. Sam and I will work out assignments.

"Willy," he added, giving his attention to his least diplomatic subordinate, "let's try to keep you clear of most of that — no teams, no interactions with the press, no task force activity with other cops."

Kunkle opened his mouth to complain, but Joe cut him off. "I want you flying under the radar. Do what you do best. Coordinate with the three of us — especially Sam — but operate solo."

Joe pointed at him for emphasis. "This does not mean you're off the leash. Is that clear? You are to keep in touch and mind your manners. You want me to say this in your language? I want you working where you can do us the least harm and the most good. I'll have enough on my hands without picking up after you."

Willy was clearly pleased. "Works for me."

"It better work for all of us."

CHAPTER SIX

Vermont's governor doesn't get a mansion. Not even a split-level suburban. The official residence is not a cot tucked into a one-window room behind the front office, as rumors have had it. But it's still just a nicely appointed apartment and office suite, located on the top floor of a high-rise, catty-corner to the gold-domed state house. In real-world terms, it's about what a junior lawyer might rate in a mid-market city.

Joe had always thought it was pretty swank. Gail, on the other hand, chose to live in a condo on the edge of town, which, to her viewpoint, was much more appealing than an empty office building after hours.

They were expecting him. A somber receptionist fairly leaped to her feet as he crossed the threshold and escorted him through to an inner office. There, a tall, slim man with graying hair and a look of permanent watchfulness was standing in the middle of the room, looking ready, to Joe's eyes, to either receive a ball or run a block.

"Rob," Joe said, extending his hand in greeting.

Rob Perkins, Gail's chief of staff, responded in kind, his body language easing. "Thanks for coming. This has really shaken her. She's a brick, normally. You know that better than most. But this came out of nowhere."

Joe was nodding sympathetically. "I understand, and I'm definitely wearing kid gloves, but you should know that I'm not just here to lend support. I have an investigation to conduct."

"Of course, of course," Rob said supportively, but Joe could see that the man's watchfulness had returned.

That notwithstanding, Perkins stepped aside and indicated an inner door leading to Gail's office. "She's waiting for you."

Joe hesitated. "You not going to join us? Or her legal counsel?"

Perkins shook his head. "Normally you'd be right. This time, she just wants you." He hesitated before adding, "You should know that she was urged not to see you alone, for propriety's sake."

Joe thanked him and entered the other room, closing the door behind him. Gail was standing by the window, her back to him, and turned at the sound of his entrance. Her face was damp with tears as she approached and buried herself into his shoulder.

"Oh, Joe. Thanks for coming."

He rubbed her back, finding his own words inadequate. "Least I could do. We're old friends, you and I."

She pulled back at the comment and studied him, her cheeks pale and her eyes red-rimmed. "We are, aren't we?"

It was phrased as a question, which he actually appreciated, given how their rapport had waned recently. They had once been very close — lovers, emotional allies, intellectual equals. But life had been hard on them, separately and as a couple. Gail had been raped many years earlier; Joe had come close to death more than once due to his job. The steady amassing of concern, paranoia, and a need for self-preservation eventually took their toll, commingling with Gail's post-traumatic need to make more of her life than she had hitherto.

She had always been a strong-minded woman — a feature Joe had enjoyed. Politics, however, and ironically Gail's uncanny success in practicing it, had, in Joe's estimation, tainted her resolve with some recent mean-spiritedness. He understood that the pressures she'd been facing — including a recent tropical storm that had inundated the state — were cumulatively more than she'd ever encountered before. But it didn't mean that her short temper couldn't hurt all the same.

With all of that crowding his thoughts, he laid a hand alongside her cheek — hoping none of it showed — and reassured her, "Of course we are."

At that, she stepped back and indicated two armchairs facing her desk, instinctively understanding — better than Rob Perkins — the double roles that Joe had to play here.

"You want to ask me questions," she said. "And I want to help."

After they'd both sat, he began with, "First and foremost, how're you holding up? This was your oldest friend, as far as I know, predating even me, and what with every-thing else this office throws at you, my guess is that you don't have the reserves you once did. I appreciate that we both have jobs to do, but how're you doing?"

She didn't answer immediately, glancing around the room first and then settling on his face before responding, "I have a broken heart."

It wasn't said without affect, as by a

woman in shock, nor did she have fresh tears in her eyes. It occupied a middle ground, at once emotional but clear-sighted, as from someone who'd come to grips with permanently losing a part of her anatomy. Joe felt his own throat tighten as a result.

"Susan was my keel," she continued. "Always there, always reliable. I'd come to see her as an extension of my own thinking, as if she was in my head. If she hadn't been so consistently supportive and selfless, I would've thought it was eerie."

She sighed and looked down at her hands. "But it never was. Hers was the kind of love they write about."

Joe exchanged the role of friend for that of the sympathetic investigator. "You were probably among the last to have contact with her, given how often you talked together."

She nodded without shifting her attention. "That's been troubling me almost most of all." Her voice had softened to a distant, far-off tone. "I keep wondering how long it was after we last texted that she was killed. Was it hours? Minutes? Did she break away from writing me to answer the door?"

"What was the nature of the text?" he asked, not revealing that they'd already downloaded the contents of Susan's phone.

She looked up to think. "Some news item she'd read from California. She was such a nerd — always fussing about things no one could control. That's what made her so good. She anticipated everything."

She stopped, arrested by the irony of her own words. "Obviously not everything," she added dully.

"When was this?" he asked.

In answer, she leaned forward and plucked her cell phone from the desk. She located what she was after and handed it over. He read the last of a text string, a cheery, "Later, girlfriend!" It was time- and date-stamped close to midnight two days earlier — the night before Susan was found.

Joe returned the phone. "And you never heard from her all yesterday?"

"No," she said simply. "I texted her a few times. I was starting to get really worried, when Rob told me she'd been found. It wasn't like her not to respond to her messages. She was one of those funny people that way: Her house was a total wreck, which made her look sloppy and disorganized, but she was a fiend about hitting deadlines, getting things done, and keeping everything in order. I couldn't figure out what had happened to her when she didn't answer my texts."

"And you called, too?" Joe asked, not having sent a text in his life, but again remembering what he'd read on the download.

"All I got was her voice mail."

"Do you know where she was when she last contacted you?" he asked. "Was it Brattleboro or here in town, or maybe someplace else?"

A crease appeared between her eyes. "I just assumed it was here, because of the legislature still being in session. But I don't know. I didn't ask, and she didn't say. You think she was somewhere else?"

"I have no idea," he answered honestly. "But speaking of the legislature, were there any ongoing issues that had really heated up?"

She stared at him. "To the point of murder? What do you think we do here?"

Diplomatically, he resisted answering.

Gail was rubbing her forehead, thinking. "The hot-button issues are about the same as always: health care, marijuana legalization, farming issues, cell towers and wind turbines, school control. There's nothing like some of the showdown issues we've had in the past, especially now that the Democrats have such a majority."

"What about the gay/straight debate?" he asked.

Her reaction mirrored Lester's earlier. "*What* debate?" Her face reddened as she continued. "What is it about this? I had no idea you were so narrow-minded. . . ."

"*Stop it,*" he ordered.

His tone brought her up short. She stared at him openmouthed as he went on, "You know very well whether I'm narrow-minded or not. Your best friend — whom you acknowledged was a lesbian — had 'dyke' cut into her chest. Don't you think that might . . ."

This time, she did the interrupting, actually reaching out and touching his mouth with her fingertips. The pain in her eyes arrested his continuing.

"I'm sorry. I'm sorry, Joe. Please."

He took her hand in his and squeezed it gently. "Of course," he said.

She retrieved her hand and covered her face, rubbing her eyes. "I don't know how to handle this," she moaned. "The phones are starting to go crazy, the press is lining up at the door, you're here asking questions, my staff wants to know the party line. And all I want to do is crawl into a hole and mourn my friend in private. It's like all the bullshit after the rape is being stirred up again. I can hardly breathe, and I'm supposed to be the cool-headed chief executive, setting the example."

He rubbed her shoulder as he got to his feet. "Well, at least I can take myself out of the equation. If anything comes up, don't hesitate to reach out, okay?"

He touched her hair with his fingertips as she remained hunched in her chair, and took his leave, still smarting from her outburst.

Parker Murray and Perry Craver were aware of the joking behind their shared alliterative moniker. Their wives had even ordered T-shirts for a squad party two years ago, reading, "I'm the other one," along with a mug shot of the man not wearing the shirt.

Kidding aside, however — and despite their names — they had first met as young men in the academy, when they were both aspiring to take the state police by storm, and had maintained a comfortable, rewarding, almost second-nature friendship that had nurtured them both through the ranks — including when they'd defected as a team to the VBI, attracted by the elite unit's looser structure and higher-profile caseload.

By now, they lived in neighboring towns,

their wives and families were friends, and when they weren't referred to by the catchy patter of their first names, colleagues often fell back onto the more predictable Batman and Robin. Regardess, the bottom line remained the same: They were an instinctively matched pair of good, hardworking detectives, which helped explain why the VBI had taken them on without a quibble.

At the moment, they were mimicking what Lester and Willy had done earlier in Brattleboro, by relieving the guard posted on the top landing of the suite of rooms that Susan Raffner had rented in Montpelier, and preparing to give it a going over.

This wasn't their first visit. When news of Raffner's death had first circulated, Willy Kunkle had called their office to at least get the address sealed off. They'd done a walk-through to check for obvious signs of violence, and to collect any computers or laptops. They'd found just a tablet, which they'd handed over to the crime lab, adding to the other electronics already gathered from Susan's car, purse, and Brattleboro home.

This second visit was to be more methodical and slowly paced. Normally, it would have been conducted by the mobile forensic lab, but they were committed to the cliff top where the body had been discovered — with Raffner's car and primary residence waiting next in line. The executive decision had therefore been made to let Parker and Perry use their training and experience to conduct the search on their own.

It was yet again reflective of a small rural state's ongoing struggle to supply at least a semblance of modern police work, but on a shoestring budget. In many ways, whatever Vermont's flashier high-tech centerpieces may have been — from state-run Web sites to supposedly universal cell service to a truly modern forensic lab — they were too frequently dogged by a quaint and ancient aura, vaguely reminiscent of the late eighteen hundreds.

The house the two detectives entered, stamping their feet free of snow, was at once charming and horrific — if your taste ran to modern spareness. An ancient, worn Victorian, the place had once been a jewel box of a building, filled with several lifetimes' worth of memorabilia. But as with all such cumbersome structures, it had also been built with a full household staff in mind — a detail it was currently lacking.

It belonged to Regina Rockefeller — the ancient, birdlike, wispy-haired homeowner

— who greeted them as she had the first time, by throwing open the heavy front door with surprising dexterity, and twisting her head around so that she could peer up at them from the permanent stoop imposed by an arthritic, hunched back. She looked as if she were forever in search of a lost contact lens.

"My goodness," she said happily. "You boys again? Come to relieve your friend? I'm afraid he's terribly bored up there. I'd keep him company, but that's why I rent the upstairs. My stair-climbing days are long gone. One reason it was such fun having poor Susan living here was that she was forever running up and down, keeping me company and keeping the place alive. This old pile is going to be like a morgue without her. Even if I can find a replacement, I'm not sure it'll ever be the same. Susan was a very special girl. She was also such a help with the snow, shoveling the walk when Useless Fred went and forgot me for the fortieth time. That's what I call him, Useless Fred, because of all the good he comes to, given the money I pay him."

She said all this as if in a single sentence, slowly backing up to allow them to enter. In fact, they imagined that the uniformed Montpelier cop who'd been asked to secure the top floor was less bored than he was frightened of being cornered by his hostess, since they could see him cautiously peering over the railing overlooking the two-story entrance hall where they were standing.

They honored his silent cowering by not waving or speaking out, instead heading toward the elaborate hardwood staircase and letting Miss Rockefeller know that they'd be back down in a while, and maybe enjoy sharing a cup of tea then.

That central hall told the tale of the house — wood panels, stained-glass windows, both soaring overhead to a vaulted, coffered ceiling and an enormous chandelier — suspended like a relic caught between the Middle Ages and *Downton Abbey*. It was all on display from a magisterial staircase that ran along two adjacent walls, leading up to a landing suitable for an operatic diva. And yet, dust covered everything, the dirty windows demanded compensatory lighting at midday, and enough bulbs were burned out in the chandelier to render such effort futile. The rugs were threadbare, boxes were piled everywhere, there was a scent of mustiness touched by mildew in the air, and Perry noticed a few rodent droppings scattered along the treads as he climbed. The hired help of yore was being sorely missed.

"Damn," he muttered. "See that? And her name's Rockefeller?"

"That means rich, bro," Parker told him. "Not tidy."

They found the patrol cop standing just out of sight from below. "You the VBI guys?" he asked.

"One and only," Parker answered. He jerked his thumb over his shoulder. "She got you cornered?"

The man only half smiled. "Pretty much. I can't use the bathroom up here, 'cause it's a crime scene, and every time I go downstairs, she's waiting with that nonstop-talking thing. She's a nice lady. I'm not saying she's not. But she just never takes a breath, you know?"

"Yep. Noticed that."

Perry was looking around, mostly studying the floor. Parker tilted his head in his direction. "He's afraid of giant rats, or maybe cockroaches."

The cop laughed. "Nah. It's better up here. This part's messy, but Raffner knew how to vacuum."

"Thank God for that," Perry said softly.

"Okay," Parker addressed the cop. "You're off the hook for a while. We're going to poke around. We'll call the PD when we're done so they can send somebody to sit on the place again. With any luck, you'll be off duty, huh?"

"Got that right," the man said, passing them by and heading for the stairs. He paused a moment to point to a door blocking the distant hallway. "That's as far as it goes, just so you know. That door's locked. This side was Raffner's apartment; past there is someone else's. The old lady rents rooms above the garage, too."

Parker nodded. "Thanks." He waited until the patrolman was out of earshot before he made an aside to his partner, "Maybe not so rich, either? I didn't know the other side was a rental, too."

But Perry wasn't so quick to agree. "Maybe that's why she *is* rich — her and the whole family." He tapped the side of his head. "Smart, if you don't mind strangers wandering around your house."

"Don't guess she does," Parker agreed as they heard Regina Rockefeller burst into a volley of chatter as their colleague hove into view downstairs.

They began from where they stood, putting down the kits they'd brought with them and struggling into gloves, Tyvek suits, and booties before spreading out and scrutinizing the worn rug of the landing, sometimes going down on all fours and using hand lights to see better. Compared to their prior visit here — to take a glance and grab the electronics — this stay promised to last a lot longer.

Raffner's rented suite came to a bathroom and three rooms, which she'd split up into a bedroom, an office, and something resembling a hodgepodge, office/living room. There was no kitchen — probably making the whole rental an illegal arrangement — but there was a hot plate in the bathroom and a microwave in the general room.

These college-style touches didn't stand out. As Willy and Lester had found earlier in Brattleboro, so Parker and Perry discovered that Susan Raffner, despite her prominence as a mover and shaker, had the interior decorative skills of a teenager.

But, to echo the Montpelier cop's parting observation, at least she'd known how to vacuum. For this, Perry was most grateful, especially as he stretched out prone to check under furniture.

They took hours, during which they collected files, boxes, letters, notebooks, notes by the dozen, and a pile of mail. They also found an ample pound of marijuana — a huge lode compared to the baggie that Willy

Kunkle had gingerly examined in Brattle-boro.

The prize, however, was something Parker found in a cardboard box labeled RECYCLE! It was a single page with a hand-printed note, folded and roughly stuffed back into the torn envelope in which it had been delivered.

"There are times I love this job," he announced, sitting cross-legged on the floor before the box, next to Raffner's desk, office paper all around him and this letter in his gloved hand.

"Got something?" Perry asked, deep into the bottom drawer of a nearby filing cabinet.

Parker pulled an evidence envelope from the pocket of his suit, but paused before filling it to show off his prize. "Read that," he said.

Perry oriented the letter right-side up. "Dykes shood die," he read aloud.

Your a disgrase to wimmen + mothers + GOD. Burn in HELL.

He nodded thoughtfully. "Not sure his English teacher would approve, but he makes his point." He flipped the page over before handing it back. "Too bad he didn't sign it."

Parker waved the envelope. "Who says he didn't? I bet he licked the flap. There's no stamp, but his fingerprints have got to be all over this."

"No stamp?"

Parker handed over the envelope, saying, "Looks like the corner was torn off when she opened it. It's pretty mangled."

Perry shook his head in wonderment as he studied it. "Unbelievable — a return address. Where do they find these geniuses?"

"I know, right? It's just a PO box, but better than nothing." He secured his find into the evidence pouch after Perry returned it, scribbling the case number on the outside, along with his name and a note about where it had been located.

"How deep in the recycling did you find that?" Perry asked.

"Near the top, which fits it having arrived a few days ago, maybe."

"You look for the torn-off corner, too?"

"Yeah," Parker said, his voice disappointed. "No luck. Probably fell on the floor and got thrown out."

"I can't believe it's Newport," Perry mused.

Parker grinned. "Yeah. You think they'd be happy to sleep with anything warm up there, lesbians included."

Parker scowled at him. "You know I come from near there."

Perry just chuckled.

CHAPTER SEVEN

Sammie Martens looked up from the paperwork spread across the dining table, her subconscious disturbed by one of those vague ripples in one's universe. She glanced at her watch. It was late. Emma had been asleep for hours. It was Willy, she realized. He was in the house, where he'd normally be tucked away, engaged in some project, but her senses told her that he was up to something else.

She rose and quietly walked through their neat, spare home, located at the top of a semicircular block of similar houses in West Brattleboro. It had been Willy's when he'd lived on his own, and in large part remained so, at least in spirit. Of Willy's multiple demons, one was a quasi-obsessional need for cleanliness and a lack of possessions, which Sam thought stemmed from his past or his occupation, or both. Either way, it resulted in an environment in which Sam certainly, and Emma by proxy, had to step with some care. Willy wasn't overbearing about it — he made an effort not to show his near-visible discomfort. But he would tidy up behind them, which in a way was a blessing. Sam hadn't touched a broom, a rag, or even washed the dishes since moving in.

A friend had asked her if any of this made her feel like a guest in her own home. But that was where Sam's emotional needs almost perfectly complemented Willy's. Given a youth of chaos, violence, and confusion, where she'd craved not being at the center of a whirlwind, here she cherished inhabiting a neutral space. For her, their neat-and-tidy home amounted to a haven of calm.

By instinct, she went directly to Emma's halfway-open door and peered in, not surprised to see Willy lying stretched out on the rug, parallel to the crib, staring meditatively at the slowly revolving mobile hanging over his daughter's sleeping form.

Without a word, Sam slipped through the doorway and lay next to him, hooking a pinkie finger around his.

He turned his head toward her. She stayed quiet, looking back. When the two of them had gotten together, years ago, no one except Joe had given them hope. Joe, typically, hadn't even registered surprise. This Sam had interpreted as the one vote of confidence she might have actively sought out otherwise. Willy hadn't expressed any need for acceptance, of course, but she thought that he, too, had appreciated Joe's blessing.

It wasn't lost on her that two grown adults had wanted the approval of a man who was not a family member and was also their boss. But such was the nature of what their small squad had become — versus their actual families.

By extension, however, it occurred to her that even Joe's opinion no longer mattered now. Emma's arrival had marked a passage toward independence and self-confidence, if one occasionally jarred by doubt. She and Willy worked hard to maintain a balance within this house, even encouraged by the challenges that had hounded them since youth.

"Ice cream?" he whispered to her.

They moved to the kitchen, where she let him prepare two small bowls — frozen yogurt for her, a cloying and layered concoction of Cherry Garcia, nuts, sprinkles, and maple syrup for him.

"How's the campaign going?" he asked,

busying himself.

As requested during the staff meeting at Joe's house, Sam was trying to organize the forces at their disposal.

"It's tricky right now," she said. "We have so little to go on, while we have a growing chorus of people demanding results."

"Damn peanut gallery," he groused.

"I've been figuring out how many people just to assign to media relations. Joe told me that the national news guys are already pounding at the door."

"Tell him I volunteer," Willy said. "And I'll do it solo."

"Right." She laughed. "Like the Unabomber, maybe."

He placed the bowls on the kitchen table and sat opposite her. "You wanna waste manpower, be my guest. Before this is done, I have a feeling we're gonna be yanking troops from media relations and putting them in the trenches."

"Really?" she asked, genuinely surprised.

He looked at her knowingly. "I'm not the only one. Why do you think the boss gave me the floater job? He's smelling a rat here, just like I am."

Newport occupies the southernmost tip of a long, skinny lake, three-quarters of which lies in Quebec, Canada, and all of which is saddled with the tongue-twisting name of Lake Memphremagog. Once a logging and railroad town, Newport is smaller than nearby St. Johnsbury, but brags of a more picturesque setting. This is a good thing, since tourist recreation has arguably become the city's biggest reason for being. Otherwise it is a blue-collar community, fortunately located near Jay Peak, the thirty-mile-long lake, and Canada itself.

It also caps Vermont's fabled Northeast Kingdom, an area whose nominal capital is Newport's aforementioned rival "St. J," some forty miles to the south. The Kingdom — labeled thus most famously in a 1949 speech proclaiming its beauties — is isolated, heavily forested, and almost empty, even by Vermont standards. It is also heralded as a bastion of sometimes eccentric or isolationist inhabitants.

Vermonters were proud of the Kingdom and its quirky lore, enjoying its hunting and wilderness offerings, while perhaps paying less attention to its financial straits and social woes. Natives eager to earn a living often moved away, while people seeking refuge from the wider world came to settle — or tried to until the harsh weather or the economy drove them off.

Finding that some anti-lesbian hatemonger had an address within the Kingdom had been disappointing to Joe Gunther, who had been introduced to the region by a favorite uncle during summers long past. But, sadly, it had not been a huge surprise.

Lester Spinney was at the wheel as the snow-covered countryside unfolded before them, the enormous white slab of the frozen lake coming gradually into view. Joe liked Lester to drive, as if the latter's steady, dependable spirit leached into how the car handled the road.

"It's fun to be back," Les said. "Remember when you and I worked that old case together? I was still with VSP and you were on assignment for the local state's attorney? That was years before the VBI was even a glint in anyone's eye."

Joe did remember, as he did so many other cases across this small state. By the time he had reached his current place in the law enforcement pecking order, it was easy to believe that he'd either worked with or met a majority of his fellow colleagues. Spinney, nevertheless, had been a standout, both because of his storklike appearance and his near-bulletproof good cheer. Native-born, like Joe, he carried a reassuring sense of being where he belonged.

"Who did you get out of our St. J office to work on this?" Joe asked.

"To convince the post office to cough up the PO box holder? Cila Lewis," Lester answered. "You know her?"

Joe thought for a moment, priding himself on knowing all of VBI's special agents. "We met a couple of times. She came from the Burlington PD, didn't she?"

"Yup. Her hubby wanted to try farming, and the best land deal he could find was up here, so rather than commute, she applied to join us. Worked out pretty good for both of them — and us, too," he added. "I hear she does a hell of a job around here. She's a tough little bugger."

The description helped Joe to sharpen his memory of her, which was a relief.

"You're an old-time farmer, Joe," Lester went on. "What chances do you give them?"

Joe glanced at him. "I'm the son of a farmer, and I got out as soon as I could. My brother did, too — became a butcher. Farming's a hard life. The long winters and short seasons this far north don't help."

Spinney drifted toward the interstate's off-ramp — two exits shy of the Canadian border. Joe took advantage of the brief silence to admire a brightly painted silo in the distance. A couple of hours earlier, they'd actually driven by where he was born and brought up.

His brother, Leo, still lived on what was left of the farm, with their ancient but spry mother. Joe hadn't mentioned it to Lester, savoring the memories in private. He might have realized early on that the farming life was not his, but that didn't mean that he hadn't loved being a part of it. His rural heritage — truly springing from the soil of this unusual, hardworking little state — had given him not just an identity, but a sense of moral sturdiness that had served him well through the decades.

"I'm starting to wonder what life isn't hard," Lester reacted, negotiating the exit ramp and aiming them down the long, broad Newport feeder road. "Not mine," he added quickly. "But certainly for most of the company we keep."

They reached Route 105, swung south and crossed the bridge at the grain elevators into the city itself, turning away from the huge lake. The modern post office was on Coventry Street — its low-slung, bland, and efficient architecture a far cry from some of the more distinguished-looking buildings farther downtown.

"There she is," Lester said, taking them

into the snowbank-lined parking lot.

A short, compact woman — her dimensions exaggerated by a bulky down overcoat — stepped away from her car and walked over to Lester's window as he rolled to a stop.

"Hey, guys," she greeted them.

"Cila," Joe replied, waving at her across Lester. "Good to see you."

"How's the farming life?" Les asked her.

"You don't wanna know," she told them.

"We get lucky with that PO box?" Joe asked, at once getting to the point and reacting to the wash of cold air that was pouring through the open window.

"Yup. Belongs to Nathan Fellows — not one of our brightest citizens, thank God."

"How so?" Joe asked.

" 'Cause I'd say he fits what we're looking for," she answered. "I ran him through Spillman and the fusion center while I was waiting, and he's up to his neck with everything from gay bashing to white supremacy to National Socialism — meaning Nazis to us lowbrows."

"He violent?"

"He's had his moments — bar fights, assaults, domestic violence, disturbing the peace. Done time for some of the above. If he's killed anybody, we don't know about it. I called one of my Newport PD contacts, and he asked around. Fellows is a known player, but mostly for being an idiot. He's got the look down." She pulled a photograph from somewhere inside her Michelin Man coat and handed it over.

"Tatts," she resumed. "Shaved head, piercings, motorcycle tough-guy clothes, complete with chains. Bad dude, one-oh-one."

Joe looked at the mug shot in Lester's hand. Lewis had pretty much nailed it.

"Where's he live?" he asked.

"Not far," she said. "Edge of town. I drove by it. It's your predictable dump, surrounded by trees, not far from the quarry. He's got maybe four Vermont planters out front, and the usual assortment of trash, scrap, and mystery piles."

Vermont planters were abandoned cars — "parts cars," in some people's parlance — but only if you like your parts corroded beyond recognition.

"He's gotta be a gun nut," Lester said.

"He's not supposed to be, legally," Cila replied. "Not according to his conditions of release. But we all know what that's worth. He could have three grenade launchers and a machine gun in there."

Joe knew that to be more than a one-liner.

"Okay," he said. "I don't really want to do a knock-and-talk — not with so many unknowns."

"And a man's house is his castle," suggested Lester leadingly.

"He work?" Joe asked Cila.

She looked surprised. "Yes, believe it or not. For a pallet- and box-making company, off exit twenty-eight, between here and Derby, in the middle of a whole miracle mile/industrial park thing."

"You think he's there now?"

"Could be. When I drove by his place, I noticed his truck was missing, and he only has the one vehicle registered to his name. If nothing else, we could check out the factory's parking lot and see what we see."

"You bring the local PD up to speed about what we're up to?" Joe wanted to know.

"Yup. They're ready if we need backup."

He pondered that a moment. "What the hell? Have 'em join us — more the merrier."

She left her car at the post office after making those arrangements and rode with them, Lester heading northeast out of Newport along Route 105. Followed by two police cruisers, they were aimed inland, however, and quickly lost the mesmerizing lake behind them, exchanging it for the flat, bland, snow-covered terrain suggestive of the Stanstead Plain across the border in Quebec.

Approaching the interstate and Derby beyond, they came upon the area Cila Lewis had described: the standard and ubiquitous American offering of mall stores, gas stations, car dealerships, and — set back from the road — small industrial operations such as the one employing Nathan Fellows. Lewis directed them down a service road between a fast-food restaurant and a gas station, toward a long, featureless, metal-sided building, its flat roof covered with a couple of feet of snow.

A low mountain range of snow had been scraped from the parking lot and shoved to the edges, where it took on the look of a row of colorless icy hedgerows.

Spinney slowed, prowled along the rows of serried cars until Cila said, "There. That's it."

Joe glanced at the two of them. "We good, then? Direct approach?"

"Works for me," Lester answered, heading for an open spot.

Aside from the usual row of loading-dock doors, there was only one entrance to the building facing them, and from its battered, half-boarded-over appearance, this company was clearly not out to impress retail customers.

Leaving the local cops outside, they found two women inside a comparatively small room, sitting at cluttered desks, and surrounded by the requisite office paraphernalia of printers, computers, copiers, cabinets, and the rest. All of it was illuminated by parallel strips of overhead fluorescent tubing, and all of it was dusty, dingy, and — to Joe's eyes at least — depressing.

But not, apparently, to the one woman who looked up as they entered. She gave them a bright smile and an upbeat, "Hello. How may we help you?"

Joe almost hated showing her his badge and watching her expression melt as she listened to him say, "Hi. We're from the police. Wondering if we might have a quick chat with one of your employees."

That caught the attention of the other woman, who had been staring at her computer screen. "Who?" she asked.

"Nathan Fellows. He working today?"

The second woman gave a sour expression, muttered, "Shoulda known," and returned to her screen.

The cheerful one answered. "Nate? Sure." She reached for her phone, adding, "I'll call

114

the floor."

"That's okay," Joe stopped her. "We'd actually prefer to just go out there and find him ourselves, if that's all right."

"I bet," the sour one said, as if to herself.

Her companion's smile became a little stiff. "Well, I guess. I mean, I don't know. We're not supposed to let people back there. You know: insurance."

"Jesus, Betty," the surly one burst out. "They're cops. They're not gonna sue us. Let 'em take the jerk out."

Lester laughed at the comment. "We probably won't go that far. We just want to talk to the guy."

"More's the pity," she growled, and dropped back out of the conversation.

Joe moved on presumption and raised the counter section that gave them access to the desk area. All three of them filed through and gathered around Betty.

"Do you have a map of the building's layout?" Joe asked pleasantly. "Just so you can show us where Nate's likely to be working." He gestured toward the door behind her.

"Oh," she said. "We have a floor plan showing the maintenance schedule for the machinery. That might work." She pulled back and opened the drawer at her waist, pawing around until she retrieved what he was after. She tapped on a section of the floor plan with her finger. "Here. At the planers."

"And where are the exits?"

She indicated a few more spots. The three cops studied the map. Cila pointed to an exit not far from where they'd parked. "I'll go around outside and position myself here. This must be how most of them go to and from the lot, correct?"

Betty nodded without comment.

"Okay," Joe agreed. "And deploy the others appropriately. I'll go in through here and work down the center aisle. Looks like it'll give me cover till I'm pretty close. Les? Why don't you take the other angle and cut off access to the bay doors?"

"Roger that."

Betty was looking from one of them to the other as if they'd just been beamed down from outer space.

Joe laid his hand on her shoulder. "Just routine," he said dismissively. "Keeps things nice and peaceful if you plan ahead."

"Okay," she said doubtfully.

Joe straightened and addressed both women. "A wild guess is that Nate is not your favorite guy on the floor."

The other secretary looked at him pityingly. "Really?"

"What's he like?" Joe asked her.

"He's an obnoxious loser peckerhead."

"Our kind of people," Lester said.

"What's he done to deserve that description?"

"He's not very nice," Betty volunteered.

"God, Betty," her friend burst out. "He's a pig. Hates women, hates minorities, hates everybody he works with, walks around with all that Nazi crap tattooed to his scrawny body. He doesn't wash, his breath stinks, he's foulmouthed and crude. I've felt more for some roadkill than I feel for him. Make sure you arrest him and haul his ass out of here."

None of the cops responded for a few seconds. "Okay," Cila finally said. "I'll circle around."

"Thank you," Joe said to the women. "We'll get out of your hair. Just so you know, chances are he won't even talk with us and we'll be back on the road in ten minutes."

They barely heard Betty's colleague whisper, "Whatever," as Joe and Lester crossed to the far door.

At the last moment, Joe looked back to ask, "What's he wearing, by the way, just so we know what we're looking for?"

"Black," was the abrupt answer. "Never wears anything else."

The contrast between the office and the manufacturing floor was abrupt and jarring. The office was a hyper-insulated shell tacked onto the building's front door like a limpet to a rock. The rest of the structure was a single large room with crisscrossing girders overhead and rows of pendulous sodium lights — all of it vibrating with the ear-splitting orchestration of dozens of screaming machines. Saws, planers, drills, pneumatic hammers, sanders, and forklift motors all contributed to the clamor. Everywhere they looked, Les and Joe saw people walking around or laboring at their stations equipped with industrial-grade hearing, head, and eye protection.

Defeated by the din, Joe signaled to Lester to head off according to plan, while he walked down an aisle between stacked pallet parts, aiming for where the planers were located.

Nate Fellows turned out to be easy to spot, even with the camouflaging effect of the protective equipment. As Willy might have observed, it probably had something to do with the large black swastika tattooed on the back of the man's neck.

Joe paused at the end of his aisle to allow

Spinney to get into position, before venturing onto the open floor, heading toward Fellows while pretending not to noticc him. Joe was too experienced not to know the consequences of prematurely revealing himself.

But his caution couldn't compete with his quarry's paranoia. Halfway into feeding a board into a howling splinter-spewing planer, Fellows looked up at Joe as if attracted by a bright light, and without hesitation abandoned the board and took off as if startled by a pistol shot. The board blew back, skittering across the concrete floor, causing several other workers to dance out of the way, their shouts overwhelmed by the surrounding industrial howl.

"Damn," Joe swore, and broke into a run, seeing Lester do the same.

The upside was that Fellows was headed toward the exit they'd anticipated him using; the downside was that neither one of them could beat the noise and let Cila know what was coming at her.

Which was when Joe saw Fellows reach under his bedraggled wool jacket as he ran and extract a gun from somewhere near the small of his back. Both cops pulled their own weapons as nearby workers began scattering in alarm.

Fellows hit the metal door like a linebacker, causing a burst of outside light to flash against the corrugated wall. Spinney got there next, pausing only a split second in case Fellows might be waiting. Joe arrived a moment later, in time to hear the stutter of two gunshots stepping on each other's heels.

He found Fellows motionless and spread-eagled on a bloodstained splash of red snow, his gun ten feet from his outstretched hand, and Cila crouched and clutching her arm, Spinney and two cops by her side and beginning to catch her weight as she slowly toppled over.

CHAPTER EIGHT

"A fucking disaster."

"The docs're saying Cila Lewis will come through without any permanent damage," Joe said.

Bill Allard glared at him, his years as a no-nonsense road trooper showing through his administrator's thin veneer. "*Fine.* Which has nothing to do with the price of eggs, as if you didn't know it. The fact that one of our own didn't get killed in this mess isn't going to make the headlines. *Her* shooting *him* will see to that."

Allard pointed out the window of his office, despite there being nothing to see besides a distant brick wall. "Have you ever seen so many news trucks and reporters camped out front of this building? Ever?"

Joe didn't respond. In truth, he hadn't. And Susan's spectacular murder combined with a related death in a police shoot-out was only part of it. Lately, Vermont had been regularly leading the news roundups — Gail's dramatic and unconventional gubernatorial victory a couple of years ago, Tropical Storm Irene's devastation of the state shortly thereafter, and several recent *New York Times* stories about Vermont's heroin epidemic immediately popped to mind.

Allard was still ranting. "And Christ knows what's next, right? I have no doubt your maniac poster child Kunkle is out there as we speak, cooking up something. What do you have him doing, anyhow?"

"He's in the trenches with everybody else," Joe answered vaguely.

Bill Allard finally calmed down. "What *are* you going to do next?" he asked, his tantrum swept away as quickly as it had arrived.

"Try to connect Nate Fellows to Raffner's murder. That would be the shortest distance between the dots. I've already got people seeing what he was doing when she was killed, as well as interviewing his pals and associates, and tearing his house apart. A guy with that much attitude is not gonna be self-effacing. If he did it, he told somebody, and we should know about it, probably within twenty-four hours."

"And if he didn't?"

Joe shrugged. "None of this has slowed

down our checking her background, associates, and activities. That's still going full guns. We are starting to run into resistance, though — just so you're aware."

Allard had settled back at his desk and now looked up at him suspiciously. "What kind of resistance? From the governor? She's the one telling us to damn the budget."

Joe was shaking his head. "Not from her. In her book, we can't do enough, fast enough. It's from some of Susan's inner circle. I know a few of them from decades back, and a couple can get pretty extreme. They're starting to suggest we're up to something more than a murder investigation."

Allard's face darkened again. "What? All this is some conspiracy? To what end? The fucking woman is *dead,* for crying out loud. Seems like her buddies ought to be pissed at whoever did it."

He rubbed his face with both hands. "Why're we never the good guys?" he asked rhetorically.

Gail scanned the faces of the key staffers gathered in her office. Alice Drim, her personal assistant, general factotum, and volunteer reelection manager; Rob Perkins, her omnipresent chief of staff; Joan Renaud, her legal counsel; and Kayla Robinson, her press secretary. Solid people, loyal and committed to her and the office she occupied. Alice and Kayla were the youngsters, both gangly and in their late twenties; Rob was tall and middle-aged, like Gail herself; and Joan was the old hand, although her looks made her appear more wizened than she deserved.

To a person, they had past governmental experience, for the pro tem or the house speaker or even some politician from out-of-state. They were professionals at what they did — and not personal friends, as Gail had been used to as a Brattleboro politician — with the contradictory effect that their skills sometimes made her feel like a virtual amateur, despite her own achievements.

Right now, for example, reading Renaud's severe demeanor, Gail knew she was in the doghouse, but in the eyes of a woman far too polite to ever voice her disapproval. Joan was old school, which struck Gail as ironic, given her own reputation as a maverick. But a smart maverick, Gail liked to think, and therefore ill-inclined to have an equally nonconformist — and possibly careless — lawyer. Still, at moments like this, following Gail's impulsive — and unmonitored —

meeting with Joe earlier, she knew that she'd stepped on Joan's sense of caution and propriety.

She wasn't really concerned, of course. She was partially indulging in body language interpretation solely to get her brain back on track. In fact, she didn't want to be here, or to be having a staff meeting. Ever since receiving the news about Susan, she'd been stuck with a humming in her head as if a bumblebee had dropped into her ear. It served as accompaniment to the steady ache in her chest.

"Governor," Rob began, "before we begin, I just wanted to say how sorry we are for your loss. Senator Raffner was an ally, a friend, and a trusted confidante."

"And pushy and opinionated," Kayla added with a supportive smile.

"And usually right," Alice finished gamely, like the second half of an amateur comedy team.

"Thank you." Gail returned with a smile, feeling its artificiality stretching her skin.

Rob got straight to his first item for discussion. "Governor, I just got a call that there was a police shoot-out in Newport. A man named Nathan Fellows was killed who the VBI believes may have had a hand in Senator Raffner's murder."

Gail stared at him, thoughts of Joe flooding her mind. "Is everyone else all right?"

"One of their agents was hit — Cila Lewis — but she'll be fine. She was actually the one who killed Fellows in self-defense. He started shooting when they approached to question him. Some neo-Nazi."

"And they're sure he was the man who killed Susan?" Gail asked.

Here, the answer was vaguer. Joan Renaud supplied it, in her legal capacity. "Governor, I was in on this phone conversation. The police are obviously keeping a lid on things for the time being — although I suspect that will only last a few more hours — but they were focusing on Fellows for largely circumstantial reasons. Now that he's dead, they're doing their best to see if they can connect him to Senator Raffner's death, but it's far from certain."

Gail absorbed this, fighting the urge to ask questions she knew they couldn't answer. She moved on, therefore, by asking, "What's next?"

Taking her cue, Rob continued. "The senator's memorial services are scheduled for two days from now — one here and one in Brattleboro. It seemed the best way to reach most of her friends without putting too many on the road."

"Letters, cards, and e-mails have been coming in like nobody's business," Alice added. "All saying how much she meant to everyone."

Kayla Robinson leaned forward and placed a couple of sheets of paper on Gail's desk, her strong, angular features poorly served by a severe haircut. "I came up with a few thoughts you might like to use in your speech. We assumed you'd want to say something."

"Which doesn't mean you're obligated," Rob said immediately. "Everyone would understand if you simply attended."

"No," Gail reassured them, picking up the sheets without looking at them. "I'll speak. Thank you."

Kayla took advantage of the gesture to say, "Governor, along the lines of dealing with the press about this, was there anything said between you and Special Agent Gunther that we should know about?"

Gail shifted her gaze back to the inscrutable Joan, who was writing a note to herself, or pretending to, eyes downcast. Gail imagined the conversation that had preceded this meeting, where they'd worked out how best to negotiate the emotional shoals surrounding her.

"He asked when Susan and I had last been

in touch. I told him it was via text and that nothing of substance was discussed."

Kayla opened her mouth to follow up, but Renaud made a barely perceptible motion with her hand that stilled her. A silence settled onto the room, obliging Gail to add, "He also asked how I was holding up. We are old friends." She hesitated, aware of the value of saying too little versus too much, but then said, "I told him that she'd been my keel — the love of a lifetime."

The stillness in the room reminded her of a time in childhood, when she'd taken a dare and grabbed hold of a rope strung horizontally over a pond. The goal had been to reach the far side dry-footed — moving hand-over-hand — but she'd tired and stopped, and gradually become aware of her ebbing strength, along with the guarantee that she'd eventually drop into the cold, dark water.

She'd been paralyzed briefly, caught between inevitability and the growing realization that — although the outcome would be the same — she did have the power to willfully open her hands and choose action over fate. The fall to the water had thus been transformed from resignation to excitement, and her surfacing from the cold depths with arms held high afterward had been accompanied by a surprising sense of self-confidence.

She watched the people before her absorbing her words, and applying their own interpretations. With the smallest click of something true falling into place, she sat back and waited, the fascination of an outside observer pushing through her grief, if only briefly.

Rob Perkins — the most seasoned of the group, and certainly the one who was most experienced with the political game's rougher aspects — was the first to speak. "Is that what you were thinking of saying at the memorial, Governor?"

His dispassionate tone notwithstanding, Gail could see the wariness in his eyes. Despite the newness of her administration — her first reelection campaign was just beginning, following the Vermont standard of a two-year term — they'd experienced a number of high-profile struggles, some of them self-inflicted.

"You have an objection?" she asked neutrally, studying their discomfort as if eavesdropping on the conversation.

But he shook his head. "Not with the sentiment, certainly." He chose his next words carefully. "But I think we all work better with twenty-twenty vision. . . . And that one's choice of words does matter."

"Meaning, was I having an affair with Susan Raffner?" Gail asked, her growing decisiveness mirroring that feeling when she'd surfaced from the pond.

"That's none of our business," Renaud said quickly. "Nor should it be of any relevance."

Gail nodded in acknowledgment. "I grant you that in legal terms, Joan. But in fairness to Rob, let's acknowledge the conclusions that've already been drawn — or which'll be drawn soon enough: Susan was a lesbian, she was murdered, and she was put on display as an antigay statement. She was also the best friend and political adviser of the single, never-married, female governor of the state. You think I don't know how many people already think I'm gay?"

"That doesn't mean you have to acknowledge the gossip," Kayla countered. "People also complain that you're rich, or from New York, or Jewish, or who knows what else. The governor is as much an institution as a person, and one thing that Vermont's always done well is to leave the personalities of its politicians at the door when it comes to public debate."

"I agree," Rob stated. "And I don't think that particular question has even vaguely reached the status of needing to be addressed. Like Joan said, it's nobody's business."

"It is mine, though," Gail told them, grateful to be taking these first steps. "Because I did love her, and we were lovers."

She noticed Alice Drim's cheeks flush slightly, and felt a sympathetic pang of regret. She'd heard through the office grapevine of Alice's recent breakup with her longtime boyfriend.

Rob recognized that they'd just ventured beyond the perimeters of mere political debate. "Are you sure that's what you want to say, Governor?"

"Susan's death is a high-profile murder case with an apparently sensationalist motive," Gail replied. "She'll become a tawdry tabloid headline instead of a life that deserved much more." She addressed Kayla Robinson directly. "You're the media expert, Kayla. What do you really think's going to be remembered about her after all the dust has settled?"

To her credit, Kayla responded with her own question: "Will your coming out change any of that?"

"It could even fuel the fire," Alice said quietly.

"My 'coming out,' as you put it, would allow me to honestly and openly speak to her qualities as a friend, a political leader, and a fellow human being, while relegating her sexual orientation to secondary status."

The group's universal body language spoke clearly of its disagreement.

Rob tried introducing a broader perspective. "Governor, I don't think there's a person here who doesn't share your view of the senator, or doubt your feelings for her. None of us wants her memory tarnished or her legacy eclipsed by the way she died. That being said, could I kick around a few purely political considerations?"

Gail's instinctive reaction was to say no. She was in no mood to be analytical about an emotion powerful enough to override all rational debate. For the first time since hearing of Susan's death, she was feeling positive. But she nodded — if just barely — and answered, "Of course." This was, after all, what remained in Susan's wake: the team that she'd helped Gail to select, and who represented the support group she saw more frequently than anyone else.

"Right now," Rob began, "there's nothing forcing us to do anything hasty — no tropical storm or breaking political scandal. I'm suggesting that we pause to weigh the pros and cons of whatever it is you may be considering." He smiled supportively. "It's not often we get the luxury of time."

But, reading her closed expression, he knew that any such luxury was provisional at best. He therefore kept going without waiting for a response. "You might, for example, reconsider using a phrase like, 'She was my keel,' which — regardless of its truth — suggests that you no longer have one. More to the point, you could voice your long-standing support and backing for the LGBTQ community, while responding to any direct questions concerning your private relationship to Susan as being just that — private."

Gail remained silent.

"Being that this is Vermont," he forged on, "I doubt the subject will even come up, but certainly that kind of statement would mark the beginning and the end of it." He held up a finger. "On the other hand, if you do choose to honor her memory as you're suggesting, I think we should be prepared for a national reaction that might do exactly what you're dreading."

"Go on," she said without inflection.

"What I'm envisioning has both good and bad aspects. People like Ellen DeGeneres will probably want to give you airtime; the Gay and Lesbian Victory Fund might offer advice and funding sources for your campaign; and others will come in to help, too. On the other hand, the Rush Limbaughs, the neo-Nazis, and whoever else you can name will come out of the woodwork and do their best to turn your loving gesture into a three-ring circus."

He kept going: "What we sometimes forget up here in our isolated woods is that on one level we're fully one-fiftieth of the entire United States. If one of our senators switches parties, like Jim Jeffords did in '01, it can cause as big a ripple as if our governor announced she was gay. People'll take notice. Keep in mind that in dozens of states across this country, you can still be legally fired if you're gay. It's a big deal, and it could completely swamp Susan's memory and your own ability to mourn her loss as you're hoping to."

As he'd been speaking, Gail's mind had wandered inward, retracing her history with Susan, with Joe, her years in Vermont, and her sometimes tumultuous journey to this office, including the life-changing rape — most of which no one could have anticipated, and none of which had been influenced by the things Rob was mentioning.

Whether it had been privilege or self-confidence or stubbornness or fate, Gail's motivators had never revolved around what people thought of her. She'd been calculating at times, even ruthless, she conceded. She recognized moments when she'd pushed Joe beyond his own moral code, and when her ego had chosen principle over ethics. But throughout, she believed she'd never weighed or protected her own image.

Perhaps noticing her distraction, Rob shifted tack slightly. "Let's talk local for a moment. I know I said that your coming out would have little effect within Vermont, but that doesn't mean we should ignore its impact. There's still a huge number of quiet, pissed off, conservative people in this state — our own silent minority — even if they often don't vote because they think themselves outnumbered."

"Like the 'Take Back Vermont' conservative movement a few years ago?" Kayla Robinson suddenly asked. "Their numbers were surprisingly big."

"Exactly," Rob seconded her. "The liberals were amazed, as if these thousands of salt-of-the-earth people had all of a sudden sprung out of nowhere." He waved his hand to encompass the room. "We liberals are constantly forgetting about those folks. We better not if you're dead set on making this move."

"When I make it," she corrected him, working to control her resentment at being lectured.

He let that one lie. "I'm talking our equivalent of the soccer moms," he pressed. "Traditionally minded, churchgoing or God-observant women who feel threatened not just by gender-bending concepts, but even the notion of a woman being unmarried after thirty. I've heard them called 'ballot box bigots,' although I think that's being overly judgmental, but they and their like-minded friends are a force to consider."

"May I ask a question, Governor?" Joan Renaud asked, her expression making it clear that she really didn't want to.

Gail nodded, meeting her eyes.

"This is not a legal question. In fact, it's none of my business, but given your apparent conviction and the fact that you seem to be inviting all viewpoints, I was wondering if you were going to announce that you are lesbian or bisexual?"

Everybody stared at her, making Renaud shrug ever so slightly and stammer, "Well, it looked like now was the time to ask."

Rob laughed self-consciously, aware of how his counsel had approached being a harangue, but not wanting it to be derailed by what he considered a side issue. "If what I'm anticipating happens, then that's the sort of question we should come to expect. Governor," he emphasized, addressing her eye-to-eye. "Some people get outed, others get caught, still others don't care about the consequences. But you are a high-profile, fast-rising chief executive. We all work for you here, and we've been in the trenches with you. Am I wrong in assuming that you are a woman of ambition? Would you turn down an offer of political advancement? Something beyond the governorship?"

Gail still didn't respond, but her lips were now pursed.

He kept at it, nearing recklessness. "I don't think so. Your ascent has been meteoric. Another reason that the national press is circling overhead — even without hearing what you're considering — is that you've already appeared on the 'stars to watch' lists of several publications. You'll have to live with this choice forever, 'cause everybody's going to be watching like you wouldn't believe. And with this, you will have given them license to talk about the one thing that's normally awkward to discuss, which is sex."

At last, he stopped. The void left in his

wake caused them all to look up, as if following the footsteps of someone who'd just left the room. Even Rob at that point muttered, "Sorry."

Gail weighed her response. She was angry, and inclined to show it, as she frequently did. On one level, what she'd just been subjected to was insensitive, belittling, and deserving of rebuke. But even with her grief having reduced her to a shipwreck survivor, she recognized the need not to lose hold of the flotsam that could save her political life — regardless of how unpleasant it might appear.

With that in mind, Gail took her chief of staff off the hook, despite her tamped-down emotions struggling hard to break loose. "No sorries. I couldn't be happier that you're all with me right now. You are my people, my trusted advisers, the reason I sit at this desk. I rely on your support, but even more on your honesty, and that's all I've heard today. I trust you. Susan used to comment that I couldn't get better than what I have in you — all of you — and this is proof that she was right."

She placed both hands flat on her desk, convinced that Susan would have been proud of her covering her emotions so well. "That being said," she went on, "I'd like to digest it for just a little bit, if you can stand it. Rob mentioned the luxury of time. I know that the police are trying to figure out exactly what happened. That'll allow us to issue no-comments legitimately at least for a couple of days, in that we supposedly don't want to second-guess law enforcement efforts."

As her staff began getting up and heading for the door, she concluded, "I do assure you that you'll know of my plans before the first memorial. No surprises. I promise."

They filed out. In the awkward and voice-less shuffling of everyone's departure, Gail's last four words hung in the air like resonant notes out of chord.

CHAPTER NINE

Standing at the window, Joe looked across the street at the St. Johnsbury Athenaeum, a Second French Empire building housing the town's library and art gallery. It had always reminded him of the *My Fair Lady* set on the inside, and the Addams family's home on the outside — complete with spiral staircases, skylights, leather books, and squeaky wooden floors. There had been times when he'd traveled the hour north from his family's farm in Thetford just to sit in the gallery, enjoy its huge Bierstadt landscape of Yosemite, and feel as if he'd drifted back into the eighteen hundreds.

But not this time. Now he was on the second floor of the courthouse opposite, in the VBI's Northeast Kingdom field office, following up on the Nathan Fellows shooting. Behind him were Lester Spinney, Bev Tetreault, and Robert Whallon — the latter two teammates of Cila Lewis, who was still recovering in the hospital. The three had been assigned to collect what they could on Fellows and see if — after the fact — he fit the bill everyone was hoping he would. Joe had just arrived to be briefed.

"Political influence might still be the force they claim it is," Les was saying. "The crime lab has come back in record time with a slew of stuff tied to Susan's death."

Joe kept studying the view, admiring how an overnight dusting of snow had made the buildings before him look like a sentimental-ized rendering of a New England long gone — at least the New England where he spent his time.

Lester continued, used to his boss's habit of staring into space when he was thinking. "In no particular order, we've got results on the rope found at the scene, the tire and shoe tracks in the snow, trace from her clothing, scrapings from under her fingernails, more trace collected from her steering wheel, brake and accelerator ped-als, and off her car bumpers." He paused, leafing through paperwork. "I've got stomach contents, blood, urine, vitreous, anal, oral, and vaginal analyses. I also have the contents of two phones and various computers. That's the majority of the scientific junk. We're still conducting

141

interviews with friends, family, and colleagues — both Susan Raffner's and Nathan Fellows's."

Joe finally turned to face them, sitting on the window ledge. He addressed Tetreault and Whallon, the first of whom was the bureau's sole transfer from Fish and Wildlife; the second yet another investigator poached from the state police. "Obviously, that's all going to take more people and more time to digest. For our immediate purposes, do we have anything connecting her to Fellows?"

Tetreault cleared her throat nervously. "None of it," she announced in a small voice. "If he'd just stood his ground and talked to us, it probably would've ended as another dead-end lead."

Joe looked at her silently, waiting.

She explained. "We compared his truck's tire treads to the wheel tracks, any rope we found to the one around her neck, all his tools for blood evidence. There wasn't a single match."

"We also found no fingerprints on the letter," Whallon said. "The one Parker and Perry found with Nate's return address. None at all, including Raffner's, which struck me as unusual, given how torn up and manhandled they both were. And the

142

same was true for the DNA test they did on the envelope flap. It was an old-fashioned lick-and-stick, but there was still nuthin — like he used a sponge or something. Who does that anymore? Oh, and for what it's worth, we also compared samples of spelling and penmanship we found in the house to the note Nate supposedly wrote. Not the same. The differences were subtle but consistent. The lab suggested off the record that it looked like someone trying to copy Nate's illiterate style. Whoever did it most likely didn't even actually mail the thing, since the stamp corner was conspicuously missing — they might've just planted it in the recycle box to mislead us."

"Fellows also carried a Buck knife at all times," Tetreault picked back up, "according to his coworkers and what we found on his body. So you'd've thought he'd've used that on her chest, but again, there was nothing on the blade. He had lists at his house — hit or hate lists, if you want, although there's nothing labeling them that. Raffner's name appears on one of them, but only once and along with most of the legislature." She paused before adding, "The governor gets more attention from him than Raffner does."

"How so?" Joe wanted to know.

"Just that her name crops up more often and in more places."

"Of course," Whallon contributed again, "what really puts the kibosh on Nate being our doer is that we found out he has an alibi for when we think she was whacked. He was in Boston, at some kind of convention for like-minded losers. The local PD're saying that from what they found, there's no way Fellows could've slipped out on his buddies and come up here to do the nasty. Times just don't line up."

"So why did he shoot it out with us?" Joe asked.

Tetreault answered, "I interviewed some of the people he hung with in Newport. They said he was pretty crazy. Talked nonstop about several of the more famous school shooters, and the guy who shot the congresswoman in Arizona. We found a sort of celebrity scrapbook at his place. His preference seemed to be the ones who died in a hail of bullets. He admired guys who didn't make it out alive."

Joe gazed at the wooden floor, weighing the implications of what he'd just learned.

"We got the wrong man," Whallon suggested during the silence.

Joe looked up. "I agree. And considering that the letter had no prints, the envelope no DNA, the handwriting was faked, and that he seems to have had a death wish, it's looking more likely Nate Fellows was set up."

Gail sat with her hands in her lap, dressed somberly, looking like the other dignitaries on stage — serious but not grim, engaged but appropriately reserved. The kind of coaching she'd received from her staff echoed in her head as she suspected it did inside most of the others slated to speak.

This was the second such event held in Susan's honor, but in Gail's view, it was the big one — the Brattleboro tribute to the fallen hometown girl. Its predecessor, in Montpelier the day before, had gone without a hitch. More than a half-dozen people had addressed the crowd, including her, the lieutenant governor, the speaker of the House, the president pro tem of the Senate, and the party leaders. They'd droned on, made all the appropriate comments, slipping in the occasional note of levity at the right times, and escaped without causing a single ripple.

Including her. Gail had spoken last — of her friendship, of Susan's energy and commitment, of her wisdom and political smarts. As Gail's eyes had moved from

145

script to audience and only rarely to her staff offstage, she'd seen universal approval among the latter, happy that her earlier admissions of love and true sexual identity had been relegated to the closet.

This, however, was Brattleboro, which, unlike other towns such as Bennington, Rutland, St. J, or even the metropolis Burlington, had an identity unique unto itself and distinct from its sisters. It had similar blue-collar, Industrial Era roots, but had deviated from the rest in the sixties and seventies — many thought because of the arrival of the interstate and the related influx of ex-urbanite hippies — and acquired a reputation for independence, daring, and outspoken liberalism.

The crowd gathered today wasn't decorously arrayed within the ornate drapings of the capitol building's House chamber; they were instead jammed together inside the local high school's largest auditorium — big, bland, and proletarian.

More important to Gail, Brattleboro was where she and Susan had met up and formed an alliance, political and personal, and where they had learned to speak their minds and act on their beliefs.

This — more than any place on earth at

the moment — was home. Where Gail's heart was, and where she'd learned to be a woman with self-respect.

As a result, when her turn finally came to speak — and having heard not a word of the preceding eulogies — she put aside her written speech, crossed to the podium, looked out onto the blur of upturned faces, and spoke from the heart, unheeding of the tension she could feel like a growing heat from her onlooking political handlers.

She began by introducing herself in local terms, as an ex-Realtor, selectboard member, and deputy state's attorney. She spoke of having been raped, and then taking to the street to protest the depersonalizing anonymity imposed on victims of sexual violence. She described her struggle to re-create herself in the aftermath of trauma, of her growing realization that she'd had it easy before, and of her need to live a different, more proactive life. And throughout it all, she invoked how Susan Raffner had been there to be relied upon — regardless of risk or consequence.

She then segued over to concentrate on Susan's characteristics — some peerless, others petty — and how she and Susan had combined strengths. But where her staff had advised her to speak of defeating Tropical

Storm Irene, of making the state more business-friendly while protecting its precious natural resources, and of how to otherwise turn this event into her first reelection speech, she did none of it.

Instead, she spoke of sex. Of its centrality in American politics, its use to skewer presidents, its hold on everything from self-image to how power can be exerted. She spoke of how it lurked beneath debates about why some leaders were unmarried, or others stayed married. She spoke of the sudden upsurge of same-sex marriage laws, of the slow lessening of sexual prejudice, and of the fact that more and more people — from professional athletes to prominent politicians — were identifying themselves sexually.

And always, throughout — her voice occasionally trembling — she spoke of Susan. Susan was proud to be a lesbian, Gail told her silent audience, but not prideful about its attributes. She saw the need for honesty and to advocate for social and cultural parity, but had no desire to claim that her choice was better than anyone else's.

Finally, her tears flowing freely at last, Gail moved to her companion's influence on her, as a friend, a politician, and as someone finally at peace with her own sexuality.

Abandoning her earlier pledge to Rob Perkins not to drop any bombshells — but carefully phrasing it along the lines of being black, or a woman, or a vegetarian — Gail declared herself to be a lesbian.

Perkins, for his part, had been braced from the start, knowing of his boss's propensity for veering off course — and surviving, even thriving, nevertheless. And once more, in the hushed silence that followed Gail back to her seat, he did the political math, aided by a subsequent delayed ripple of applause that quickly swelled into a cheering, foot-stomping, standing ovation.

She'd done well. She had couched her revelation in humanitarian terms, making future negative reactions seem small-minded and vindictive. She'd also used her murdered, martyred friend as an example of why such issues as sexual orientation had by now become as antique and horrifying as lynching or witch burning — and why a disclosure like hers should have by now become as irrelevant as right- or left-handedness.

It had been, Perkins grudgingly admitted, a masterful political performance. And — he knew by the same token — the beginning of another roller-coaster ride.

■ ■ ■ ■

Willy Kunkle wasn't surprised when he heard of the lack of evidence against Nate Fellows. He hadn't needed an Agatha Christie list of missing clues to doubt whether Fellows was Raffner's killer. For Willy, it had been instinctual. There'd been no logic to the chain of events from the start — Susan's disappearance in the night; her ghoulish reappearance, but minus any fanfare claiming credit; her conveniently available murderer found at work, as if completely clueless; and now, whatever evidence that had led to Nate's doorstep coming abruptly to a halt. It struck Willy as it had Joe earlier: a collection of feints hiding something as yet undecipherable.

Part of their problem had been the speed with which they'd been delivered the case. From the flashy hanging to the political pressure and media attention, it had come at them too fast to allow them to simply study its component parts, as Willy was doing now.

Typically, of course, he was not at the office in this pursuit. He was again lying flat on his back in his daughter's bedroom, in the middle of the night, pacing his thoughts to her gentle breathing just above.

As Sam had discovered, this had lately become a habit, born of a developing shift in Kunkle's view of the world and his place within it. For decades he'd trained himself to see love, charity, kindness, generosity, and the like as human weaknesses — and had coated his armor against their corrosion through alcohol, anger, violence, and cynicism. He'd also chosen two careers, the military and law enforcement, to reinforce his dark convictions about humanity's baser instincts — earning the wasted arm as a visceral reminder.

Therein, however, had also lurked the crucial flaw in his strategy. As irony would have it, the more he found his outlook rewarded, the more he'd had to admit that a parallel human decency must exist for it to be true. As proof, instead of the forecast grim reward at the end of a hopeless tunnel, he'd found instead Gunther, Sammie, and — most poignantly — Emma.

This had presented him with a true dilemma. The promise these people represented should have made him feel relieved, especially since it suggested that he'd been receptive to salvation all along. But he'd struggled for too long, had accumulated too much emotional and physical scar tissue, and was experiencing the kind of exhaustion that doesn't see the adage, "There's light at the end," with anything approaching joy.

Nevertheless, with all his resistance, he was becoming aware that the good things in his life might not have been random, might have been as much his due as the unhappiness preceding it, and might just possibly continue to happen.

The latest evidence of this had been drawing him to this room ever more frequently.

He shut his eyes briefly and listened to Emma sleep, allowing her universe of warmth, comfort, peace, and love to soak in a little.

So — he now considered from this unusual viewpoint — what of the world of Susan Raffner?

An active, restless, independent woman; impatient, demanding, intolerant of resistant ignorance; and as prejudiced against the prejudiced as the most partisan among them. Willy had seen Raffner in action for as long as he'd lived in Brattleboro, which by now went back decades. She'd forever been at the forefront of protests, marches down Main Street, and demonstrations of civil disobedience. She'd regularly attended selectboard meetings as a citizen, had been a town meeting representative for years before joining the board, and had monitored even the most obscure subcommittees over time. Long before he'd learned her name and categorized her in his mind, he'd come to recognize her grim expression in the crowd, floating among the front rows of angry-faced protesters against which he'd stood alongside his fellow cops.

But what in addition, he asked himself, thinking of his recent tour of her now-abandoned home? What had been going on behind that attention-getting façade?

He ruled out the sexual orientation with which she'd literally been stamped. To his thinking, it was an arguable distraction. He would consider that later. Instead, he opted for the path he and Lester had physically taken through her Chestnut Hill house, and which had only ended in her bedroom. The overflow of magazines and newspapers had come first, using that approach. That and the computer printouts. There had been piles of them, everywhere, and filing cabinets jammed full. Not many books, though — just the opposite of Joe Gunther's place, Willy thought.

So, articles — articles of staggering number and variety, covering current events, political debates, differing viewpoints, and researched analyses. The environment, poverty, racism, sexism, immigration, pollution, privacy, labor, education, domestic violence, slavery, genital mutilation, agricultural industrialization, gender bias, and even the fate of the panda had featured among the stacks and bulletin boards and heaps of folders that had transformed most of Susan's supposedly conventional home into an activist's library.

The sole exception had been the kitchen and that bedroom, Willy conceded. Could it be, he considered — now that Nate had been discarded as a decoy — that the next red herring was to be hidden within the mass of causes with which Susan was associated?

Putting that aside for a moment, and sticking to his own orderly procedure, he considered the kitchen — another reflection of Raffner's all-inclusive personality. Her kitchen had been stuffed with a surfeit of whole grains, local products, organic fools, and, as Spinney had pointed out, vegetarianism. It had displayed a whirlwind brio similar to what they'd seen in her filing system. Willy didn't doubt that Susan's political correctness as a consumer was as hallowed as the Pope's faith; he also suspected that her actual consumption of those products was more haphazard than it was healthily balanced. Her good intentions, he imagined, were probably matched by the amount of mold growing in the back of her refrigerator.

He paused again to weigh what he'd pondered so far — and what among it might have stimulated a homicide.

Along those lines, he returned to her activism. The irony, he was beginning to think, was that she'd been so all-inclusive with her criticisms and protests that she'd reduced herself to more of a predictable, general nuisance than a threat deserving of retaliation. By being everywhere, she'd lessened her value as a target.

Of course, he admitted, that was an ex-sniper's viewpoint.

Emma shifted in her crib, sighing peacefully, making Willy smile. He thought of what he knew of Susan personally. He'd never liked her. That wasn't a shock. She was perhaps as driven and intense as he, but without a glimmer of humor, as far as he'd ever seen. The woman had been all indignation and simmering fury.

Which told him what? He slipped his good hand behind his head as a cushion and gazed down his body toward his socks. Sometimes, he knew too well, people were killed simply because they drove others to murder them — they didn't know when to quit.

Intrigued by that notion, he moved forward in his mental tour and proceeded upstairs to Susan's sanctum sanctorum: her bedroom.

The love nest of Lesbos, Spinney had called it.

Willy pushed out his lower lip thoughtfully. That became interesting, put in this particular context. If Susan had been a humorless harridan of obsessively left-wing causes — as he'd just painted her — what had she been in that bedroom?

What was interesting to him was less the sexual orientation they'd discovered there and more the room's pure sensuality. While lesbianism and eroticism had become a porn industry standard, Willy had found that most gays of his acquaintance — male and female — placed sex on roughly the same platform as did straight people. It was a gender preference, not one based on uncontrollable appetite.

Which told him that Susan's bedroom, rather than being an extension of her public lifestyle, in fact represented a personal contradiction. In Willy's experience, Raffner had been about as sensual as Susan B.

Anthony or Ralph Nader. The fact that a select few only had enjoyed her charms within a seductive den of tantalizing offerings suggested that she'd both needed such an outlet, and had kept it confidential for some reason.

For Willy — a hunter of human beings — that unusual self-restraint indicated a break with the established norm of the rest of her life, introducing a wild card to the cipher that had become Susan Raffner — and which may have played a role in her demise.

He sensed before he saw a movement at Emma's bedroom door. Sam glided over the threshold, dressed only in a T-shirt. She slid down beside him, still as warm as the bed she'd just left, and draped one bare leg across his thighs.

"Figuring things out?" she barely whispered.

He brought her close enough that she half covered him. "Trying to."

She passed her hand across his chest, feeling him respond against her inner thigh. She chuckled quietly. "Why, Mr. Kunkle. What're you doing down there? What *have* you been thinking about?" She reached down to confirm her suspicion and dawdled a bit, encouraging him.

He kissed her neck. "Homicide, actually,"

he said, and then pointed at the door, and by implication their bedroom down the hall. "But you know how one thing leads to another."

Joe handed Beverly a glass of chilled white wine, which he'd begun to make sure he had available for her occasional trips to Brattleboro. Given the nature of their jobs — his frequently putting him on the road; hers usually keeping her in the lab — it made sense that he most often slept over at her house. That made the rare exception all the more appreciated.

Except when the phone inevitably rang.

He glanced at the device's small screen and grunted.

"What?" she asked. "Duty calls?" She wasn't upset — another thing they shared was a fatalistic acceptance that most of their plans would be upended without notice.

"It's Gail," he said in a neutral tone.

"Answer it," she said, a rueful smile growing. "I can take a walk around the block. I imagine the two of you have a few things to discuss."

He grimaced. "Oh, no. I'll let it go to the answering machine."

Beverly's smile faded. "Joe, answer it. She's not only in pain, she's taken a huge step into the unknown. It's the right thing to do."

He conceded. "Okay, okay, but stay. Please." He suddenly reconsidered and added, "Unless you'd prefer to leave."

She shook her head, but rose and headed for the bathroom. Joe hit the Receive button.

"Hey there, Governor."

"Hi, Joe." Gail's voice was strained and oddly flat. "You got a minute?"

Joe glanced at Beverly's departing back. "Sure. You okay? I mean, all things considered."

"You heard about the memorial?"

He was struck by the roundabout reference. "I heard about the only memorable thing said there, if you can forgive the near pun."

He could tell from her hesitation that he'd caught her by surprise. "And you're okay with that?" she asked.

He'd had time to consider the question in the few hours since her eulogy. He hadn't attended, not wanting that much proximity to either her or her supporters, especially on the home turf he and Gail had once shared. But he'd listened to it on the local radio, thankfully in the privacy of his car.

Beyond the initial shock of hearing

159

something suspected said out loud, he wasn't sure he was truly surprised. Knowing both women for as long as he had — and despite sleeping with one of them for most of that time — he'd always found their friendship similar to that of a long-married and compatible couple.

It had never bothered him, although he'd never suspected a sexual liaison. He'd respected Susan, even if he'd never warmed to her — which was clearly mutual, as she'd made clear — and he and Gail had physically lived together only briefly, for a short time following the sexual assault. It had struck him, nevertheless, that in a way, Susan and he had shared the same woman.

What he'd heard over the radio was therefore more of a confirmation than an announcement out of the blue.

"You suspected," she said to fill the silence.

"Only that she fulfilled a need I never could," he said. "I didn't know the nature of it. I didn't need to. When you and I were at our best, I was a happy man."

Here, he thought of Beverly, still tactfully out of the room. It struck him that while he should have felt embarrassed, he didn't — instead enjoying at last the proximity of a nonjudgmental and supportive close friend.

160

"Oh, Joe," Gail uttered wistfully.

He resisted the old impulse to travel to her side, hearing such sadness.

If he, Susan, and Gail had in fact once been an oddly closeted trio of sorts, he was no longer in the mood to act the hero upon the death of one of them. It was one thing to understand and sympathize — entirely another to rush to the rescue of someone whose emotional makeup he was no longer sure he understood.

Especially now that he'd found his own happiness with a woman he trusted entirely.

"What do you plan to do next?" he asked, mainly to move the conversation along. "Rob and company must be running around in circles. Had you given them a heads-up? What you said at the memorial didn't sound like it came from a speech."

"I told them about Susan and me, but I promised not to torpedo them in public, too."

"Wow," he said. "They must be looking up the meaning of the phrase."

She laughed despite herself. "I'm afraid you're right. I did mind my manners during the Montpelier speech."

"Right — be sure to remind them of that. What's their reaction been so far?"

"They're balancing the pros and cons of

saying I'm bi versus a committed lesbian. Your name came up in that regard — not that you need to worry," she added hastily. "It's all typical what-the-governor-meant-to-say crap. It's not gonna happen."

It struck him how they'd instinctively steered the conversation toward the practical, letting the emotional eddies in the wake of her announcement settle down to mere ripples, if that. These were times when New England's famed taciturnity came in handy.

"Where do you stand there?" he asked along those lines.

"I've always thought the bi position to be wussy," she stated flatly, sounding more like the Gail he knew. "It's like saying you're a vegetarian because you don't eat red meat."

"It might be accurate, though," he countered, not sure why he was bothering. "I wasn't the only man you knew in that way."

As soon as the phrase left his mouth, he winced.

But Gail didn't react to the Victorianism. "I owe it to Susan," she said. "And to myself. She was so comfortable in her skin. I was too worried about the implications to be that honest."

He couldn't avoid seeing the self-flagellation in that statement, which also didn't mean it wasn't true.

"There's bound to be a shit storm," he counseled. "At least from out-of-state. National media's still in the neighborhood, especially since the Newport shooting was also announced this afternoon."

Bringing up the point made him wonder if she hadn't factored it into the equation. She was a politician, after all, and not without a natural wiliness.

He was glad when her reaction seemed to lack that level of cynicism.

"Rob made the same point," she said. "I know I have him around for just that reason, but right now, I'm pretty sick of what's supposed to be right or wrong politically. I just know my heart's been broken, and I wanted to honor the reason why." Her voice cracked as she added, "Joe, you've known me almost as long as she did. Both of you were there after I was raped. You know what it did to me — how I had to start from scratch. I don't want to forget that, and I sure as hell don't want to betray the vows I took — and that you both witnessed — to get where I am now."

Joe let the air clear a moment before he said, "Then it sounds like you did the right thing. That's got to be a good feeling — even with all the hurt you're carrying."

He could almost hear her mulling that over. "It is." She then said, "Was that man the one who killed her, Joe?"

"I shouldn't say," he told her honestly. "Except through so-called proper channels. But it's not looking good. That's not to be shared with anyone, okay? Act surprised when they break the news to you."

"Okay," she said. "But what does it mean?"

"More digging for us and probably more ducking questions by you. You're going to have your hands full with so many other things, though, that it probably won't matter. We are taking what happened in Newport as a clue, by the way, and not as a screwup, like they'll be saying in the papers. We have a feeling there was more to it, but that's all I want to say."

"Sure, sure."

"The people around you doing more than just handing out political advice?" he suddenly asked, despite his earlier instincts not to prolong the conversation. "You have anyone who actually cares about you?"

He was thinking of the near posse that Susan had kept by her side virtually around the clock, including people like Alice Drim, who'd come to Gail from Susan's entourage. "You have no support group nearby?" he asked. "Like Alice or Kayla?"

Gail sighed. "No, they're all here. Alice has been very sweet, but she's up to her neck raising money for the coming campaign. Plus, she's been having romantic problems. Kayla told me that Alice also has a brother or something in the hospital. Both of them are nice enough — I don't mean that — but they're young, distracted, and not as comfortable to be with as Susan was. It's just . . . not the same."

Joe didn't respond.

"Thanks, Joe," she finally said. "For listening. And everything else."

"Anytime, Gail. Call whenever you want."

He hit the Off button on the phone and gently laid it down.

"Oof," Beverly said, stepping in from the next room, where she'd been keeping out of sight.

He tilted his head slightly and smiled at her. "Have I told you how happy I am we got together?"

CHAPTER TEN

Kunkle was taking his freelance assignment to heart, unconcerned that Joe had probably handed it out to keep the office loose cannon far from the media limelight. For one thing, Willy didn't care; for another, he agreed with the decision.

The man at the wheel of the car offered him a stick of gum.

Willy shook his head, his eyes on the motel across the parking lot.

In the driver's seat was Bob Crawford — not undercover tonight, but nevertheless ponytailed, bearded, with a tattoo on his neck and a single small hoop hanging from one earlobe. He led the Vermont Drug Task Force, a state police–run unit so established and effective that when the VBI was chartered, draining the state police's plainclothes ranks, no one had even considered challenging the task force's primacy. As Joe and Allard had urged at the time, it was good at its job and had been at it a long time. Why mess with success?

There were doubters. Other cops and a few politicians who thought that the task force had lost its edge through a lack of imagination and a rigidity of style. But Willy was not among them.

He also liked Bob Crawford, who probably wouldn't have survived in the state police if it hadn't been for this unit. The length of his hair and beard indicated how long it had been since he'd last worn a uniform. He'd resembled a biker for years by now, and while such single-mindedness wasn't truly the state police way, his bosses had realized that cutting a little slack was the only way to keep such an asset employed. Even better, by promoting him to lieutenant, they'd effectively made him the unit's leader — a convincing show of support.

"When you called," Bob now said, his eyes straight ahead, "you said you were looking at how marijuana is being run nowadays. What're you working on? I just ask 'cause if it's drug-related, we're supposed to be inside the loop, given what we do." He held up a hand to stop Willy from responding right off, adding, "But keep in mind that I know how you work. If this is just you being you, then this conversation never happened. I got that."

Willy nodded, having just entered the car. They were in Brattleboro, which is why Bob had told him to come by. On any given night, Crawford could be anywhere in the state, watching out for the welfare of his multiple teams.

"Okay. Thanks," Willy said, holding off on answering right away. "Who're you staking out tonight?" he asked instead.

His companion didn't mind. "Just documenting a buy. It's the bedrock of our business — knowing who's who and what they're up to."

He paused to reach for a long-lensed camera as a car stopped in the motel's parking lot. A thin man in a hoodie got out and looked around. Crawford took a shot of the car and its license plate. He also murmured into his portable radio that he'd done so, hearing the reply over the earbud he had shoved into his left ear. Elsewhere in the darkness, members of his squad were in a van, running the audio and video equipment that was recording this transaction's every moment.

Willy stayed quiet as Crawford tracked the man walking over to the motel's exterior staircase and eventually climbing to the second floor.

"Come on," Crawford urged softly, "pose for the camera."

Almost on cue, as the man reached the balcony, he turned to check the parking lot again, exposing his face to the light — and Crawford's lens.

The camera fired. "Nice. You got real stage presence."

"You know him?" Willy asked.

"One of our CIs. Solid guy, considering how he started. Used to be a real loser; he's one of our best now."

The informant continued to the door they had under surveillance, knocked, waited a moment, and was caught in silhouette as the door opened and his profile was highlighted by the room's interior glow.

Crawford continued shooting as a second man filled the doorway, stepped out onto the balcony, also looked around, and then invited the newcomer in.

"Gee," Willy commented with false amazement. "That's really subtle."

"Doesn't have to be," Crawford said. "The amount of this kind of activity, compared with the number of us that're out here tryin' to stop it? His chances of being caught are like one in fifteen thousand."

Willy stared at him. "No shit."

"No shit. We got this mope in our sights, so he'll be goin' down soon enough, but there are dozens like him who have about as much chance of being busted as I have of being hit by lightning."

He reached again for the radio and asked, "Everything okay?" He disconnected the earphone so that Willy could hear the reply over the speaker.

"Right as rain," came the response. "He's broadcasting loud and clear, and he should be comin' out now."

True to form, the distant door reopened and the informant stepped back out onto the balcony, appearing as empty-handed as before.

"Light shopping day?" Willy asked.

Crawford chuckled, plugging into the radio again. " 'Cause he's not carrying a grocery bag? This is not a weed buy. We don't give a shit about that anymore, unless you're talking pounds of the stuff. Nobody does." He jutted out his chin toward the motel. "We're hitting this loser for smack." He tapped the earphone with his fingertip. "And from what I heard, we just scored fifty bags."

As they saw the skinny man return to his vehicle and drive away — around the corner to meet up with the task force van and hand over his wire and his heroin — Willy watched his colleague visibly relax. Bob Crawford had been at this long enough to sound casual and disengaged, but from Willy's own field experience, he knew that Bob's nerves had been on edge from the start.

"You'll bust him later tonight?" Willy asked.

"Probably," Bob said lightly. "We'll let him and the girlfriend he has in there get nice and sleepy first."

Crawford placed the camera into the back and shifted more comfortably in his seat, at last making eye contact with his guest. "So — what *are* you after?"

"A way to trace dope," Willy explained. "We found a lot of it when we processed Susan Raffner's two homes. I'm just wondering where it came from."

Crawford studied him for a moment. "I thought that was a hate crime," he said. "You guys shot someone and everything."

"Looks that way," Willy replied.

The drug cop smiled. "And looks can be deceiving. I get it."

Crawford was enjoying himself. He glanced toward the motel parking lot, to make sure there were no unexpected movements. His own documented buy was concluded, but that didn't preclude someone else worth photographing dropping by for a score.

"Okay," he said. "The feds have some detailed databases for tracking pot — brands, contents, level of THC, even packaging. Routine stuff, but sophisticated. But it's not like it is with heroin, where the dealers actually stamp their product like trademarks. Marijuana is tougher. It's grown locally, or it comes out of Canada or Mexico or who the hell knows where else, and it shows up in generic supermarket baggies. I have a long list of different types and origins that runs for pages. Still, you might be able to tell local from Mexican, if you're lucky."

Willy pointed across the parking lot. "Does this guy sell it?"

"Most of them do. If you're in business to make money, you mix it up, right? Word on the street is that the drug you use is the drug you can afford. But why all this about the lowly marijuana plant?" He laughed. "If it's okay to ask."

Willy shook his head. "The hate crime connection with Nate Fellows is wrong. We're either missing something, or we're being jerked around. Anyway, I took a step back, looked at everything we got so far on the victim, and began to wonder about the pot. She was a serious user. Not that there's anything indicating a drug angle here. There's not. But it is a curiosity, and right now, we don't have anything else to go on. You ever meet her, or see her in action?"

Crawford shrugged. "Raffner? More like read about her. Got the feeling she was a real fire-breather."

"She was that," Willy agreed. "But you know how it goes — you start looking at a frustrating case's bits and pieces, till you get stuck on the one that looks like it might have some meat on it."

Crawford was nodding agreeably. "Cool. I know the feeling."

"Well, with her," Willy continued, "or maybe I should say, to me, it was her grass stash that struck a chord. Almost everything in her life was controversial, from her politics to her sexual orientation. But the grass was flat-out illegal. That struck me as an anomaly — not because it didn't fit her character, but because it introduced a different world from hers — of crooks, drugs, and illegal deals."

Bob snorted. "It's just pot, Willy — it's not like she was shooting smack."

Willy didn't react, staying on track. "It reminded me how in the old cocaine days, a huge number of U.S. dollar bills became tainted with minute traces of coke, regardless of whose pocket they were in — including little old ladies'. It was crazy how that shit got everywhere, just from money changing hands, day to day."

"Okay," Crawford said, by now mystified by his friend's line of thought.

"Well, what you were saying made me think: If a dealer peddles heroin and marijuana, both, is it possible that a trace of the first could end up contaminating the packaging of the second?"

Bob's expression cleared. "Which would give you a double trail to follow: the marijuana inside a baggie and a dusting of heroin on the outside. That's neat. You're saying she was maybe done in over a drug deal, and not over her politics at all. I didn't think of that. Never needed to, since we're not murder police like you boys. But I like it. And the contamination angle's very CSI.

"Of course," he continued after a moment's reflection, "identifying that tiny amount of heroin — minus its own stamped packaging — isn't going to be easy. You'll have to focus on things like purity and adulterants before you can maybe guess where it originated. On the bright side, connecting that both marijuana and heroin came from the same place would make you more interesting to federal prosecutors and might help in identifying some of the people involved — or in ruling others out. Now *that* could be useful."

"So it is possible?" Willy asked, sounding to Bob unusually tentative.

"Sure. Why not? These bozos aren't neat freaks. Most assembly spots I've seen have drug dust all over the place. I'd give it a try, if I were you."

Willy nevertheless pressed what he sensed was a reservation. "You have a problem with it, though."

"I wouldn't say a problem. Maybe I been spending too much time chasing morons, but I was just thinking there might be a simpler way: Why not just go after all of Raffner's friends till you find the one who smoked with her, or maybe even supplied her? Spare yourself all the super-scientific mumbo jumbo."

Willy pulled a face and stared glumly out the window. "I thought of that. But her buddies're starting to get wound up, wondering why this wasn't solved three minutes after we found her. They're already growling about how we're trying to make Raffner the criminal instead of the victim. It's just paranoia, but it's closing the ranks

175

of the faithful."

"Ah," Crawford muttered sympathetically. "And shooting that guy up in Newport didn't help, I bet. Assuming," he emphasized, "that he's not your guy."

Willy looked at him. "What makes you say that?"

"You told me as much, and I trust your instincts. Besides, if he had been, it would've been plastered all over the five o'clock news." He paused before adding, "Something tells me you haven't been able to connect the dots — not to mention that you're sittin' here playing twenty questions with me. You guys are up shit creek without a paddle."

Willy wasn't going to argue otherwise. "We could do with a break."

Sam checked the nightstand clock. Three-seventeen. She barely glanced across the bed, knowing that Willy wouldn't be there. He was sometimes, usually lingering after they'd made love. But generally, he wandered around the house like a cat or dog, finding opportunistic spots to make a temporary bivouac. That's how she'd known to find him beside Emma's crib.

It was part of the PTSD — what he called his "war thing." It made him restless, a poor and sometimes terrified sleeper, and directed him to sit with his back to all walls, to work alone if he could, to avoid creating predictable habits, which in turn dictated that he almost never slept twice in a row in the same place. Those and about fifty other eccentricities.

Tonight, they hadn't started out in bed together anyhow. He'd left home earlier to do "some poking around" — his favorite pastime. The Raffner killing had made him more restive than usual.

Sammie rose, not feeling like returning to sleep, and slid into a long, warm, flannel robe. She didn't worry about waking him up, wherever he was. The nearly inaudible sounds that she'd made getting out of bed were guaranteed to have alerted him.

Perhaps it was an indicator of the many quirks that kept them together, but she enjoyed the occasional night when she went hunting for him, trying to figure out where to start. Surprise was clearly not a factor — all the better since he never went anywhere without a weapon, including to the bathroom — so the challenge boiled down to determining his predictability. She gave herself bonus points for locating him on the first try — almost as much as he saw it as a sign of personal weakness.

This time, however, she didn't stand a chance. She hadn't reached the end of the hallway when his quiet voice crept up behind her. "Got the midnight munchies?"

She turned to find him leaning against the wall, a shadow in the distant night-light's glow. He had a pickle in his hand. She walked up to him and took a bite.

"Why not?"

"That's what I thought."

Perhaps disturbed by their quiet voices, or more probably because she was due, Emma began crying softly from down the hall. Both parents moved into her bedroom.

"Hey, little girl," Sam cooed as Willy picked the child up. He shifted her expertly to the changing table against the wall, and swapped out her diaper with practiced skill — all with one hand.

"Wanna spoil her a bit?" he asked her mother, tucking Emma into the crook of his arm. "A few minutes on the couch?"

Sam, always impressed by his easy dexterity, led the way to the living room.

"You got something on your mind," she stated as they all three settled down. Through the broad window facing the street, they could see snow falling under the streetlamps posted along the horseshoe-shaped street outside their home. "I can hear the gears going 'round. You find anything interesting on your outing?"

She drew a blanket from the back of the sofa to cover their shoulders, bringing them under a tent. This was a proximity she knew he never would have tolerated a couple of years ago.

"I went to see Bob Crawford," he said. "To spitball a few things."

She nodded, letting Emma curl her fingers sleepily around her extended thumb. She trusted Willy to explain when and if he was ready. "He doing okay?"

"Yeah," he replied distractedly, before asking, "You're the air traffic controller on this case. Where do things stand?"

"Not good. We either have no planes to land or they're all crashing like in Newport. The press hounding us and interviewing everybody before we can get to them isn't helping, either."

"What about any Raffner-related evidence?"

She leaned into him slightly and looked him straight in the eye. "No change, as you very well know. Everybody's still digging through it like tunnel rats. What're you really after?"

He liked that. "You *are* getting to know me."

"I better be. Spill."

"Such a hard-ass. You hear of anybody looking at the drug angle?"

She smiled broadly and poked him, making Emma gurgle happily. "Aha. Bob Crawford. Things're coming clear. Do tell."

"The dope Raffner had in Montpelier and Brattleboro. There was a major bag of low-grade marijuana in her apartment and what looked like a travel supply in her love nest at home. Got me curious about how she scored her stash, and who from. Old-time doper like her probably had a regular supplier. I wanted Bob to give me an update on the state of the trade, just in case it could give us a trail to follow. God knows, a little progress would be nice."

Sam had been nodding throughout. "I made sure we got the baggie and both samples up to the lab, but I'll ask 'em to step up the pace a bit. Given all the headlines around this case, they'll probably cooperate — happy to see the last of us, sooner the better."

Willy extended the pickle to her for a second bite, which she accepted. "Thanks."

She spoke again as she chewed. "One thing you might want to consider."

"Yeah?"

"The governor coming out at the

memorial'll mean we'll have to watch our step more than ever."

"Why do we give a rat's ass about that? We knew she had no taste in men after she dumped the boss."

Sam burst out laughing. "Well, I'll be damned. He'd take that as a total compliment, if I repeated it to him."

"Which you won't, knowing me to be the vindictive, unstable person I am," he said in a threatening tone.

She shook her head. "God, do I ever. I am serious, though. Zigman doing what she did makes Raffner a romantic partner, which for us means that what's good for the goose might've been good for the other goose, too."

Willy gave her an appreciative look. "You're saying the governor of our fair state and her girlfriend smoked dope together."

Sam went further. "I'm saying that's what the tabloids, the talking heads, and the headlines'll be screaming if we don't keep this little inquiry under wraps."

She reached up and touched his cheek. "I'm saying, Willy, that for once in your life, keep an eye on the politics here. We're the governor's special unit. If she's part of this somehow, and we make that connection — and I mean more than sharing a joint in bed — then we better make damned sure we have a rock-solid case, 'cause our employment could be on the line."

This time, he leaned over carefully and kissed her cheek. "I love it when you talk dirty."

"You hearing me, Mr. Kunkle?" she asked, her expression serious.

He saw the look in her eye. "I hear you, babe."

But the look wasn't reserved solely for him. His mention of the marijuana and wanting to chase down the connection between it and Susan Raffner had revived a ten-year-old, still-open wound in Sammie's history — which made her think that Willy might not be the only one on the team who should start indulging in a little freelance investigating.

CHAPTER ELEVEN

Across the board, there are roughly eleven hundred fully certified police officers in Vermont — compared to some sixteen thousand in Massachusetts and sixty thousand in neighboring New York. It's the lowest number among all fifty states. Even largely rural New Hampshire has over twice as many cops.

That boils down to the Vermonters being a pretty tightly-knit group, regardless of uniform.

Sammie Martens counted on that when she traveled to the state's forensic lab in Waterbury a few days following her late-night conversation with Willy. Given the above statistics, it wasn't long before every plainclothes investigator got to meet at least a few of the crime lab scientists.

Sam, given her energy and overall style, had made a point of going beyond mere chance encounters to make friends with several of the lab's personnel. This was practical — the efficiencies of asking a favor of a well-placed pal being self-evident. But Sam's interest in forensics was also genuine, and appreciated by the people she befriended.

The lab was located where it had always been — attached to the building housing the Department of Public Safety and the Vermont State Police, among other agencies. But where in the past it had occupied the top floor only — in what had resembled a 1950s high school, complete with lockers lining the hallway — it was now a wing unto itself, modern, up to the latest rigorous standards, and a monument to a small group that had dedicated itself to making this lab one of the best in the nation, despite its small size and budget.

Sam signed in at the reception desk and was met by Christine Hartley, one of the lab's senior chemists, whom Sam had first met ten years earlier.

They exchanged hugs at the door, before Chris escorted her into the facility's bright and spacious embrace.

"I guess you're earning your big bucks on this case," she commented, leading the way.

"If only," Sam replied. "I'm not complaining. It's a lot more interesting than the domestics and juvie crimes I used to handle at the PD. But if we get one more major headline thrown at us, we may have to bring in the National Guard just to reach the office. The boss has taken to either meeting in weird places at odd hours or calling us on the phone instead of holding staff meetings. It's gotten a little strange."

"We get the same thing with the occasional high-visibility murder or kidnapping," Chris commiserated. "The advantage here is that it's a secure building." She jerked a thumb out one of the large windows they were passing. "They get stuck out there in the weather; no wandering the halls unescorted. I do love that."

She opened the door to an airy lab room, empty aside from another white-coated employee, working at something in a far corner.

Sam looked around admiringly. "God. I still can't get used to this building."

Chris smiled broadly. "Neat, huh? So much space. I can't, either."

She sat down at a counter strewn with folders and paperwork — her workstation, which Sam supposed doubled as an office.

"Okay," Chris then said. "Let's talk drugs. That's what you mentioned on the phone, right?"

Sam parked herself on an adjacent stool.

"Right. Did you get a chance to check out the marijuana we sent up?"

"I did. And you were right. There was some trace on the packaging, and it did test for heroin."

"Could you tell anything from it?"

"Like did it have additives or dilutants mixed in?"

"That and anything else," Sam said. "Could you tell where it came from, for instance?"

Chris frowned. "You know that most of the time we get that from what's actually stamped on the baggie, right? Horse from Hell, Dragon Tattoo, etc. I've even had 'em with Snoopy on them, which I thought was a goddamned sacrilege."

"I know, I know," Sam told her. "But I thought you could identify a geographical source from the chemical makeup."

"You can," Chris agreed. "That is, other people can, using what they call stable isotope ratio analysis. We don't do that kind of work here. Don't have the equipment, the expertise, or the money. The DEA's who you want there — but bring a lot of time to kill, 'cause they're wicked backlogged. I also guarantee that they'll rank the request pretty low on their priorities."

Sam was disappointed. "What about the

weed?" she asked.

"Same thing," Chris replied. "I mean, I can tell you it's terrible stuff, if that's any help — full of dirt and twigs and crap like that. 'Course," she added with a smile, "that's what I know from the literature — not from personal use. But that being said, I have no idea where it's from. Used to be that most of our marijuana was locally produced, but times have changed, as if you didn't know. Now it's a wide-open market and we're getting product from all over the place — including our own backyard."

Her friend's disappointment prompted Chris to add, "I did run it through the mass spec, just to see, and I can tell you it's clean in the sense that nothing's been added to it. There was a craze awhile back when they soaked it in nutty additives like PCP. But not this load. It actually reminded me of the kind of grass they'd rake off the production room floor and sell for cheap to idiot teenagers. Before everybody wised up."

That did little for Sam's mood.

Chris tried another tack. "There were fingerprints on the bag."

That helped. "Whose?" Sam asked hopefully.

Chris hedged a bit. "Not my department, but they *are* being analyzed by the latent print folks. I can find out for you, outside normal channels. Be a lot quicker."

"Would you?"

"Of course," Chris promised. "I'll get right on it. The stable isotope ratio analysis I mentioned might be worth a look, by the way. It's something they were starting to apply as part of the Marijuana Signature Project, around 2006 or so — in Utah, I think — with good results. The nutshell explanation is that plants grown in different settings or regions have different and distinct signatures based on the isotopic composition of a particular region's water. It's like a fingerprint from nature herself. You can see why so many people are using it to trace marijuana." She made a sad face. "Except us, natch. I am sorry about that. Is it very important?"

"It's so low on the totem pole," Sam conceded, "that Willy and I are the only ones looking into it. Between you and me, we're kinda stumped on all fronts right now, so we were hoping this might help."

"As in finding a source for Raffner's stash," Chris sympathized. "I can see where that might be useful."

"Is this isotope thing hard to do?" Sam asked.

Chris laughed. "Can't be too hard. My

188

brother does it in California. Actually, he's tons smarter than me — he sure as hell makes more money. But I'm the bratty little sister, so I have to dis him, right?" She let that go, seeing that Sam's smile was forced at best, and resumed in a more serious tone. "Okay, basically, base elements like carbon, hydrogen, oxygen, and others are in almost everything on earth, albeit in multiple forms. But each form has a specific atomic mass. You remember that from chemistry class?"

"Can't say I do," Sam murmured, having never sat in a chemistry class, much less retained anything said in it.

"Never mind," Chris said. "What matters is that they're called stable isotopes, as against unstable ones, which of course are radioactive. Anyhow, isotopes are attached to everything in the plant world and therefore used to do ecological research. That's what my brother's been doing for years."

"Sure," Sam said, barely following.

But Chris needed no prompting, informed or otherwise. "If you and Willy raid a dope-dealing operation in the Northeast Kingdom, say, you might expect to find all local product. But test what you grabbed for its stable isotopes, and voilà," she said, throwing up her hands. "Turns out some of it's from California or Mexico or Washington State. That would probably be an eye-opener, no? Is that what you're talking about?"

Sam gave her a rueful smile. "Exactly why I'm here, Christine."

Her friend stared at her, slightly embarrassed. "Of course you are. Okay — a compromise: If you get the proper blessing or Hail Mary or whatever from your prosecutor — SA, AG, whoever's on this case — I'll send a sample to my brother and ask him to give it top priority. Turnaround time should be a few days, tops, and I'll ask him to waive the cost as a family favor. Would that do the trick?"

As a response, Sam leaned forward and kissed her cheek.

Chris patted her back. "Cool," she said. "And once we get that data, we can run it by the DEA's index of drug profiles, which is growing weekly, and see if we get a match — that should be virtually instantaneous. Drug dealing is becoming so organized by the crooks that there's an impressive amount of product consistency — at least compared to the old days. It'll end up being like quality control in the legal pharmaceutical market. Who knew?"

"Who, indeed?" Sam agreed.

Twenty minutes later, Sammie hit the Off button to her smartphone and let her hands drop to her lap. She'd pulled off the road in Middlesex — almost to the interstate that would return her to Brattleboro — in order to get authorization for Chris Hartley to send her samples out for testing.

It felt odd to be delving back into illegal drugs. Sam hadn't ventured there since she'd gone undercover to shut down what she'd thought was a major drug operation in the making.

It hadn't been, as events had later proven. She'd been an unwitting pawn in a turf war originating in Holyoke, Massachusetts, and acted out in Rutland, Vermont. She'd feared that she'd stumbled upon an assault by drug traffickers on the little-exploited Vermont market, and had seized on an opportunity to infiltrate one of the warring parties, posing as a local dealer.

But it had been a disaster from the beginning. She hadn't cleared her actions with Joe or anyone else, forcing him to rally a support operation too quickly and with too little information. She'd also completely misinterpreted the true intentions of her supposed partners and had almost gotten herself killed not once, but twice. More personally — and never revealed to a single soul — she'd become too close to her partner-in-crime, a smart and urbane man named Manuel Ruiz, and had almost gone to bed with him.

It had all collapsed on her with devastating effect, keeping her on the job, but reducing her self-esteem to levels she hadn't experienced since childhood. The survivor of a home wracked by alcoholism and abuse, Sam had grown up fearful, angry, and doubtful of her potential. Her almost merciless journey through her teens, a brief career in the military, and then her early years as an overachieving cop, resented by many of her male colleagues, had almost been destroyed by what she'd interpreted as a public humiliation.

Joe, as usual, had smoothed things over and salvaged the good from the rubble of her ambition. Furthermore — and most crucially — neither he nor any of her colleagues had ever expressed anything but support thereafter, allowing her time and space to heal in private.

By the same token, she'd steered clear of drug cases from then on, and — she'd noted ruefully — Joe had never assigned her to one. He was a supportive, caring, and considerate leader. He was also no idiot, as this delicate reprimand had proven — although, in his defense, she'd never asked him if her interpretation was accurate, or a figment of her paranoia.

Life had therefore carried on. The VBI — then virtually an experiment — had earned its keep. She and Willy, who'd just started seeing each other romantically, had moved in together and formed a family with Emma. Manny Ruiz — who'd escaped capture — had slipped from the forefront of her memory, as had his embarrassing effect on her emotions.

The corrosive irony of all this — and perhaps one more reason it had struck her so hard — was that she'd rarely enjoyed working a case more than she had that one, perhaps even because of how intimate she'd become with Ruiz. The adrenaline of flirting with exposure while constantly adapting to changing events had been intoxicating, and had left her as euphoric as she imagined many combat vets were after surviving a close encounter. As a result, a persistent, oddly empty sensation had haunted her ever after, and continued to tug at her imagination. Equating her attraction to undercover drug work with the appetite that rules an addict was an overstatement, but with resonance, nevertheless.

Of course, there was also the argument that her longing was based on the need for personal redemption. That possibility hadn't escaped her, either.

Ever since Willy had first broached the topic of drugs, following his meditation on Raffner's sensual needs, Sammie had wondered if this was what she'd subconsciously hungered for — a chance to succeed where she'd once stumbled, achieve absolution, and even put to rest her dormant remorse over having almost cheated on Willy.

The cell phone in her hand disturbed her reverie. She was surprised to see Chris Hartley's name appear on its screen.

"Hi. You forget something?"

"Just the opposite. I wandered down the hall to consult with my latent print colleagues, and they actually had the results."

"You're kidding."

"Crazy, right? Anyhow, there were two sets of identifiable prints on the larger of the two bags of marijuana — one belonging to Susan, no surprise there — and one to someone named Margaret Kinnison. That one may be a surprise, huh?"

"Why was she on file?"

"Pure quirk," came the answer. "Her

prints were collected years ago for exclusion only — an embezzlement case where all the employees were printed in order to find the on-staff thief. But the prints were never thrown out, as they should've been. Dumb luck, huh? Gotta love it. Of course, you know you can only use them for investigative purposes — they're inadmissible as evidence. But it shouldn't be too tough to get a separate set on your own if and when you meet her. Anyhow, I thought it was such a fluke, I couldn't resist telling you ASAP."

"Totally." Sam matched her enthusiasm, feeling the very rush of adrenaline she'd been contemplating earlier. "You are too much. Thanks, Chris. I owe you big time."

"I've always wanted to hear that one." Chris laughed before hanging up.

Sammie glanced at her watch and began heading for Montpelier as she auto-dialed her phone.

"How's the road trip goin'?" Lester asked as a greeting.

"Not bad. Can you take a look at that list kicking around the office? The one with the names we've associated with Raffner so far?"

There was a pause before he announced, "Got it. Who do you need?"

"Margaret Kinnison."

"Yup. She's here."

195

"Any context given?"

"Just that she works at the State House, is listed as a staffer in the Senate secretary's office, and therefore must've worked with Raffner."

"Outstanding. Thanks."

"She a lead?"

Sam laughed dismissively. "Right up there with looking for Jimmy Hoffa's killer."

She hung up before he could press her further, her hopes overriding a nagging undertow of guilt.

CHAPTER TWELVE

The Vermont State House is a curious combination of elegance — complete with gold dome and classical columns — and lopsided quaintness, because of its small size and oddly imbalanced proportions. But it is pleasingly placed before a broad, snow-covered slope, flanked by the appropriate cannon and statuary, and is a perpetual favorite among camera-toting tourists.

Unless they want to park. On that score — at least while the legislature is in session — Sam found the capital to be the single most irritating place in the state. As she always did when in town, therefore, she abandoned her car at the first illegal spot that she happened upon, threw her credentials onto the dash, and walked to the capitol building.

There, just inside the heavy front doors, she introduced herself at the sergeant-at-arms's office, and asked where she might find Margaret Kinnison.

In terms of efficiency and protocol combined, Sammie knew that she shouldn't be here. Parker and Perry included this town in their territory, after all, and were already fully engaged in the investigation. Vermont cops had jurisdiction wherever they went within the state, and certainly any VBI agent was free to act wherever he or she chose. But there were rules of etiquette, which Sam had already bruised by traveling to see Chris Hartley. Coming here, to meet someone with whom she had no personal connection whatsoever, was a more flagrant affront — and one about which she couldn't have cared less. It was becoming increasingly clear that the influence she and Willy had on each other was happily cross-germinating — good news for him, more complicated to define for her.

She ended up on the first floor, amid a tangle of offices and cramped hearing rooms, fed by an inexhaustible flow of people moving at high speed and either talking to each other or muttering on cell phones. Sam felt like a teenager on her first day in high school, scrutinizing door numbers and labels to find out where she needed to be — hoping not to be run over. The capitol is reflective of the sobriquet "the people's house" in quite concrete terms — for the most part, its elected residents don't have offices. They are therefore readily available to their constituents, unless they're hiding off campus in their cars or at a bar. Everyone tends to mill about, as a result, either on a mission or hoping to find a quiet corner to do some work. It makes the efforts of the shared secretarial and support staff that much more challenging.

At last, Sam found herself in the doorway of a small subcommittee room, overfilled with a long table and a cordon of empty chairs. It was populated solely by a short, sturdy, nervous-looking woman, standing at the table's head and gathering together a thick sheaf of loose papers left over from a just-concluded meeting.

She looked up as Sammie entered. "May I help you?"

Sam showed the badge on her belt by opening her coat. "Margaret Kinnison?"

The woman's expression didn't change, but her hands froze in mid-motion. "Yes."

"You available to answer a few questions?"

"What about?"

Sam kept her voice at a near monotone — neither threatening nor comforting. "A couple of things, starting with Susan Raff-

199

ner's murder."

Kinnison straightened. "Me? What would I know about that?"

Sam barely smiled. "My very point."

In the brief silence following her one-liner, Sam watched the other woman lower her eyes, swallow hard, fiddle with her papers without seeing them, and then say, "I don't know anything."

Sam stepped farther into the room and shut the door behind her, severing the hubbub outside as if with a guillotine. She asked, "We gonna be left alone here for a few minutes?"

Kinnison checked her watch. "We should be."

Sam gestured with her chin toward the chair at Kinnison's waist. "Sit."

She did so as Sam removed a small recorder from her pocket, laid it on the large table, and removed her coat. "You got a problem with me recording this?"

Kinnison was sitting down awkwardly, bumping her knee against the table's skirt board. "No, no. That's okay."

Sam sat nearby. "For the record," she intoned, "I'm Special Agent Samantha Martens of the VBI, and I'm with" — she looked directly at her subject — "would you state your name for the record?"

"Margaret Kinnison."

"What is your date of birth?"

Kinnison recited it, followed by Sam's informing the recorder of the day's time and date, and their present location.

"What do you do at the State House, Ms. Kinnison?" she then inquired.

"I'm a senate liaison. Kind of a glorified secretary, really," Kinnison threw in with a sad smile. "I and people like me keep the paperwork moving in the senate and between the senators and others in this building."

"Did you know Susan Raffner?"

"Sure. I know all the senators."

"Some better than others?"

"I'm not sure what you mean. I work more for some than for others. A few of them are well enough organized that they don't need much help."

"And Raffner?"

Again the nervous half smile. "She was one of the needy ones. Very nice woman, and supersmart. Not so good keeping everything in order."

"So you spent a lot of time with her."

It wasn't a question. "I guess I did."

"Outside the building, too?"

"We go over to the Pavilion next door sometimes, if we have to coordinate

201

something with the governor's office."

"How 'bout beyond there, maybe for personal errands?"

Kinnison repeated the eye shifting and paper shuffling. "I guess," she replied in a lower voice. "Maybe."

"What for?"

"You know, normal stuff. Get a sandwich for her."

"Did you ever see her socially?"

That response immediately invoked a rare flash of direct eye contact, quickly broken off. "Oh, no."

"She draw the line there?"

"Not in so many words, but she was nice to us, generally."

"You're suggesting a have/have-nots division."

"I guess," she said again.

"How did that feel?"

"Okay. They're the bosses. We just work here."

"Did you have contact with her only during office hours?"

"No."

"So how did that work?" Sam pressed her. "She call you?"

"She gave me a pager."

Sam scowled. "She do that with the other staffers?"

"No."

"How did you rate the extra attention?"

"I . . . don't know."

Sam placed both forearms on the table. "What did she have on you, Margaret?"

Kinnison remained tucked in, with only the crown of her head showing. "I don't know why she was killed."

"I didn't ask you that. Why did you say that?"

Long pause. "I don't know."

"I think you have your suspicions, Margaret. She was a powerful, influential woman. She pissed off a lot of people. Did she piss you off, too?"

Surprising to Sam, Kinnison did not look up. "No."

"Then what?"

No response. Sam reviewed what she'd just heard, comparing it to what she knew of Susan Raffner.

"She scare you?" she asked.

The head nodded wordlessly.

"That's 'yes'?"

"Yes." It was barely a whisper.

"To the point where you thought you might lose your job if you didn't cooperate?"

"Yes."

"Was that because of something she said to you?"

"No."

Sam fought to control her frustration. This woman was making her think of a small animal, responding to threats real and imagined without discrimination.

"Margaret, I think I'm getting it," she said in a gentler voice. "Susan Raffner was like a force of nature, expecting a response whenever she made a suggestion. Did you find that both attractive and maybe a little scary?"

"Yes."

"And it made you feel important and invisible at the same time?"

"Yes."

"Did that make you volunteer more than you might have for somebody else?"

This time, it was just the head nod again, which Sammie didn't ask to be verbalized. She'd abandoned any notion of a clean and forensic interview by now, opting instead for leading questions only. She was impatient enough that she no longer cared how well this recording would hold up to legal scrutiny — and by contrast, sure enough from her subject's compliance that she'd get what she was after.

"Let's focus on what she asked you to do when you were off the clock, Margaret," she said. "You said you'd go out for food sometimes."

"Yes."

"What else?"

"Groceries. Dry cleaning."

"Buy some drugs."

The muted noise from the hallway slowly took over the long silence in the room. Sam became aware that Kinnison was crying, her tears dropping on the backs of her clutched hands.

"Tell me, Margaret."

Nothing.

"We have your fingerprints on a bag of marijuana."

Still, silence.

Sam changed directions slightly. "What do people call you? Is it Margaret?"

"Maggie."

Sam rose, her chair screeching on the floor. She leaned across the space separating them, her hands flat on the table. "Maggie, if you were worried you might lose your job because of pissing off Susan Raffner, I guarantee you a lot worse if you don't start talking. Tell me how your prints got on that bag."

At last, Kinnison looked up, her cheeks damp. "She said her regular supplier had been arrested, and that she needed a refill."

"How did she know to ask you?"

"She got me talking one day, about when I was younger and a little out of control. She could be really persuasive and nice when she wanted to be, and I was trying to make a good impression. I told her I'd done some drugs but had managed not to get busted. It wasn't then, but maybe a few weeks later, she brought it back up, and told me how I could help her out. Not 'if,' but 'how.' That was the way she put it. I didn't feel like I had much choice."

"Plus," Sammie suggested, "you were still doing drugs, even if only now and then."

Kinnison hesitated.

"About which I couldn't care less," Sam told her. "Keep going. You got hold of your source?"

"Not really," she answered slowly. "I don't smoke marijuana — never have. I had to find somebody else — sort of a friend-of-a-friend thing."

"Go on."

"Well, that was it. I found the source, Susan gave me money, and I bought it for her."

Sam settled back into her chair, her prayers of the past twenty-four hours answered. Whether it ended up having anything to do with Raffner's death or not, at least she was getting some traction.

"From the top, Maggie. Who was the source? How much money changed hands? Where did it happen? Don't leave anything out."

Maggie's face creased with anxiety. "I don't know names. I only know my guy."

"What's his name?" Sam almost shouted. "For Christ's sake, Maggie. Get your head in the game. This is a murder investigation. We don't give a shit about you unless you start ticking me off. Then I'll cut you down like grass in front of a lawn mower. Is that clear enough for you?"

There was a knock at the door and a young woman poked her head in. She opened her mouth to say something, but Sam interrupted her with, "Get out. Police business."

The door shut.

"Talk," she ordered.

By now, Kinnison was sitting back in her chair, her hands in her lap, openly crying. "His name is Brandon Younger. He lives in Hartford, Vermont. But he gave me the number of somebody in Rutland. It was a TracFone, though, so the number's long gone, and I never was given a name. I called it, said I had a thousand dollars for the best weed he had, preferably Canadian hydro — which is what Susan had asked for — and could we meet up? He said sure, and that's what I did."

"Alone, or with Susan?"

She shook her head. "No. That was the whole point. Susan didn't want to take the risk, now that she was a senator. I was to be her buffer. That's what she called it. And she paid me, too."

"How much?"

"Three hundred dollars."

"Okay, so you go to Rutland and meet this guy. Where? What were the details?"

"I think it was South Street, but I'm not sure. An area they call the Gut. I was told to drive slowly, until I saw a boy wearing a top hat, and then I was to pull over and park. It was night, a little scary, and that part of the block was really dark, as if on purpose. I rolled the window down and stayed in the car, like I was told. That's when some man came up from behind, like cops do when they pull you over, and we did the sale — the money for a really big bag of grass. After that, he disappeared and I drove away. That's all there was to it."

"What did you see of him?"

"Nothing. His belt buckle. It had the word 'Indian' written on an Indian's war bonnet, like in profile."

"He was alone? What happened to the kid?"

"I never saw him again. But there was somebody behind the man with the belt buckle, in the dark. I could just see his outline, but that was all."

"What was said?"

"Not much," Kinnison said, calmer now. "Belt Buckle asked if I had the money. I asked if he had the dope, and we made the exchange."

"That was it?"

Maggie thought back. "The man behind Belt Buckle told him to make sure it was all there, and Belt Buckle got angry and said that he had it."

"What did he say — specifically?"

" 'Fuck, Stuey, I got it, okay?' I think that was it."

Sammie felt the blood drain from her face. "He called him Stuey? You're sure?"

"That's what I heard."

Sam pretended to check the recorder, making sure it was still running, while actually processing what she'd just heard. That decade ago, when she felt she'd so badly dropped the ball going undercover in Rutland, the man who'd come close to killing her after recognizing her as a cop had been Allan Steward Nichols, always called

Stuey. Only Willy's timely arrival had saved her life.

"Do you think you'd recognize Stuey's voice if you heard it again?"

But Kinnison shook her head. "I barely heard it then, and I never really saw him. He was just a shadow."

"No problem," Sam reassured her. "So you drove out and delivered the bag to Susan. Is that correct?"

"Yes, but she got really upset with me a day later. She told me that I'd been ripped off and that what I'd bought was garbage. That was the word she used." Kinnison's voice rose into a whine. "I told her from the start I didn't know anything about weed. How was I supposed to know if it was any good? Plus, it was all wrapped up. Did she really want me to sample the stuff? She would've yelled at me for *that,* then."

"I hear you, Maggie," Sammie soothed her. "She put you between a rock and a hard place. What happened after she confronted you?"

"Nothing, as far as I know. She asked me what you just did, for names and places and the rest, but I forgot the Stuey part 'cause she was so mad, and that was it. I said I was sorry a few more times, till she made it clear that it was a closed subject and that I was never to mention it again. That's when I really got the feeling that my job here was sort of hanging by a thread."

"She threatened you?"

"No. But I could tell she stayed pissed off. She was much cooler to me from then on. And she took her pager back."

"How long ago was this?"

Kinnison thought for a moment before stating, "A week? Maybe less."

Sam let some thirty seconds elapse while she reflected on what she'd gathered. She then had Maggie swear to the truthfulness of her statement before ending the recording, told her to stay available for further conversation, and let her leave.

After the door closed once more, however, Sammie remained seated, caught up in a swirl of emotions.

In terms of facts, all she had was corroboration of something they already knew: Susan Raffner had been in possession of illegally purchased marijuana. Sam had now learned how that had come about, but it still didn't connect to Raffner's murder. Raffner hadn't been at the point of sale, hadn't known the seller, and hadn't been given Stuey's name afterward. According to Margaret Kinnison, she'd merely been angered by the transaction's outcome, and then had dropped the matter.

Which left Sam in a private quandary.

She could report what she'd learned — as immaterial as it seemed — and fold it into the overall investigation, where everyone else would then learn about Stuey Nichols's resurfacing in such a coincidental fashion.

Or she could hold off on the revelation and spend some personal time checking into what more might be hovering just out of sight.

Nichols could well be clear of anything related to Raffner, but he was obviously back to dealing drugs — if via a surrogate. And — she rationalized — despite the magnitude of this homicide investigation, it did not preclude other cases from being pursued. That was part of any cop's job description. Thus, went her thinking, she wouldn't be emulating Willy by going solo on this — she was simply being thorough.

She might even bring Willy into it. That way, she wouldn't actually be keeping Stuey to herself — or the baggage he represented.

Chapter Thirteen

Gail looked up from the stack of papers she'd been pretending to read. Alice Drim was standing in the doorway, more paperwork in her hands.

"What is it?" Gail asked.

Alice smiled sadly. "You look wiped, Governor."

Gail shrugged. "Yeah. Well . . ." She indicated the pages Alice was carrying. "That for me?"

Alice approached and laid the pile on the desk between them. "Just for signing. They've all been checked and double-checked. Most of them are thank-yous for contributions."

"How're we doing there?" Gail asked. "The war chest getting close to deserving the name?"

Alice's face cleared. "Oh, Lord, yes. We already have over a million in the till. Your handling of Tropical Storm Irene was right up there with putting a printing press in the basement."

"Even with the lesbian fallout?"

After a moment's hesitation, Alice conceded. "Even with. A lot of people are behind you on that."

Gail nodded thankfully. "Thanks. I know you weren't so sure about it yourself."

Alice pursed her lips thoughtfully before responding. "I don't have your courage. You keep doing amazing things, and even though they don't always work out, I think people respect your willingness to try."

She stared at the floor for a moment, as if struggling with how to broach a new topic.

"What?" Gail asked.

Alice looked embarrassed. "It sounds stupid. But out in the front office, we heard that Ellen DeGeneres's people had called about an interview. I guess somebody heard Kayla talking on the phone. Are you going to say yes?"

Gail laughed despite her weariness and grief. "You think I should?"

The young woman's face opened up. "Absolutely. Are you kidding? I mean, self-ishly, as your reelection coordinator, I strongly recommend it — the money'll start really pouring in if you do. But it's also just awesome. Ellen DeGeneres? That would be so amazing."

Surprisingly charmed by Alice's eager naivete, Gail shook her head. "Okay. I'll give it serious consideration. You hear what Rob has to say about it?"

"I think he's pretty psyched, but he'll tell you himself. And he'll probably try to make it as boring as he can. You know him. But don't let him fool you. I mean, what's the downside?"

"What, indeed?" Gail agreed, adding after a pause, "How're you doing, Alice? I heard you've been having a hard time."

The young woman shrugged. "No secrets in this office, right?" She hesitated before admitting, "I have a brother in the hospital. We think he'll be okay, but only time'll tell. Not like Kayla's grandmother, though. She died. Did you hear that?"

Gail shook her head, forced to consider all the lives around her, so often taken for granted, but each burdened with its own troubles and heartache. "No. I'm sorry to hear it. Thanks for telling me. I'll be sure to ask her how she's doing."

Alice walked to the door, flashing a sudden smile before leaving. "Sure. Don't forget about Ellen. I hope I get to meet her."

Willy groaned. "Stuey's back? Proof there's

no God."

Sam passed him a piece of the pizza she'd brought home from her field trip north. "I considered not telling you."

"Really? Just because I almost killed him last time? How long you think I bear a grudge?"

She answered by laughing with her mouth full.

He smiled back. "Point taken." He took a bite and chewed thoughtfully. "How'd you find out?"

"He had something to do with selling Susan Raffner that crappy grass," she explained, before giving him details of her interview with Maggie Kinnison — and of the conversation she'd had with Chris Hartley before then.

He didn't interrupt, or do more than work his way through a second slice. After she'd concluded, however, he adjusted Emma's pacifier — she was sitting in her carrier, on the table, watching them intently — and sat back.

"What're you looking for?" he asked.

She placed her own unfinished wedge on the plate before her. "Looking for?"

He chided her gently. "I know you, Sam. You're working an angle. You want to tie Stuey into this?"

"Isn't he already there?"

"No more than the guy who filled her gas tank that morning."

She was struck by the pure logic of the comment, and with the fact that he'd been the one to make it.

"You don't want a piece of this creep?" she asked.

He then gave her the look to which she was all too accustomed — and which, this time, she'd been so fervently hoping he'd deliver. "I didn't say that."

"Anything?" Joe asked.

Lester looked up from peering inside a box on the table before him. The basement room they were in was filled with similar containers — piled five deep in some cases — all brought in from Susan Raffner's Brattleboro home, and all being pawed through laboriously by a half-dozen weary VBI investigators. Joe had just descended three flights from his office to see how they were doing. Earlier, he'd phoned Parker and Perry in Waterbury with the same question, since they were doing roughly the same thing with the contents of Susan's apartment in Montpelier.

There were also several computers open and running, so that they could pore over what had been collected from her electronic devices.

Joe raised his own much smaller — but, he hoped, more appreciated — box into the air. "Doughnuts," he announced to a generalized if feeble cheer. "I tried to make them as unhealthy as I could."

He placed them on a counter running the length of one wall and stepped aside to chat with Lester, whom he knew wouldn't indulge.

"The tough part with all this," Lester was saying, waving a hand at the room and its contents, "is that there could be a hundred potential killers lurking behind the reports, letters, e-mails, memos, and everything else we're digging out."

He pointed at the ten-foot whiteboard hanging on the opposite wall. "We're logging each of them in, cross-indexing names and organizations, assigning threat levels as we go. But it's starting to numb the brain and make me think it's all basically canceling itself out."

"How so?"

"She picked a fight with everybody," Lester exclaimed, his frustration peaking. A couple of people near the doughnut box laughed and one of them chimed in, "A total pain in the ass."

"But no one who stands out."

Lester perched his long, skinny frame on the edge of the nearest table, which still left him virtually eye-to-eye with Joe. "Nobody who says, 'That does it, bitch. You're toast.' But like I said, that doesn't mean somebody in this mess didn't finally snap and want her dead."

Lester pointed toward the exit. "How 'bout in the field? Anyone getting a good interview somewhere? What's the weather like, anyhow?"

It was in fact a spectacular day — sunny bright, with a cobalt blue sky, making a fresh overnight snowfall dazzle the eye. "It's okay," Joe reported instead. "But there's no joy anywhere in Mudville. The local cops in Montpelier and Bratt are helping out, along with the troopers. So we've got, grand total, anywhere up to twenty-five people working this from all angles. But still, like here, we're only getting a picture of a woman who worked nonstop to right every wrong she could find."

"Whether it was a wrong or not," Lester added.

Joe smiled. "There is that. She was opinionated, if nothing else."

The phone in his pocket began vibrating, and he took it out to read its screen. It was

David Hawke, the crime lab's director.

"Speak of the devil," he told Lester. "This, I'll take." He stepped out into the hallway for more quiet.

"David," he then said, looking around to make sure he was alone in the gloomy municipal building's virtual crypt of a basement — usually a safe bet.

"Considering how you guys have been bugging us up here," Hawke said, "I thought I'd give you a sneak peek at something we just found, before I send out official notifications."

"I am sorry about that, David. This thing is driving us nuts. What've you got?"

"As you know, along with all the other junk that's been dumped on us, we ended up with Susan Raffner's vehicle."

"Right."

"Well, we've started going through it, and I thought you should know that we found a fingernail in the rearmost storage area — behind the wire dog partition. The DNA says it's hers."

"The right index," Joe guessed, recalling the autopsy.

"Yup, along with the smallest hint of blood, implying a violent and painful removal."

"Where was it — specifically?"

"You might ask," David reacted approvingly. "I did, too. It was wedged in between the bottom edge of the rear hatch and the hinged floor cover, as if someone had been trying to access the lock release."

"Trying to get out, you mean?"

"Indirectly. It's a little tough to explain without the car, but both the Prius's toolbox and mechanical door release are tucked in under a trapdoor in that rear floor. Nice idea, making everything neat and tidy, and maybe even accessible to an athletic leprechaun who's crawling into the back from the inside after dropping down the car's rear seats. But not so easy if you've been dumped on top of the very trapdoor you're trying to pry open. Plus, that wire partition was professionally mounted. It's solid. From the hair samples we gathered, I'd say she had a Corgi. Does that fit?"

"Yes," Joe told him. "She loved that mutt. Yapped constantly. One of her friends has him now, from what I heard."

"Well, anyhow," Hawke resumed, being thorough, "none of this absolutely indicates that she was reaching for the release catch. She might've also been going for Toyota's version of a tire iron, or maybe she just caught her nail at a different time for some unrelated and completely innocent reason

— although the freshness of the nail fragment implies otherwise."

"What you're saying," Joe suggested, "is that it's consistent with someone having tossed her into the back of her own car — basically into a cage."

"It is."

Joe let the image sink in for a second. "You still working on the rest of it?"

"You know we are."

"Thank you, David."

Joe could almost hear the smile over the phone. "You're welcome, Joseph."

"Oh. Wait. David?" Joe suddenly said.

"What?"

"You said we'd been bugging you about results. That's not supposed to be happening. Who's been on your case?"

"Nah," the director conceded dismissively, "I wasn't complaining. I know how something like this gets everyone's engine revving. No big deal."

"Still . . ."

"I saw Sam in here yesterday, chatting with Chris Hartley. They may've been just catching up, but the conversation looked pretty intense, and I know Sammie can get like a dog with a bone. I was just yanking your chain, though, so don't jam her up, okay?"

"Got it, David. Thanks again."

"You're welcome."

Joe hesitated, sensing that his friend had something more on his mind. "What?"

"It's probably nothing. Well, it's certainly nothing I can do anything with," Hawke admitted. "But the footprints that were photographed at the scene of the hanging?"

"What about them?"

"I can't really put this in scientific terms, but they're a little odd. In and of themselves, they're just rubber-soled, size-eleven boots, from all appearances — standard Vibram soles, available at any Walmart. But I think the person wearing them had something physically abnormal going on. Call it an irregularly irregular gait."

"A limp?"

Hawke laughed self-consciously. "I knew I shouldn't've brought it up. It's too vague. A limp would be regularly irregular. What I'm talking about isn't that. It's more subtle — call it a randomness in structure. It's as if the footprint owner had a bilateral leg tremor that made each foot land ever so slightly differently every time he stepped on the snow."

"But you can't say for sure that he has a disability."

"No. In fact, what I'm seeing might have

been induced by stress or weight. Could've been that he was carrying something that made him stagger erratically — but just a bit."

"All right," Joe said after a pause. "Thanks. If inspiration strikes in the middle of the night, don't hesitate to call."

He pocketed the phone thoughtfully and noticed Lester standing in the open door of what they were calling the Case Research Room.

"Everything okay?" Lester asked.

"Hypothetically," Joe posited, as if resuming a different conversation, "if Nathan Fellows was framed, it had to have been by someone who knew him."

Lester went along. "Maybe not. They could've just heard about how mouthy he was."

"They had his return address — or at least his hometown."

Spinney nodded. "Okay. Yeah." He indicated the room behind him. "So far, except for the one letter supposedly written by him, we've found nothing. Not from him, not about him, nothing."

"But there wouldn't be, would there?" Joe countered. "That's the point — to send us in the wrong direction."

Lester blinked slowly. "Where're you going with this, boss?"

Joe pursed his lips before replying. "Guess I'm just trying to find a loophole somewhere. You kill someone because you're really pissed off at them."

"Or you're drunk or on drugs," Lester added, "and you have no idea what you're doing."

"Okay, but let's assume it wasn't that spontaneous, mostly because everything else about this seems well thought-out."

Lester wasn't giving up so easily. "But it could've been spur-of-the-moment. That letter from Fellows could've been planted after the fact. Remember: It didn't have a stamp, and therefore no postmark showing when or if it was actually mailed. We might be dealing with a quick thinker — he kills Susan, says, 'Oh, shit,' and starts building his beaver dam with the few hours he's got before the alarm is sounded. Then he sits back and watches us run all over the place."

"Meaning he's watching us now?"

Spinney shrugged. "Could be. You wouldn't do this unless you were stuck in plain sight. On the other hand, given how many people knew or worked or fought with Susan Raffner, we're talking half the state's population."

"That call I just got was David Hawke,

saying they found Susan's fingernail in the back of her own car."

"So she was stuffed away, still alive, and driven somewhere?"

"Yeah, but only partway. The tire tracks at the hanging didn't belong to her car, so her killer had to have switched. Not only that, but Hillstrom said the second head injury killed her instantly, which suggests she received it *after* being confined."

"Fitting the scenario that she was grabbed, pushed around, and hit on the head earlier, maybe rendering her unconscious. Could be she woke up in the car and tried to get out."

"Which," Joe explained, "she couldn't because of the dog cage she'd had fitted in the back — a detail I hadn't thought of. She was probably yelling at her attacker as they drove."

"That may've been what bought her the second blow on the head," Lester mused.

They paused, considering the variables. "That bruise across her back," Joe suggested softly. "You could get that from the edge of a car trunk."

Spinney didn't respond, since each of them knew that was but one possibility.

Instead, he asked, "Hawke have anything else?"

"Not that he shared. He did say they were still processing the car, which — given the fingernail — I'm glad to hear. *Somebody* drove the damn thing at the end. We know that for a fact. Susan did not park it in a junkyard herself."

Lester glanced over his shoulder, prompting Joe to say, "Go back to it, Lester. Thanks for hearing me out."

"You got it, boss. I'll let you know when we find the signed confession."

He closed the door behind him, leaving Joe in the semi-gloom of the hallway. The basement of the municipal building also made him think of the bowels of some pre–World War I ocean liner — not that he had any vast experience with those. But it was high-ceilinged and tenebrous and long and narrow — not to mention imbued with just the right aura of decay. It seemed a perfect match for his increasingly pessimistic mood.

He reviewed his seemingly random and largely pointless exchange with Spinney, returning to his question at the beginning of it.

Why and how, specifically, had Nathan Fellows been made the patsy in all this — assuming he had been?

Joe checked his watch and decided to

drive back north, to revisit Nate's old neighborhood.

CHAPTER FOURTEEN

For Joe, one of the enduring attractions of being a major crimes investigator was the freedom to follow his hunches. After decades of trying on most jobs that his profession had to offer — at least within Vermont's limited sphere — he was where he'd always aspired to be, which was neither the top honcho, assailed daily by media types and hand-wringing politicians, nor among the rank and file, having to spend days in a windowless room raking through a dead woman's files.

As he eased out of his car in the Newport police department's parking lot on Field Avenue, he was once again struck by his good fortune — especially having just left Spinney in that Brattleboro basement.

A redbrick building among a cluster of similar brethren — the library and the courthouse among them — the PD was the clear winner for ugliest duckling. Not that it didn't have some historical gravitas, assuming one's taste ran to the flat-roofed, heavy-browed, nineteenth-century armory look.

A man in a black overcoat and leather gloves exited the building and waved to Joe as he was halfway across the lot. "Hey, there. Long time, no see. What's it been? A few days? I don't see you for five years. Now I can't get rid of you."

Following Cila's shooting, Joe had seen police chief Bill Mares, but only on the fly, as Cila was being prepped for transport via helicopter to the hospital.

They shook hands, and Joe's companion took his elbow and steered him toward Main Street at the corner, explaining, "It's colder than a witch's tit today and I'm hungrier than hell. Grab an early lunch? That work for you? On the phone you said you just wanted to pick my brains — always better when they're being fed."

"No problem," Joe agreed, not seeing much option anyhow. "You guys busy this time of year?"

"Aside from police-involved shootings?" Mares laughed. "Not too bad. The weather's a trade-off — we get more domestics when everyone's cooped up, but I can't complain. How're you coming with the case? Oh" — he suddenly changed tone — "and how's

Cila doin'?"

"She's fine," Joe told him. "From what I hear, there won't be any permanent damage. The case . . . I can't say that's as healthy. One of the reasons I'm here."

"Yeah," Mares sympathized. "I figured as much." He guided them across the street and down the block to a small restaurant with partially steamed-up windows.

"You'll like this," he said. "Quiet, fast, cheap, friendly, and you can pronounce what it serves."

He navigated the length of the place with the ease of a man at home, and settled into the last booth of a long row, facing the door. The booth having high bench backs, Joe didn't mind settling in opposite him, conceding that since it was Mares's patch, he was entitled to choose the catbird seat.

The chief called out to the woman behind the counter, "Shirley, we might need a menu for my friend."

Joe turned to add, "Just a bowl of soup and a Coke will do me. Your choice on the soup."

Mares said no more to her, and Joe surmised that he'd long ago settled on a meal that he enjoyed every time he dropped in.

He wasn't wrong. With Joe's fresh-from-the-can New England clam chowder came a thick Reuben and fries for Mares, along with a thermos of black coffee.

"Why're you still looking into Nate Fellows?" Mares asked as he wrapped his thick fingers around the Reuben. "I thought you'd written him off as a fall guy — at least, that's the rumor."

"It's why, and if, he was chosen that's got me curious," Joe explained. "It's like an itch I can't reach."

Mares took a large bite and chewed meditatively. "I hate those. Who iced the senator if not him?"

Joe brushed the question away. "We've got a small army working on that."

"And a checkbook from heaven to pay 'em," Mares commented with envy.

Joe couldn't argue. "I haven't heard any grumbling about expenditures. Were you able to poke into Fellows's background?"

Mares took a swig of coffee as Joe sampled his soup. "Yeah. 'Course I have no clue what you got already, which is probably everything."

"No," Joe reassured him. "Once we started thinking he'd been set up, we pretty much dropped him, which may've been a mistake."

"Oh, I don't know," Mares tried setting

him at ease. "Nate was a dime a dozen. Maybe more over the top with all the Nazi crap, but otherwise your average brain-dead, wife-beating, beer-guzzling, jail-happy piece of shit who couldn't keep his act together if you gave him a million bucks. No mastermind — that's for sure — so you were probably right not to give him much thought."

Joe was used to the dismissive litany dear to the hearts of so many cops — also sometimes a cynical mantle worn out of self-protection and pride. But he was actually struck by one detail he hadn't heard before.

"He had a wife?"

"Yeah, not that he acted like he knew it. Kids, too. Of course, they got farmed out to foster care years ago. I called DCF just before you got here, to brush up. Our interactions with Nate hadn't involved family stuff in a long time — just the usual drunk and disorderly, disturbing the peace, DUIs, license suspended, and the rest." He paused to take another bite. "Anyhow, records say he was married to a Stacy Barton."

"But this is ancient history."

"It is if your average life span is thirty-two, like for most of these geniuses. I'd guess Nate and Stacy went their separate ways ten years ago or more. I wouldn't swear they haven't been in touch since, though. A lot of these girls are like moths to a flame. You tell 'em they're flirting with disaster, the evidence piles up — with trips to the emergency room or detox or jail — and it still does no good. It's like a kinky attraction. I know nothing about this couple, but we've all seen it before, haven't we?"

"Sad to say," Joe agreed. "Okay, then, what about someone else? A new girlfriend, a regular drinking buddy — someone here in town he hung out with?"

Mares's face brightened, while he paused to eat some more before responding. "Wylie Dupont. You'll love him. Complete opposite of Fellows. Nate was all 'tude, all the time. In your face, 'Whatcha gonna do about it?' Fight first and ask questions later. Wylie? A real doofus. Kinda sweet, pretty stupid, and totally harmless. For a paranoid like Nate, Wylie must've been perfect — no threat whatsoever."

Joe pushed away the soup that he'd been working on throughout and pulled out his notepad. "You got a location on him?"

Mares rattled off a Bay Street address. "He rents a room. It's a flophouse. He's been there for years. That's where I'd start.

He works odd jobs — burning burgers, pumping gas, bagging groceries — but only when he has to. He also steals. We've caught him a few times, but he's good enough to get away with it most of the time — doesn't take too much, doesn't brag when he does, doesn't flash the cash or go crazy to attract our attention."

"Okay," Joe said. "How 'bout anyone who hated Nate's guts?"

"Ah. Less easy to define. We did — I can tell you that. You know how it goes — you get a population of a few thousand people, you tangle pretty much all the time with the same fifty or a hundred badasses. And inside that group of frequent flyers, you get the select few who just bust your balls like clockwork. That was Nate. And we weren't the only ones. He just had that effect on people."

"And yet he was employed when we found him," Joe commented.

"Yeah," Mares agreed. "Recently. He was smart enough, and capable. Good with his hands. But it would never last. On that level, he was like his buddy Wylie, but where Wylie can never qualify for much more than taking out your garbage, Nate could sell himself — until he actually got the job, of course. Then he'd turn into a jackass and get himself canned. Regular as rain."

"Okay — that's his institutional reputation. What about one-on-one? Did he ever send anyone to the hospital or get into a feud or target somebody for special attention?"

"Like gays?"

"No. Someone specifically, who might've decided to pay him back."

Mares poured himself a third cup of coffee, having demolished the sandwich. "Oh, I get you. Huh. God, the guy was so busy pissing everybody off, I'm having a hard time picking out just one." He paused to think and take another sip, before admitting, "Nothing stands out, Joe. I'm sorry. Maybe that's where Wylie'll come in handy, specially now that Nate's dead. I would guess he's dyin' for company."

Sammie Martens pulled into the Rutland Plaza shopping center's vast parking lot, its stark modernity at odds with the row of ornately decorated, turn-of-the-century buildings directly across the street — standing shoulder-to-shoulder as if in defense of an older, less efficient, but more artistically sensitive time.

She was feeling forlorn, unsure of her motives or even her loyalties, amid the ghosts of her decade-old fiasco. Back then, the generalized relief over her survival had allowed everyone to more or less move on. But now, once more in Rutland — to which she hadn't returned since — her adrenaline of a couple of days ago, stimulated by hopes of redemption, had yielded to a fear that she might be not only repeating history, but involving the father of her child in the process.

She checked her watch. She was here to meet Willy, who was coming from another direction. She'd actually cooked up an excuse not to ride with him, in order to arrive sooner and allow some time to drive around the city, reacquainting herself with the geography.

Rutland was not a complex socioeconomic puzzle. A working-class, ex-railroad and marble quarrying center, it had the standard big-town skeleton of rich and poor neighborhoods, historic downtown, and a couple of tacky commercial strips. It also had the railroad, was the state's third largest city, and a major urban hub.

And it was home of the Gut, a mysteriously named neighborhood, literally located beyond the railroad tracks, that had long been the recipient — often unfairly — of people's disparaging comments. Nevertheless, the Gut had historically attracted most of the city's more active drug business, which had only grown as of late.

That last development had only further darkened her mood, seeing her old stomping grounds slip by. The so-called war on drugs had been invoked enough times to drain the phrase of meaning. Which didn't mean that Vermont's recent headlines for heroin abuse weren't well deserved. The forces that Sam had tried to staunch had only expanded, and their lethality had spread with heroin's increasing purity and affordability.

Was it therefore wrong of her to have seized on a vague connection between the high-profile murder of Susan Raffner and the overall drug trade, possibly to the benefit of addressing both?

It was a stretch. She knew it. But with Willy's help and encouragement, she'd been loath to resist the temptation to coincidentally correct an old embarrassment, while making some headway on a stalled case.

Some old impulsive habits were harder to break than others.

"If I'd wanted you dead, you'd be dead."

She snapped out of her reverie at Willy's voice in her ear, and twisted around to find him inches away from her side window.

She rolled the glass down. "Jesus. How long you been there?"

He jerked his thumb to the back of the car. "I parked right behind you. Where were you?"

She rubbed her forehead. "Wondering if this is such a great idea."

He walked around and got into her passenger seat. "Ah, scruples," he sighed. "I always wondered what it was like to drag those around."

"Fuck you," she said. "You got more scruples in that stupid arm of yours than anyone I know. You just pretend you're a tough guy."

He didn't argue the point. "You wanna call this off?"

She cut him a look. In the old days, he would have been all derision and taunting. Such a question now reinforced her high opinion of him.

Which didn't mean she was buying it. "So you can turn cowboy and maybe get yourself killed? I don't think so. If we're about to end our careers, I'd just as soon do it together."

"I doubt it's that hairy a deal," Willy commented. "By following Raffner's stash to its source, we're just following a lead."

"Without telling anyone," she countered. "That shows the courage of our conviction."

Willy laughed. "Hey. I'm covered. I'm the official stray bullet — per the boss. You're the one feeling like you're playing hooky."

"Thanks a lot," she muttered.

He grinned. "I'm here, Sam. So what's your plan?"

"You ask Bob Crawford to hook up with us?" she asked.

"You command, I do," he replied.

"You are such a bullshitter." She smiled. "Well, Bob *is* my plan, since you already briefed him on the Newport mess. There've been a lot of changes in this town since I was under — the drug squad's been disbanded, a new police chief's taken over, the community's more involved than it was. Crawford has his eyes open. I'm hoping he'll give us a lay-of-the-land snapshot. I don't want to cold-call Stuey without knowing what he's been up to and who he's allied with nowadays."

Willy checked his watch and slouched down in his seat. "Okay — hurry-up-and-wait time."

Joe slowed just shy of Wylie Dupont's address on Bay Street. Mares's description of the place as a flophouse had been charitable.

It was a two-story, small-windowed, sway-backed, ex-barn wrapped in peeling Tyvek sheeting. It looked as if someone years earlier — fueled with ambition and few funds — had begun a restoration project with no skills and little hope of success, and had met his expectations.

The irony of the setting's misery lay across the street, which was a beautiful and uninterrupted view of a finger inlet of Lake Memphremagog, now a slab of frozen water cloaked in snow. The juxtaposition made a lie of the premise that all waterfront property was pricey, while saying a great deal about Newport's relative isolation from the commercial mainstream.

Joe found a spot at the foot of the poorly plowed driveway, and gingerly ascended its slippery incline, his hands out to his sides, fully prepared to suddenly find himself extended flat out in midair like a cartoon character in mid-pratfall. Considering that he thought himself on little more than a minor inquiry, it figured that this would be how he'd wind up in the hospital with a broken leg.

Such, thankfully, was not to be. He reached the building's tilted front porch, weighted down by cordwood, and seized its railing like a drowning man reaching shore.

Not minding the clumps of frozen snow glued to each step, he hauled himself up, reached the apartment building's front door, and stepped inside after seeing no doorbells or signs to direct him.

He found himself inside a gloomy central hall constructed of unfinished drywall and scarred plywood flooring, facing a barely visible array of metal mailboxes. Pulling out his small flashlight, he studied the names labeling each box — several of which were illegible — until he spotted a cramped "D'pon," which he took to be the best effort of Wylie Dupont.

He did not press the buzzer mounted above box number six, not only convinced that it didn't work, but also not wanting to give Wylie a heads-up.

Number six, on the third floor, unsurprisingly faced not the photogenic view, but the rear of the building, where Joe had earlier noticed a caved-in, ancient horse stable, now filled with abandoned trash and rusting metal equipment.

He paused to catch his breath, unzipped his parka, and knocked on the flimsy door.

Without warning or approaching footsteps, it opened within seconds, revealing a young bearded man with long hair and slightly vacant eyes.

"Hi," he said without expression.

Joe responded with a friendly smile. "Hi, yourself. You Wylie?"

The young man seemed to consider that for an instant, before saying, "Yeah," and then turning on his stockinged heel to leave the doorway empty and Joe standing by himself. Joe's built-in caution loosened another notch.

Wylie's greeting had been neither hostile nor welcoming, but oddly neutral, as if he were simply too distracted by something else to make an effort either way.

Leaning forward at the waist to better see ahead, Joe slowly crossed the threshold.

Unexpectedly, Wylie Dupont was indeed otherwise occupied, delivering worms one-by-one to a box turtle housed at the bottom of an old fish tank. Looking around, Joe took in a single room with one window, no closet, and no bathroom — a communal lavatory presumably being located somewhere on the landing.

The place struck Joe as a large closet, converted into a bedroom, if only through the application of a number on the door. He did discern, spotting it through the mess, what he thought might be a bed — or at least a thin mattress — along one wall. But otherwise, the tiny space was filled with an upended stack of two-by-fours, half of a bicycle, a collection of empty picture frames, several plastic garbage bags, an assortment of dropped clothes, tools of all kinds — in various states of disrepair — and three broken TV sets. From waist height on down, the place was a jumble; from there to the ceiling, it was as if the room was empty. The fish tank was spacious and upscale by comparison.

Wylie seemed to have forgotten him.

"I'm Joe," he said. "You live here alone?"

His host didn't respond, intent on his mission. The turtle's neck was fully extended as he reached for the dangling prize Wylie held above him.

Joe tried again. "I wanted to talk to you about Nate."

"He's dead." The reply came fast and without inflection.

Joe kept addressing the young man's back. "I know. That must've been tough. You were good friends, weren't you?"

"We were friends." Same toneless high-speed delivery.

Joe paused, considering the value of continuing the conversation. Mares had implied that Dupont might be a worthwhile witness, but so far, the evidence was lacking.

"I'd like to ask you a few questions about him, if that's okay," Joe tried, mostly to be thorough.

The turtle finally took hold of the worm, allowing Wylie to turn around. He looked happy with his success.

"Sorry," he said, smiling. "Jack comes first when it's lunchtime. Who're you?"

Joe hesitated at the startling change. This was evidently a one-thing-at-a-time sort of guy.

"My name's Joe. I'm hoping to learn a little about Nate. What kind of person he was, who his other friends were. That kind of thing."

Wylie seemed confused. "Why?"

Joe decided to begin again. He opened his jacket to reveal the badge attached to his belt. "I'm a police officer," he began. "And I'm trying to find out . . ."

He stopped in mid-sentence, brought up short by Wylie turning red-faced and bunching up his fists.

"You killed him," Wylie growled through clenched teeth.

"No, no," Joe tried placating him, holding up both hands. "I want to find out why that happened."

But the transformation was complete and irreversible. The gentle, childlike man of moments ago tucked down and charged Joe as if wishing to spear him with his body. Joe had only time to catch his head like a basketball as it careened into his midriff and propelled him backward toward the half-open door.

Wylie's fury turned him into an irresistible force, as brainless and direct as an attacking bull. Joe's shoulder struck the edge of the door, pivoting him slightly as they both blew out onto the landing. For a split second, Joe saw the yawning top of the staircase approaching at speed — along with the good chance that he was about to become a human toboggan — before he twisted violently in the same direction that he'd already begun. He used Wylie's momentum against him by grabbing his ears and throwing him forward as if passing a ball, reversing their positions just as they flew into the void and down the staircase.

The next few seconds became an explosive ecstasy of arms, legs, glimpses of passing stair treads, and a rapid succession of painful and jarring body blows. It ended as abruptly as it had started, with both men in a heap at the bottom.

Half-conscious, his head ringing and his body throbbing, Joe gasped for air as he kept slapping at Wylie and trying to push him off, only slowly becoming aware that his attacker had become a dead weight.

With that, he stopped his efforts, hearing shouts as from a great distance, and lay back against the wooden floorboards, caving in to an overwhelming urge to rest.

He shut his eyes, he thought for just a moment, and passed out.

CHAPTER FIFTEEN

"Joe."

He kept his eyes closed, half hoping he was still dreaming.

"Joe."

The dream had been negligible, but it had helped dull a pain in his head of staggering intensity. Not so the man's voice.

"Wake up."

He opened up just enough to see Bill Allard's familiar shape looming over him. "Jesus," he muttered. "Give it a rest."

"I'm supposed to find out if you've been brain damaged."

Joe widened his eyes. "By yelling at me? Who told you to do that?"

He raised a hand to test his throbbing head and found his forearm tethered to an IV tube and one finger capped by a pulse monitor.

He looked around slightly, trying not to move. "Where am I?"

"Dartmouth-Hitchcock Medical Center," Allard answered him. "They brought you straight here after the downstairs neighbor found you in a pile in Newport." He added with an edge to his voice, "Where you'd gone to interview a dangerous half-wit on your own with no backup and without telling dispatch. Congratulations. Pure dumb luck you made so much noise going down — imagine if that lunkhead had just cut your throat and then dumped you in the lake. You're supposed to be influencing Kunkle — not the reverse."

Joe used his other hand to massage his forehead, to no effect except to discover that it was covered with a bandage.

"Was Wylie Dupont found with me?"

"Yeah, with a broken neck."

"He's dead?"

"No. He might wish he was when he comes out of his coma — assuming he does."

Joe scowled. "He just blew up. It was crazy."

Allard's tone hardened again. With his vision clearing, Joe could see that Bill looked like he should be in the adjoining bed. He was obviously exhausted. "What's crazy is that there're enough TV trucks dogging my heels to document a shuttle launch. We were just starting to think they might find this whole mess too boring to stick around, when you decided to go commando on us."

"I thought that meant you weren't wearing underwear."

Bill glared at him. "Don't fuck with me. What the hell were you doing, anyhow? What does Dupont have that's so valuable?"

Joe blinked slowly a couple of times. "That's the worst part — probably nothing. I was just hoping for some sort of break."

Bill shook his head. "No one ever told you to beware what you wish for?"

Bob Crawford got out of his car and crossed over to where Sam and Willy were sitting in her vehicle. He settled into the backseat.

"Nice heater. Mine only goes up about half-power. They can't figure out why. Gotta drive around dressed like an Eskimo." He began struggling out of his parka as he spoke. "You hear about your boss?" he asked.

They both turned to stare at him. "What?" Sammie asked first.

"He's at DHMC with a bump on the head. Got ambushed in Newport by some buddy of the late, unlamented Nate Fellows. Guess he was flying without a wingman for some reason." He waggled his eyebrows at

250

them. "What're you two up to?"

Sam wasn't ready to move on yet. "How is he? Is he okay?"

"Fine, far as I know. He went down a flight of stairs. The other guy came out worse, so there may be some justice in the world."

"Spare me," Willy grumbled.

"How did you hear all this?" Sam asked, still struggling with her surprise.

"The hospital is media storm central, but my source is a nurse I know on the floor. You guys should play the radio more often."

Willy shifted his attention to his partner. "You wanna go rushing off to his side — hold his hand?"

Of course she did, which heightened her anger at his attitude. "Damn. You do have a gift."

Crawford weighed in. "Wouldn't make any difference. You know he's got hot- and cold-running medical care. You can't beat that. Plus, it sounds like your boss-of-bosses is with him anyhow."

"Allard?" Willy was caught off guard this time.

"That's what I heard. He's probably reaming your boy a new one."

Willy tilted his head appreciatively. "Could be," he agreed. "I'll remember that next time he beats up on me."

Sam scowled at him. "You poor baby. You do suffer."

Willy laughed. "I do. I do."

"So," Crawford asked, "you going or not? We can do this another time."

It was Sammie who chose for them. "No, you're right. Sounds like he's fine. We can catch up with him later. Or I can," she said darkly to Willy.

"Okay then," Bob resumed. "What d'you want from me?"

"For starters, what've you heard about Stuey Nichols?" Willy asked.

Bob nodded in acknowledgment. "Allan Steward Nichols. Lives in the Gut somewhere. Moves around, like most of them, so I don't have a specific address."

"And?" Willy pressed.

"Not much else. Local loser doing pissant deals — making ends meet. Not a major player. Why?"

"Sam's got a source who says he was in on a deal to supply Susan Raffner with weed through an intermediary."

"No foolin'? I get why you're interested."

"But you don't know his whereabouts?" Sammie confirmed.

"Not exactly. I can find out — just by taking you up the street."

252

"Good," Willy encouraged him. " 'Cause if we're real lucky, this might be the back door into what got Raffner killed. Bob, if you don't know where Stuey lives, you know at least where he's getting his supplies? It was Holyoke, back in the day."

"Still is," Bob said. "The powers change names now and then — the top dog right now is somebody named Manny Ruiz. If we could land him, that would be a major home run. But it's not likely. Too well protected."

"Whoa," Willy reacted, tapping Sam on the arm. "He was your squeeze back then."

Sam shot him a withering look, surprised by her own anger. "That was the cover. Glad it was convincing, even after all these years." She shifted to Crawford. "How big is Ruiz?"

"Top ranks. It's a more open marketplace than it used to be, now that Vermont's a ripe-'n'-ready consumer state. The last bunch of hotshots were out of New York — the Bronx, to be precise — but even they weren't cut from the old cartel model, with the strict pyramidal, top-down, Mexican drug lord structure. The action's shifted to what used to be the runners and lieutenants — like a middle management thing now, 'cause the money's so good and the risks so minimal."

He jutted his chin out the side window at the town around them. "That's partly why the shift in policing in this town."

"I was telling Willy that they discontinued their drug unit," Sammie said.

"Correct — for local departments, it's less about interdiction now, and more about making your town an unappealing marketplace. You wanna meet with the local expert on that, I know where he is right now — regular as rain every day. He might also be able to tell you about Stuey."

Sam and Willy exchanged a glance. "Sure," Sammie told Crawford.

It was late at night when Joe saw the door to his hospital room swing open without a sound. He was awake, reading a history book. His sleeping schedule had been knocked off-kilter by the visits he received around the clock from doctors and nurses, not to mention the spontaneous naps he fell prey to.

Adding intrigue to this interruption was the fact that he recognized the wary business-suited man who entered as Gail Zigman's head of security, John Carter.

"John?" he said inquiringly.

Carter finished his survey of the single-bed room, also glancing into the small bathroom. "Hey, Joe. How's the noggin?"

"Not a vital organ, so all's well. What're you doing here?"

"On the job," was the answer. "You up for a guest?"

Joe guessed what was next. "Absolutely." He marked his page and rested the book in his lap.

Gail entered as John left, closing the door and leaving them alone.

Joe smiled. "Just so it's on the record, I know that you know that we shouldn't be meeting without a witness in the room, unless I've been taken off the case."

She smiled back tensely and crossed over to him to administer a kiss on the cheek and an awkward hug. "I know you know that I know — and that I also don't give a good goddamn." She sat in the chair next to his bed and slipped off her coat.

"How goes the battle?" he asked. "You've had more press coverage recently than most natural disasters."

"Interesting comparison. I'll tell you about it in a couple of minutes, but it's not why I came." She laid a hand on his and looked him straight in the eye. "I want to know if you're okay. Really. And please — none of the New England macho crap you just gave John. I want the truth."

He turned his hand over so he could interlink fingers with her. "I'm fine. I promise. They're holding me overnight to be safe, but every test and scan and blood draw they've done shows nothing wrong. Apparently, I bounce as well as when I was a baby. I'd tell you if it was otherwise. Speaking of bouncing, though, how're you holding up? I don't guess you've fit much governing in with all the junk that's been flying at you."

She forced a smile. "You've been keeping company with Kunkle for too long."

"Oh?" he asked.

"My coming out has been called a lot of things lately, but 'junk' isn't one of them — or my grieving over Susan's death."

He tilted his head slightly at the rebuke and looked at her without comment, forcing her to respond apologetically. "But there you have it. Sad to admit, Kunkle is usually right. So, yes — all PC aside, I've been drowning in junk, most of it coming from beyond our borders."

"You were warned about that, if I remember."

"I was. Rob foremost among them was quick to point that out. Thankfully, he hasn't now been saying, 'I told you so,' for which I am very grateful. And my staff in general has really been great."

"Nevertheless," Joe asked her, "any regrets?"

"No. I followed my conscience. Maybe not good politics, at least outside Vermont, but I can live with it."

"From what I've heard, it's not hurting you nationally, either, except among people who would never agree with you anyhow."

Her mouth tightened slightly before she commented, "Implying it was smart politics after all?"

He squeezed her hand. "Can we stop this? We used to be best friends. I'm not sure what made me a bad guy, but I've never sniped at you or disrespected you or talked behind your back or — ever — doubted your integrity. And your being here now tells me you know that to be true."

She was crying, her head tucked, her other hand wiping her nose. He let her be, not offering platitudes or empty soothings. He made it a point to never say, "I'm sorry for your loss," and he didn't try for an equivalent phrase now. She had come to him, across the state border and near the middle of the night, and he half suspected it was in part to do exactly what she was doing now. He wasn't about to stop her.

"We were lovers, Joe," she finally said,

extracting a tissue from her pocket and blowing her nose before continuing. "We might as well've been married. We saw each other through my rape and your almost getting killed, and your mom and brother nearly dying in that car wreck — just for starters. I come out and tell the world I'm gay, and all you say is that we better be sure to follow protocol and talk through channels. I mean, shit, Joe — I got that much out of fucking Rob Perkins or the ice queen Joan Renaud."

Joe felt a surge of anger. His entire life — from watching his taciturn father while a child, to absorbing the deaths of comrades in battle, to letting invective slide off him in mid-interrogation in order to secure a confession — Joe had practiced self-control. Denying himself the short-lived pleasure of an emotional outburst had become as natural to him as his advice to others to let their feelings run free. In most people's eyes, he knew this paradox made him something of an Obi-Wan — useful, he conceded, but largely untrue. He hurt and pined as much as anyone. His instincts to lash out and curse and complain were no different from anyone's. He'd merely trained himself to rein them in, to process in private, and to counsel on the basis of what he learned, rather than on how he felt.

As he did now, instead of arguing with her. Wronged as he was, he tamped down his protest, and said, "You know me better than that, Gail. You're in pain you hoped you'd never feel again, and you're swamped by what everybody's throwing at you. Susan was someone you loved, along with being the best counselor you ever had, and you're beating on me hoping I'll get pissed enough to maybe justify our breaking up in the first place."

She opened her mouth to react before he cut her off. "The point is, life sometimes sucks and makes us doubt our decisions. But you were right to leave me, and right to run for governor, and right to open your heart to Susan. You don't need to kick me in the shin while you're legitimately and lovingly wishing me well."

He propped himself up on one elbow to lean closer to her, making himself dizzy in the process, but feeling relieved nevertheless. "Take a breath, Gail. Accept the pain and the grief and — most of all — the help that people are offering you. You have a right to be angry. Just don't use it on the rest of us."

He didn't expect her to respond one way or another, and was grateful that she didn't, instead merely tucking her head in deeper and completely yielding to her sorrow.

He lay back against his pillows and let out a breath, struck by the contrast between the two most recent victims of catastrophe that he'd encountered: Vermont's chief executive — ambitious enough to make the governorship a mere launching pad for higher national office — and Wylie Dupont, lying in a room down the hall, barely aware of what had befallen him, or why.

There wasn't much to be made of it, he decided, aside from the usual tired aphorisms concerning life's odd quirks. Decades ago, he'd been offended by first hearing the phrase, "Shit happens." Now, possibly aided by his proximity to Willy, he was finding himself hard-pressed to improve upon it.

He watched the woman with whom he'd once shared a life, and who'd left him in pursuit of things still in development. Her action had made it possible for him to connect with another woman he believed might be the companion he'd longed for since seeing his young wife die decades earlier. What cancer had taken then — and Gail had stewarded for as long as she could — was a quality of love that Beverly had met and matched with generosity and grace. Who was he to complain now?

Bob Crawford got Sam and Willy into the Rutland City police department through the back door — a clear indicator of his close ties to the building's occupants. Emphasizing the fact, he led them through a couple of hallways and up a flight of stairs, casually greeting people along the way, explaining, "When they built this place, the sheriff was on the top floor, making the whole law enforcement thing look neat and tidy. But he took off for bigger quarters, and for a while, the town politicos were licking their lips about what to use this for." He opened a door at the top of the stairs and ushered them into what resembled a string of offices and cubicles better suited to an insurance agency than a police department. It was quiet, gently lit, fully carpeted, and tastefully decorated.

"That was before Peter Quayles signed on as chief," Crawford said, laughing. "No one was expecting him."

His guests had heard of Quayles, but had never met the man. His PD being responsible for its own major crimes investigations — as were several of Vermont's major towns — the VBI was rarely contacted for assistance. Sam and

Willy knew he was British-born, U.S. urban-trained, and had overcome a lot of initial resistance. But he'd also hit the ground with an energy and enthusiasm rarely seen in this state.

"He's a big believer that it's better to have people pissing outside the tent than inside," Bob explained, waving his arm around. "So before the town fathers could preempt this space, Quayles moved in almost everybody he could think of who had anything to do with his own law enforcement mission. He's got so many agencies and organizations represented up here — social services, mental health, mediation, victim's advocacy, women's protective services, early intervention, the AG's office, Department of Corrections — that I figure the public defender's office has moved in, too, but I just haven't noticed them yet."

"But no drug squad?" Willy asked. "Rutland's problems are in the *New York Times,* for Christ's sake."

Crawford's voice became studiously neutral. "We still off the record, like we were the other night in Bratt?"

"Sure."

"Remember I was telling you about how all our running around making busts basically amounts to a mouse fart in a high

262

wind? Well, that's partly what's making Quayles stick out around here. He's cooked up something different."

"What's he done?" Willy asked, sounding dubious.

"I don't know what to call it," Bob admitted. "They have a catchy title for it, of course, which tells you next to nothing, but I see it as replacing the old combat model with a social revolution one. In a nutshell, it's a civilian take-back-the-streets concept, where the cops act less like paratroopers and more like local service providers with guns, backing up the church groups, the community organizers, the special advocates, and the state outfits like DCF and Probation and Parole. Even the prosecution's on board, cutting deals that hold people accountable." Again, he indicated the offices and cubicles up and down the hallway. "Like I said, he brought 'em inside the tent."

"Cool," said Sammie.

"Useless," said Willy.

Crawford led them around a corner, heading for an open door on the right. "In any case, everything revolves around what Quayles would probably call the crown jewel, which — surprise, surprise — is a computer."

"Naturally," Willy said under his breath.

They arrived at the door and Bob stepped aside to introduce the man sitting before a wall-sized screen, reminding Sam of Captain Kirk facing the forward display of the Starship *Enterprise.*

"Sam and Willy, this is Bruce Steinmetz — the PD's primary intel man."

The young man in question rose quickly and shook hands, a beaming expression on his face. "Welcome, welcome."

"They're from the VBI," Crawford went on. "I'm giving them a once-over-lightly of how things have changed around here."

Sam pointed at the huge screen. "That what you were talking about?"

Steinmetz smiled broadly. "We've worked to get as many of our statistics collected in one place as we can, from dog complaints to sightings of drug deals to shoplifting calls, and everything in between. We call it RutStat."

"You're kidding," Willy groused.

Steinmetz sat back down and began to scroll through a variety of color-coded displays and map overlays, speaking as he proceeded. "The idea was to get a real-time and historical picture of what's happening in the city. When are most of the retail thefts occurring and at what time of the day or week? What part of town suffers most from open drug sales, and how are they related to things like the bus and train schedules? Where are we getting the most complaints about vagrants and what can we do to address them?"

"Meaning you can get your people there to head off complaints instead of reacting to them afterward," Sam said enthusiastically.

"Right," Bruce replied, matching her tone. "We can be seen stopping problems before they start, proving to the community that we can all work as a team."

"This the guy who can tell us about Stuey?" Willy asked abruptly, tiring of the dog-and-pony show.

"Bruce," Crawford addressed him. "These two flew a name by me while we were chatting outside."

Sammie finished for him, "Allan Steward Nichols, nicknamed Stuey." She rattled off his date of birth from memory.

"I didn't have any way to check it out," Bob finished, pointing to the computer, "being shy one of those."

Steinmetz entered the inquiry so rapidly, his fingers blurred against the keyboard — a happy man in his element.

"Here he is. Alive and well and living in

the city." He paused, reading on, before he added, "No fixed address. He moves around town."

"He had a family," Sammie said.

"No mention of that here," Bruce responded. "How long ago?"

"Ten years."

"No arrests?" Willy asked.

"Sure, but not recently."

"You have anything like 'known associates' on that thing?" Willy persisted.

"Sure — all part of the RutStat design," Bruce said, typing again.

"RutStat," Willy said, as if to himself. "Sounds like a bull breeding program."

Bruce seemed immune from sarcasm. "That's good. I like it. We're just starting, but already numbers are exploding with people calling us for service. Before, they either saw us as the bad guys or were just resigned to having dealers and gangs own their streets."

"Rah, rah," Willy said in a flat voice, checking his watch. "You get that info yet?"

"Yeah. Sorry." Bruce rolled his chair back slightly and indicated the page he'd brought up. "There's not much, since he's been under the radar, like you guessed. Still . . ."

Willy was leaning forward to better read the information, and relayed to Sammie,

"Now we're cookin': Best bet looks like someone named Jackie Nunzio."

"She's consistent for at least the last few months," Bruce added. "You want a printout of her last-known address? It's a motel, not where you or I would ever spend the night. But it's home-sweet-home till they evict her or the state snaps out of thinking they're doing her a favor by paying the rent."

The printer to Bruce's side spat out a sheet, which he handed back over his shoulder. It included Nunzio's latest mug shot.

"What about some guy who wears a belt buckle labeled 'Indian,' like the motorcycle?" Willy asked, taking the sheet and recalling what he knew of Maggie Kinnison's Rutland dope transaction.

Bruce gave him a round-faced blank stare. "A belt buckle?"

"Yeah," Willy said hopefully. "You got that kind of stuff, don't you? Crazy hats, cowboy boots, tattoos, Afros — shit like that?"

"We collect tattoos," Bruce replied hesitantly, knowing that wasn't enough. "But we're still ramping up, like I said. Those kinds of details are coming next."

Visibly disappointed, Willy stepped back without comment.

They chatted a little longer, if only to make Willy's obvious desire to leave more gracious. But as the three of them hit the parking lot outside, he immediately asked Sam, "You up for checkin' out a fleabag?"

Crawford laughed. "Always charging ahead."

They'd driven over in separate cars, and Crawford was already beside his. "You all set with me?"

Willy shook his hand. "Yeah, Bob. Thanks. This was a big help, and all the social mumbo jumbo notwithstanding — and Rut-Stat's dumb name — that was interesting."

Crawford nodded and opened his door. "Wave of the future, Willy. Thought you'd get a kick out of it — even a dinosaur like you."

CHAPTER SIXTEEN

"This is not fun."

Beverly paused from rubbing Joe's neck as he lay on his stomach. "Too hard?"

He reached back to touch her hand. "No, no. That's wonderful. I meant how this whole thing is going."

"You didn't enjoy being pitched down a staircase?"

"I can't complain about the therapy." He twisted around enough to catch her eye.

She was naked under a silk robe, straddling his back as she worked, which had caused the garment to open.

She laughed and turned his head forward. "You are feeling better."

He took advantage to roll onto his back and look up at her, his hands now resting on her bare thighs. "That a medical opinion?"

She adjusted herself on top of him, being careful of the low ceiling just above her head. They were in the sleeping loft at Joe's home in Brattleboro, where she'd driven him after his discharge from the hospital. "More empirical. So, what's not fun?"

"The damn case. Being turned into a basketball by a half-wit and landing in the headlines is par for the course by now. I think Bill Allard would be delighted if a jetliner fell out of the sky and hit the capitol, just to get the spotlight off of him."

"It must be frustrating," she sympathized.

"I don't even know how many people we have working on this anymore," Joe told her. "We even have four guys who're only studying surveillance tapes."

"From where?"

"You name it. Turns out Vermont's lousy with video cameras. They're in banks, parking garages, retail stores, ATMs, grocery stores. We've done our best to track every place Susan might've been for the couple of days before she died, and combed each area for cameras."

"But nothing so far," she said, slipping off to one side and stretching out beside him, pulling her robe closed and flipping a quilt over them.

"Nope. And nothing from all the document searching and interviews. I do still have some hopes there, but she never threw any of it away, which means we have to paw through everything. Basically," he concluded, "we're dead in the water."

"All while the reporters and politicians clamor from the sidelines," she commiserated.

He was silent for a moment, staring at the wooden ceiling. "Let's talk about the body a little. That okay?"

She smiled. "I don't know, Joe. Dead people? Really?"

He stuck a finger into her ribs, making her squirm. "All told," he said, "she had bruises, the carving, a torn fingernail, a shattered skull, and a ligature around the neck. Is that about it?"

"Yes," she replied without hesitation, while waiting for him to continue.

"What's been rattling around my brain," he went on, enjoying — as always — their easy exchange, "is that according to your report, some of these were premortem, some perimortem, and some committed after the fact."

"That's my conclusion," she confirmed.

"Okay. All that implies a progression that mirrors Susan's last movements."

"A geographical progression matching a chronological one?" Beverly asked.

"Yes. And we can say this because of the

fingernail found in the back of her car." He suddenly glanced at her. "You can state for a fact that the nail wasn't torn off after death?"

"I can and do."

"So," he said, "whether the car ride came before or after the bruising, it definitely happened before she was killed by the second blow to the head."

"Okay," she said noncommittally.

"Well," he said, coming to his point, "there's the thing: For some reason, her killer wanted to take her to that cliff from someplace else, and it looks like he did so while she was still alive."

"Why?" she asked.

"Exactly," he mused. "Why that particular cliff? It was dramatic, which is what we thought was the whole point, but why not just hang her from a rooftop or a tree or dump her in the middle of the interstate?"

"Because it was theatrical?" Beverly suggested.

"Yes," he agreed. "But it may have been familiar, too. We canvassed the whole region, asking people if the cliff had any special attraction, and found that a few kids had once risked their necks climbing the steel mesh, but that was it."

"You've also got where the car was

abandoned," Beverly said.

"Right," he agreed. "Another indicator of preplanning — and local knowledge. There's so much maneuvering about this murder. We usually find them dead where they were killed. This one's just so . . ." He hesitated before adding, "Fussy."

"Maybe not," Beverly suggested. "You might move a body around to avoid detection, meaning that the killing or kidnapping may have occurred in a place lacking in privacy."

"So I grab you, I shove you in the trunk of your own car, and I drive you to the cliff . . ." Joe interrupted himself.

"What?" she asked.

"That's not right," he explained. "Susan was grabbed and transported in her own car, but the tire tracks belonged to something like a pickup truck."

"A vehicle swap," Beverly said.

"Right, which possibly means another person was involved."

"Or the killer just used the Prius to drive to the truck, possibly killed her at that point — perhaps because of the lack of a containment area like the Prius's dog cage — and then drove to the cliff in the truck. Of course, for that to work, the truck had to have been parked at the junkyard."

"True. But why use the Prius at all?" Joe asked, rubbing his forehead in frustration.

Beverly remained silent.

"They must've been together beforehand," Joe said tentatively. "Maybe carpooling."

"In *Susan's* car," Beverly emphasized.

"And then pinning it all on Nate Fellows," Joe said softly.

She remained silent, waiting.

He slipped an arm around her shoulders to draw her closer. "Okay — there's a big 'if' here — if we're right that Nate was framed, the killer would've had to have known him, or at least about him in some way. He knew where Nate lived, and he knew about Nate's prejudice."

"If that's correct," Beverly said, "then connecting the dots gets a little easier, mathematically speaking."

"But," Joe countered, "where *is* the connection between Susan, her murderer, and Nate? State politics? Some activist forum or protest group? A newspaper article referencing Susan and hate crimes? A drug angle? A large quantity of marijuana was found at her place."

Beverly snuggled up to him. "You'll get it," she said comfortingly. "You just need that first domino tile to tip over to start a pattern running."

But he was having his doubts.

The motel that Bruce Steinmetz sent them to was a sad blemish lining one of the major approaches to Rutland, flanked by a familiarly numbing succession of gas stations, restaurants, and convenience stores. It was barely a motel at all, having taken on the more profitable and less demanding role of a way station for welfare recipients — individuals or families tangled up in the system, and needing housing "temporarily."

Willy drove them across the marginally snowplowed parking lot, edging by a few cars that hadn't been moved in months — and were planted like empty, ice-slabbed igloos along the fringes of the central driveway.

"Cheery place," he commented, glancing up at the low, dark, snow-clotted clouds whose arrival forecasters had been anticipating for days.

He nosed the car into a slot opposite the reception sign and killed the engine. "Time to meet the woman in Stuey's life," he said sourly. "This should be a treat."

They both swung out and entered a lobby that — had they actually been searching for overnight accommodations — would have made them feel that they'd stepped into a chain-saw murder movie.

"What?" asked a short bearded man from behind a cash register.

Willy sidled up to the counter. "That your version of 'Welcome. How may I help you?' Jesus, man, you need inspiration."

The man's face was unchanged. "What I need is a break from jerks like you. What d'you want?"

Willy revealed his badge. The man snorted. "I knew you were cops before you got out of your car. I see you people more than I see my tenants. Who're you after?"

"Jackie Nunzio," Sammie told him, impressed that he hadn't even glanced at the badge, much less asked which department or agency employed them.

"Twenty-four," he said instantly. "Second floor. That way." He pointed behind them.

Willy reached into his pocket and pulled out a mug shot of Stuey Nichols. He was about to show it to the counterman when the latter stepped back, waving both pudgy hands. "No, no, no. Do what you gotta do, but I ain't lookin' at no pictures. People come, people go. I don't give a fuck who they are."

Willy replaced the photo and said in a sweet voice, "Thank you for your courtesy, then. Do you have a feedback card I can fill out, to let your bosses know what a great job you're doing?"

The man gave him a pitying look. "Have a nice day."

The balcony servicing the second floor was crusty with frozen snow, plastic bags of garbage, and a few scattered chairs, toys, and personal belongings. Sam and Willy picked their way with care, hearing — behind a procession of closed doors — a series of muffled arguments, crying children, blaring TVs, and the occasional instance of almost ominous dead silence. The latter was what they found at door number twenty-four.

Sammie knocked loudly. "Jackie?"

There was no response.

She tried again. The next door down the line opened and a woman with hair dyed bright red stuck her head out.

"Who're you after?"

Willy was about to answer when Sam cut in, not interested in a repeat exchange of attitudes. "Jackie Nunzio."

"She's there," the woman said. "Maybe in the bathroom."

"Thank you so much," Willy said.

The woman glared at him. "Whatever." She slammed her door shut.

Willy made a face and crossed to the

window beside the door, cupping his good hand on the glass to shield his eyes from the daylight.

"She's down," he said, and reached for the doorknob.

Sam understood instantly and pulled her weapon as Willy pushed open the unlocked door and stood aside to draw his own gun. The two of them swept inside and spread out against the inner wall.

Before them was the body of a motionless woman, facedown on the floor at the foot of an unmade bed. The room was a shambles of things dropped without thought. It smelled of unwashed humanity, hopeless endeavor, and poverty.

And of death. A small pool of bloody purge fanned out across the cheap carpeting from beneath the woman's flattened cheek.

Willy gestured to Sam to proceed as he kept his back against the wall and covered the room — a well-trained team with plenty of past practice. She silently skirted the body, approached the bathroom, and cautiously checked it out.

"We're alone," she announced in a calm voice.

Willy reached behind him and gently closed the door. "Bed?" he asked quietly.

She squatted to look. "It's on a pedestal. No room to hide underneath."

She straightened as they both holstered their guns and looked around.

"No obvious signs of violence," Sammie said, not moving.

Willy also kept his ground, not wanting to contaminate the scene any more than necessary to secure it. "In the corner, hanging from the hook, men's jeans?"

She followed his look. "I'd say so, plus, there're items on both night tables — his and hers."

"Kids, too," he said. "At least a boy and a girl, judging from the toys and clothes."

She checked her watch. "School should be out, but who knows? Could be at day care, DCF, a special after-school program, or a half-dozen other things."

Willy broke ranks and began walking across the room, picking each step carefully, heading toward the near side of the bed. "Assuming the male of this tribe is our pal Stuey, he maybe left something interesting in his side drawer. I'm sure he'd want us to have it before we call the cops on this. Protect his privacy, you know?"

She barely shook her head, smiling as she did — his obliging straight man. "I'm sure he'd appreciate it."

Willy crouched by the night table and eased the drawer open with his pen after taking inventory of the ashtray and scattered belongings under the bolted-down lamp. For her part, Sammie straddled the dead body and compared the face pressed into the carpeting with the printout from Bruce Steinmetz.

"It's definitely Jackie Nunzio," she said, "and the blood's from her mouth. She's been here long enough to decomp— a day or more."

"That much, I could smell," Willy said, before pulling on a latex glove with his teeth. "There're about six empty bags of what looks like heroin here on the table, and a couple more on the floor. She could've overdosed."

Sammie was still looking, without actually touching the body. "That's what it looks like. Her arm's a mess. You can totally tell she was right-handed from the track marks, and there's a syringe half hidden under her torso."

Willy turned toward her, a scrap of paper in his fingers. "Two phone numbers, one with a Massachusetts area code."

Sam got out her cell phone and tossed it onto the unmade bed near him. "Take a picture. If they're not burner phones, maybe

Lester can tell us who they belong to through that super-snooper reverse finder program he got from the feds."

Willy flattened the piece of paper out and positioned her smartphone over it, saying, "Guess we better call the locals. Don't want the desk clerk saying we spent half an hour up here before blowing the whistle."

"What about Stuey?" Sammie asked.

Willy gave her an all-too-familiar look. "I think I have a plan B for him."

Gail gave a final wave to the cheering group at the curb and climbed into the back of her van, waiting for the door to slide shut and the tinted windows to block the view before tilting her head back and moaning, "My head's about to explode. Who's got some aspirin?"

Alice immediately stuck out her hand, two pills cradled in her palm. "I thought I saw that look on your face," she said sympathetically.

The van had been rigged out as a mobile office, with two captain's chairs facing the back bench. As Gail reached for the aspirin, she noticed that her usual entourage of a security driver, Alice, and Kayla Robinson had been joined by a fourth woman of distinctly urban, tailored appearance.

"Governor," Kayla said. "This is Maureen Bentsen, of the . . ."

Gail swung around to shake hands, ignoring the pills. "I know who you are, Maureen. I wasn't expecting you until later — it's so early in the campaign. I am truly honored by your interest in us."

Bentsen represented a group of Washington, D.C., political consultants, with a special interest in gay and lesbian issues. She had approached the campaign just two days earlier, asking if she might be of service.

Bentsen shook hands but then indicated Alice's offering, as the van pulled into traffic. "The honor is mine, Governor, but please take your pills. I know what it feels like to be under such pressure."

She continued speaking as Gail reached for a water bottle. "I'm sorry to drop in so unexpectedly, but things worked out that I could get here sooner than I thought."

"No, no," Gail countered, wiping her lips. "I'm delighted to see you. You're doing us a real favor here, so please — no apologies. How do you think we're doing? If that's not too abrupt?"

Bentsen laughed, her eyes remaining watchful. "I think I can be of some help, if that's your question. Which isn't to say that you're not doing a great job so far."

"For a rookie out of her depths?" Gail asked.

"Not a rookie," Bentsen differed. "Maybe a renegade, which can be good or bad. You are certainly in unknown waters since your announcement at Susan Raffner's memorial."

Gail nodded. "Point taken. I have been surprised at the variety of outside . . ." She hesitated.

"Offerings," Kayla diplomatically suggested.

Maureen Bentsen nodded wistfully. "Ah, yes. Nothing to beat this for getting all vested interests and almost every nut job to express an opinion. I heard that Ellen DeGeneres reached out, speaking of the good guys?"

"And *The Daily Show* people, along with a couple of Boston talking heads," Gail confirmed.

"There'll be more." Here Bentsen looked at Kayla. "Those two are obviously fine, but I recommend you tread carefully as the offers mount up — which they will. By accepting too much visibility, I guarantee that you'll be accused of thinking beyond the governorship and aspiring to greater office. Which could cost you the election. It points out the real need for you and your staff to absolutely focus on your constituents — especially in independent Vermont."

She switched her attention to Alice, who was sitting in one of the captain's chairs. "How's the money coming in?"

Alice looked slightly ill at ease. "I'm so sorry I don't have the figures right here. I wasn't expecting you. But, as I told the governor a couple of days ago, we're right at the million-dollar level."

"Any noticeable change since the memorial?"

"Not really."

"What's that mean?" Gail asked.

"It's not surprising," Bentsen told them. "People vote with their wallets as much as with their ballots. What you've done is being seen by your base as brave and honest and worthy of support, but there are plenty of others who are less enthusiastic. The plus side is that your numbers are good, meaning that the respect you earned from past leadership will hold back the resentment or fear or whatever it is that turns people against gays."

Bentsen shifted slightly in her seat to better address Gail directly. "I need to ask you a personal question, along those lines, and — believe me — it is relevant, given the circumstances."

Gail looked at the others in the vehicle. "I trust Alice and Kayla implicitly," she said. "Ask away."

Bentsen nodded once. "Okay. How are you dealing with the death of your best friend? You came out as a lesbian after her murder. Not as a bisexual, but a lesbian, despite a long history of heterosexual relationships. People are going to connect the two and challenge your motivations."

"What are you asking?"

"What you've done is make a commitment. It's caused a lot of people, including my organization, to lend you support, give you publicity, and contribute money. And this is just the beginning." She gestured to the aspirin bottle. "But it's going to make your current headaches seem trivial in comparison, because the opposition hasn't even warmed up. What I'm asking is whether you've looked long and hard into your soul about what you're doing."

"I have," Gail said forcefully. "With every passing day, I'm more sure of it. Susan and I talked about this before she died, in part because I do have thoughts about higher office. She was the one who counseled that I ought to consider coming out, if for no other reason than to be centered and balanced as the woman I feel I am — before entering the national political arena where they take no prisoners, as you've been implying."

Gail gazed out the front window as she continued, "I actually reached out to the man to whom you're referring. He's a highly placed Vermont police officer and a truly good guy. I told him, in effect, that I'd never felt more solid as a result of all this, and I sensed he completely understood and was supportive. It hasn't been easy getting here, and I haven't always treated him or others in my life very well."

She returned to look at her guest. "I am angry at Susan's death, and devastated that she's no longer nearby. But I've done what I've done out of honest self-respect."

Maureen Bentsen smiled and reached out to pat Gail's hand briefly. "Then we'll see what we can do to keep you in office, Governor — and maybe more."

CHAPTER SEVENTEEN

Hartford, Vermont's name may have been inspired by its muscular, urban cousin in Connecticut, but if so, the two stopped speaking then and there. The sole similarity was that they bordered the same river. Otherwise, the northern namesake was a spread-out jumble of unincorporated villages — Hartford, Quechee, West Hartford, White River Junction, and Wilder — containing a small fraction of the original's population. The larger Hartford's "metro area" census, in fact, exceeded one million people, or almost double Vermont's entire tally.

For that matter, the town that Sam and Willy entered — after handing over the scene containing the late Jackie Nunzio to the Rutland police — had always lacked a robust identity. This was perhaps helped by its straddling the junction of Interstates 91 and 89, which made it by default a major temporary stopping-off point for people with intentions both pure and otherwise. Additionally, Hartford's longing for homogeneity had suffered from the extreme contrast between its two most opposite municipalities, Quechee and White River Junction. The first was well known for boutique stores, an expansive golf course, upscale condo clusters, and proximity to affluent Woodstock; the second for being a down-on-its-luck railroad town, surrounded by economic vitality but possessing only a faded, funky charm that it touted with heartfelt, slightly winded zeal.

The two cops were here to find Brandon Younger, Willy's plan B.

Sam was of two minds about this, torn between her initial instinct to salvage her self-perceived damaged reputation, and worrying that Willy's help might create a mess that would turn her first transgression into a minor misstep.

It didn't help that the conclusion she and Willy had reached concerning Jackie's fate hadn't dovetailed at all with their homicide investigation — reducing their field trip to Hartford to a possible wild-goose chase. Jackie's autopsy and tox exam were yet to come, of course, but there was no indication that they'd change what was safely

288

looking like an accidental overdose.

That heightened Sammie's quandary, in her view. As Willy had said, Joe had assigned him the freelancer's job — not Sam. Willy could poke around and pursue leads to his heart's content, as long as he stayed under the radar. Sammie, by contrast, was the Raffner case's coordinator, responsible for making sure that all the cops working this case kept on task, didn't bump into one another, and processed everything properly.

Messing about with Willy on a persistently weakening tangent was guaranteed to bode ill for her.

Willy, unsurprisingly, showed little concern for any of this.

"What was the address Maggie gave you?" he asked, straining to sce the passing street signs in what was becoming the worst snowstorm of the season. It had already taken them twice the normal travel time to get here, and the snow had only started falling an hour ago.

Sammie told him. Securing the address had been simple. Once Willy had revealed his strategy — to locate Stuey following the same route Maggie Kinnison had taken on Susan's behalf — Sam had merely called Maggie up, hoping the pressure that she'd applied in person would still yield results. It had. In a monotone, Kinnison had recited Younger's address and phone number, and agreed to not give him a heads-up, although Sam wasn't putting much faith in that part. Presumptions notwithstanding, almost everyone lies to the police, from the hardened criminal to the little old lady caught speeding to church.

She and Willy were fully prepared for Brandon Younger to be either expecting their visit, or conspicuously out of town.

"There." Sam pointed down a narrow side street, lined with three-story, industrial-era worker's housing, called triple-deckers for their stacked exterior staircases crisscrossing from one balcony to the next. In these near-whiteout conditions, they looked vaguely like a flotilla of ancient, beached riverboats, left to rot by the side of a stagnant stream.

"How the hell're we gonna know which one's his?" Willy said mostly to himself, struggling not to sideswipe any parked cars. "Can't see any house numbers."

Sam glanced at her notepad. They'd gotten dispatch to retrieve Younger's registration earlier. "It's this one. That's his car."

Willy pulled over, more or less. As soon as he killed the engine, the windshield was covered with a screen of white snowflakes.

They struggled with gloves and hats to better protect themselves from the elements, knowing the wind would seek out any exposed skin for a painful bite.

"You set?" Sam asked.

Willy zipped up his coat. "You do know it sucks to live up here."

She laughed. "Yes, dear," and she opened her door.

In contrast to the car's combination of heater fan, engine noise, and the police radio murmuring under the dash, what they stepped into — even with the wind — was an eerie, all-enveloping, world-sized cotton ball of sound-absorbing silence.

Stumbling in the gray light, slipping and catching their boots on unseen obstacles, they made it to the sidewalk, up the swaybacked building's uneven steps, and onto the porch.

Willy leaned in close to Sam's head. "What floor?"

"First," she answered in a low tone, feeling oddly exposed in a sound vacuum with no visibility.

"There's gotta be a back entrance," he said. "If he spooks, I don't wanna go after him in this shit."

"You want to go 'round?" she asked.

He mulled it over before nodding. "Give

me five minutes and then pound on the door."

"Roger."

Back outside, Willy realized that five minutes wouldn't give him much time. The narrow passage between the buildings was plugged with a Dumpster, two vehicles, and piles of trash, all cemented in place by past snowfalls and ice from the roof high above. Giving up discretion and even safety, he stumbled, lurched, slipped, and staggered through the barricades, cursing nonstop all the way, until — breathless and sweating — he reached what passed for a backyard.

There, simultaneously, a ground-floor plywood door flew open and a heavyset bearded man burst out onto the back porch, wearing only jeans, a T-shirt, and sneakers. He gave Willy a quick glance, cut in the opposite direction, and made to vault over the railing ahead of him to escape across the yard. He didn't make it, catching a foot as he leaped and sprawling onto the thickening snow with a resounding thud.

Struggling with his own footing, Willy tried reaching him before he got back up, not counting on the man finding a chunk of cinder block in the snow, which he hurled at Willy's head with surprising ease and accuracy. Willy dove to one side as his attacker made for an opening in the gaping wooden fence surrounding the yard.

Awkwardly regaining his footing, Willy glanced at the back door to see Sam appear, quickly assess where Brandon was going, and vanish again, presumably to circle around from the front to cut him off. Encouraged, Willy continued his chase.

Beyond the gap, he found himself in a narrow alleyway filled with more obstacles and hemmed in by more fencing. Ahead of him by a dozen yards, but already more ghost than man, Brandon was using his familiarity with the terrain to make good headway. Willy began ruing that he hadn't kept his gun in his hand from the start, and shot the bastard when he'd first caught sight of him — counterproductive, maybe, but much more satisfying.

Gasping for air, constantly reaching out for support, Willy found his physical asymmetry costing him distance, to where all he was doing finally was running in the same direction as his quarry, without actually seeing him anymore.

That was explosively remedied when Younger sprang out like a pit bull from behind a stack of garbage cans and caught Willy from the side, lifting him up and smashing him against a tree trunk, wrenching his back and banging his head — the sounds of their bodies colliding and the wind escaping their lungs the only things breaking the universal silence.

Dazed by the blow, Willy struggled against his pummeling opponent. However, it was the dull crack of a gun barrel striking the back of Younger's head, accompanied by Sammie stating, "You move, you die, motherfucker," that finally did the trick. Willy dropped his arm, fell back, and exposed his face to the falling snow, letting out a groan. "Damn, girl. You do know how to make an entrance."

Brandon Younger lived alone in a barely furnished ground-floor apartment dominated by a huge, stained couch, an arena-sized flat-screen TV, and little else. Her rage compensating for their difference in size, Sam almost threw the wounded man, covered with snow, onto the couch and stood over him, her gun still out. Behind her, Willy shut the back door and quickly checked the one bedroom and bath for other residents. There were none.

"You are some piece of work, you know that?" Sammie asked their reluctant host. "What the fuck were you doing?"

Younger was rubbing the back of his head.

"This really hurts."

Willy pulled out his own gun and pushed it between Younger's eyes. "You know I can take care of that, right? You resisted arrest — I got the bruises to prove it — so I shot your pathetic ass to save my life. That work for you?"

Younger looked from one to the other of them. "I thought you were cops."

"We *are* cops, stupid," Sammie told him. "Pissed-off cops." She leaned forward and placed the barrel of her gun next to Willy's, pinning Younger's head to the back of the couch.

"You guys are crazy," he said timidly. "I could get you in trouble."

"Not if you're dead," Willy said menacingly.

"This won't hold up in court," Younger tried one last time.

"It's never going there," Sam assured him.

The man's body deflated as he sank into the stained cushions. "What d'you *want*?"

"Stuey Nichols," Willy said.

His eyes widened. "Who? You did all this for someone I never heard of? You're kidding me."

Sam rapped his forehead with her gun barrel, making him wince. "Let's try Maggie Kinnison."

This time, they got somewhere.

"That crazy bitch?" he said. "Did she put you onto me?"

"Not even close," Sam lied, straightening and holstering her weapon. "What's she to you?"

"She *used* to be a customer. *That's* over with, for sure. I don't need shit like this."

Willy was still standing over him. "Are we gonna have to start all over again?"

Younger scowled. "Give it a rest. I get who's the alpha dog." He shifted his glance to Sam. "Maggie dates back to the old days. But I haven't sold her dope in forever. People move on, or I thought they did. Now, I can't get rid of the bitch."

"What's that mean?" Sammie asked.

His face displayed amazement. "Well, damn. First, she calls me outta the blue and asks where she can score some weed, then some crazy queen bee wannabe shows up and demands to know what I told Maggie, and now it's you two. Fucking Maggie Kinnison is like comin' outta the walls. I never made a cent outta any of it, and now I'll probably have to go to the hospital for my head."

"Not unless you want a brain transplant, moron," Willy said. "You're not even bleeding."

"Fuck you."

"Shut up," Sammie yelled at him. "Will you focus for one goddamned minute? Who's this queen bee you're talking about? What was her name?"

"Right," Younger retorted. "Like she told me. I don't know your names, either. Good thing, too, considering the lawsuit I could throw at you."

Willy flicked his hand at him, which made the big man cower. "Don't even think about it."

"Describe her, then," Sam persisted.

"Don't have to. She's all over the news. Got herself strung up, which she totally deserved."

"The woman hanging over the interstate?" Sam asked.

"That's her. The politician."

"She came here?" Willy asked.

"That's what I said."

Sammie sat on the couch arm next to him. "What did she want?"

"To know what I'd told Maggie, duh."

This time, Willy did hit him across the head, albeit with the back of his gun hand. "Manners, asshole."

"What did she want?" Sam repeated.

"Like I said," Younger replied in a whine.

"She just wanted to know what I told Maggie."

"Why?"

"She was pissed, is why. She said she'd been ripped off, and nobody does that to her, and heads were gonna roll, and shit like that. It was crazy."

"How'd she been ripped off?" Sam pressed him, not revealing what she knew.

Younger rolled his eyes. "Well, *weed,* of . . ." He broke off to cover his head as Willy raised his hand again, still holding the gun. "Okay, okay. I'm sorry. She was complaining about the weed she got — or Maggie got for her, or whatever. She wanted her money back."

"And you told her . . ."

"I told her she was outta luck, that I'd given Maggie a phone number that didn't work anymore."

Willy did one better than Sam, and sat beside Younger on his other side, so that his body was pressed up against him. The big man pulled himself together, trying to appear smaller.

"Don't give me that, Brandon," Willy said, dragging out his name. "There is no way in hell she took that, said, 'Thank you very much,' and walked out of here empty-handed. How'd you get her to leave?"

Younger hesitated, struggling to come up with something plausible. Willy leaned into him, his face inches from his ear. "We could've killed you back then. We can sure as shit throw you in the can for resisting arrest, attempting to escape, and assaulting two police officers, not to mention what we'll find when we toss this dump and discover what you've got for sale."

"Oh, no," Sammie added. "It's worse than that. He's directly tied to a homicide. His ass is ours."

Younger began struggling to get up, which met with Sam pushing him back into place. "You can't do that. I only read about it in the paper. I didn't even *know* that broad."

"So, tell us how the conversation ended," Willy told him in a reasonable voice.

"I gave her a name," Younger finally admitted.

"How'd that happen?"

"She told me she wanted to talk to the guy with the Indian belt buckle. Well, I know who that is. I mean, everybody does. That's like his calling card. They even call him The Indian. Kinda stupid, you ask me, but to each his own."

"You're killin' me," Willy almost whispered.

At last, he gave up the rest of it. "His

name's Buddy Ames," Brandon sighed.

Joe sat at his desk in Brattleboro, staring out the window, the falling snow drawing his attention with the mesmerizing appeal of a fire in a grate.

Sam stood before him, studying his profile, her emotions still sorting through the tangles of Brandon Younger's revelation. From a nonsanctioned side action with Willy in Rutland, urged on by the ghost of a ten-year-old failed covert operation, she'd become the bearer of what Joe had just enigmatically termed "the domino we needed" — a solid lead connecting Susan Raffner's last few hours with something that might explain how and why she'd died.

Joe's silence, however, had her worried. The light was fading, they were alone — Willy had gone home to Emma — and Sam had been hoping for her news to be met with actions and commands, or at least enough motion and noise to cover the unconventional nature of her information's journey to his ear.

But he was too experienced a cop to not consider precisely that, and therefore to ask, "What were you and Willy doing in Rutland?"

"Like I said, Maggie Kinnison set that going."

"To a motel room with an overdose?"

She hesitated. "Stuey Nichols came up as a possible involvement. The girl's place was the best we could figure as his last known address."

He kept staring at the snow. "So Willy then thought of Younger when the girl turned up dead."

"Right."

"And Younger in turn just gave you Buddy Ames."

Joe swung around enough in his chair to fix her with an unblinking gaze.

She felt her face warm under the scrutiny. "Yeah — eventually. You know how it goes. Back and forth."

"This was recorded?"

"No. Willy and I can both vouch for what was said, though. And it's in our written reports."

"And Younger? What will he vouch?"

She swallowed hard. He could vouch, she thought, that we hit him, intimidated him verbally, and probably made what he told us inadmissible — if it ever reached court. Instead, she said, "He's cool. In exchange for what he told us, we let him walk on attempting to escape and assaulting a police officer."

He looked at her for a couple of seconds in silence, their shared knowledge hanging between them of how often these types of encounters could quickly morph into something beyond a conversation. As boss and subordinate, mentor and acolyte, Joe and Sam had long walked a road lined with mutual respect, shared allegiance, interdependence, and even love.

Moments like this, simmering with unspoken truths, could take time to be absorbed through such layers of trust.

Time that Joe now mercifully brought to a close.

"Okay," he said quietly, as if accepting not just her version of events, but — by having granted a risky player like Willy such independence to begin with — his own collusion in their retelling. "Let's see if we can find Buddy Ames." He then smiled slightly and added, "Because regardless of what really happened between you and Brandon Younger, you two may have given us the kick-start we've been looking for."

CHAPTER EIGHTEEN

Rutland Police Chief Peter Quayles was angular and hawk-nosed, with a penchant for moleskin trousers and tweed jackets. The look, combined with his British accent, made for a caricature of a 1940s Pinewood Studios actor. His actions and demeanor, however, spoke otherwise. The man was businesslike and direct, if a little flowery with his syntax. Joe was delighted he'd chosen not to invite Willy Kunkle to the meeting.

In fact, Joe had brought along only fresh faces — and certainly not the same two people who'd prowled around Quayles's building without introducing themselves.

Instead, it was reliable Lester Spinney who accompanied him into the chief's office, along with Bob Crawford, of the drug task force, with whom Quayles was comfortably familiar.

"VBI, eh?" Quayles said as he shook

hands and bowed toward a cluster of chairs in the corner. "I've been hearing about you boys — and about you in particular, Special Agent Gunther. You are a highly respected man. Very flashy initialization, by the way — VBI. Does it earn you much respect?"

Joe was used to most variations on that comment. He tried deflecting with, "Most people think we deliver packages."

"According to my man Bruce," Quayles countered, his smile fading, "you recently helped to deliver a dead body."

"We did discover one — sadly," Joe readily admitted, wary of what their host thought of outsiders poaching on his territory.

But the chief surprised him by replying sympathetically, "Sadly is the word. Despite our attempts to address the ills of this beleaguered city, I remain staggered by its daily heartbreak. The poor woman had three children. Did you know that?"

Joe opted for playing it straight. "No. After my people briefed your response team, they took off. Jackie Nunzio had been mentioned as a conduit to another source, which obviously didn't pan out. I don't think they actually learned a great deal about her."

"And yet" — Quayles looked him straight in the eyes — "here you are again."

Joe nodded. "Yes. The other source turned

out to be Buddy Ames — otherwise known as The Indian. That sent us full circle, back to Rutland."

Again, the chief shifted moods, his expression creasing into a broad smile. "Indeed. Thanks so much for sending us his name." Quayles reached out with one long arm and retrieved a file from his nearby desktop. "Bruce tells me that Buddy has quite the history around town. Bit of a swaggering brute, from what little I read — complete with that belt buckle trademark."

He switched his gaze to Crawford, who was there mostly to smooth out this initial meeting, being a trusted ally to both parties. "You are acquainted with Mr. Ames, Bob?"

"Historically, yes," Bob replied. "Not lately, though. Has the PD had any recent dealings with him?"

"Not according to this." Quayles hefted the file before replacing it on his desk. "But," he continued, "inferring from your presence here, he may be facing some new entries, is that correct?"

Joe waggled his hand from side to side. "Maybe. Maybe not. First, we just want to find him."

"Concerning Susan Raffner?" Quayles almost interrupted. He laughed at his own cleverness, and filled in, "Hardly Sherlock Holmes, Mr. Gunther. You are the VBI's field force commander. Why else would you be slumming on my patch rather than pursuing the senator's murderer?"

"We don't have a direct tie-in between Ames and her death," Joe quickly clarified. "But his name came up in a way that's giving us hope."

"Very carefully put," Quayles complimented him. "Can you tell me what to expect in terms of what they call blowback? The Raffner investigation could no longer be called low-key by even the wildest imagination. As soon as word leaks out that you're in Rutland, I'll be receiving phone calls."

Joe and Crawford glanced at each other.

"Ames has never been violent in our experience," Bob said, only indirectly addressing the chief's concern.

"All the same," Joe added more expansively. "The common thread between Raffner and Ames is drugs — specifically marijuana."

"Really?" Quayles reacted, startled.

"Yes, but it should be stressed that we have no idea where this might lead, if anywhere. To be safe, you might want to appoint someone as a liaison to keep us from stepping on any toes, and maybe to help us with local intelligence. From what I was told about your RutStat program, you have quite a finger on the city's pulse."

Quayles laughed again. "Flattery will get you everything. Well, if you know about Rut-Stat, then you probably also know that I prefer an all-inclusive form of management. We have invited several federal agencies to stretch their muscles down here in the past, and Bob will attest to our being open to his task force operating in town when they need to. I only ask that if any actions are contemplated that might alienate the local citizenry and imperil our community polic-ing efforts, I be advised. Is that acceptable?"

"Of course," Joe replied immediately.

Peter Quayles crossed his legs and steepled his fingers before him as he concluded, "If, in exchange for my support and co-operation, a few kind words could be dropped into Governor Zigman's ear, I would be extremely grateful. I hope that's not too forward of me. She has not hesitated to make Rutland the state's poster child for drug-related misfortune, and yet financial or even logistical support has been thin."

Initially, Joe was struck by the almost oily suggestiveness of the comment. But in fact, it was a practical request. If this man was as devoted to his cause as he claimed to be, could he be faulted for using every avenue available?

"I'll do my best," Joe promised him.

Willy stepped into the VBI office on the Brattleboro municipal building's second floor and looked around, stamping his feet free of residual snow.

"You could do that in the lobby," Sammie suggested from her desk.

Willy ignored her. "The boss around?"

"He and Lester're in Rutland, rubbing noses with the chief there. Why? You got something?"

Willy hung his coat on a hook near the door with a well-practiced gesture. He reached into his pants pocket and waved a small piece of paper at her.

"Remember those two phone numbers I photographed at Jackie Nunzio's?" he asked.

"Yeah. Did Lester kick something back?"

Willy made himself comfortable behind his desk, which he'd positioned to face the rest of the room in instinctively paranoid fashion. "Never sent 'em to him," he replied.

She wasn't surprised. That, too, fit the man's style — never show your cards if you can avoid it. Even — or sometimes especially — to your own colleagues. She sighed inwardly, the anxiety that had lessened when she'd mostly come clean with Joe earlier returned as a twinge of dread. What the hell had Willy done now?

"Okay," she said suggestively.

He tilted his head and smiled. "Well, you know. Don't give away what you got till you know what it is, right? That's my motto."

"Really," she said sardonically. "I had no idea. So, what's on the piece of paper?"

He was going to milk this a little more, enjoying himself for no reason she could ascertain. "I know Lester's got his magical websites and all, but it wasn't rocket surgery to figure that the numbers were related to drugs somehow."

"Rocket surgery?" He had made her smile with that one.

"I got in touch with a pal of mine at Homeland Security," he continued. "A sort of under-the-table request. He ran both numbers. I chose HSI over DEA 'cause I like 'em better, but also 'cause they're getting all the funding and most of the toys lately. Anyhow, the opening news flash was hardly earth shattering: Both numbers are disconnected. But it turns out that the feds, with all their snooping hardware, keep an archive of old drop phone numbers. Christ knows why. But he called me back after a bit and said that while one of the numbers was a dud, the other had once been associated with your old sweetheart, Manuel Ruiz."

Despite her best efforts, Sammie's face flushed. "You can't help yourself, can you?"

He laughed. "Relax. You're the only one who carries around that ancient baggage. No one else cares."

She left it there, grateful for his evident lack of interest.

"It got me wondering about what old Manny was up to, which Bob Crawford hit on the head — the man's turned into a big wheel. You trained him well."

Sam became genuinely curious. "Bob talked about how the business had stopped being so top-down — that the previous underlings were now moving and shaking. Is that where Ruiz fits in?"

"Not exactly," Willy said. "Those were mostly New York guys. Manny is still operating out of Holyoke, for some reason, maybe because of Hispanic traditions, or family, or who-the-hell knows. He's still pretty old-school. Again — supposedly. But you're probably not gonna see him around Rutland anymore."

"Meaning what?"

"He's an executive nowadays. Money's his

thing. Never touches the dope. Did he dabble in the product when you worked with him?"

"No," she said, thinking back. That had been one of the appealing things about Manny. He'd seemed more like a young company man on the rise — little violence, no drug use, minimal alcohol, gently spoken. Of course, later — after he'd escaped and the Rutland operation had been shut down — it turned out that he'd actually killed people to serve his double game. To Sam's way of thinking, that had only qualified him as being typical of the sort of boyfriend she'd sought out most of her life.

Until now, she liked to think.

She shook her head slightly at her own thoughts. "Does your source know if Manny's tied to our case?"

"He could be," Willy admitted. "Rutland only got bigger for him over time."

Sam's phone began buzzing. She picked it up off her desk and glanced at the screen. "Cool," she told him. "It's Chris Hartley, from the crime lab."

She put the phone where Willy could hear it. "Hey, Chris. You're on speaker. Willy's with me."

"Hey, yourselves," her friend responded,

sounding upbeat. "I heard from my brother. He really came through — record time for those laid-back academic types. Must be I have some pull after all."

"What did he find out?"

"In a word? Mexico. That's where your marijuana came from. . . . Well," she interrupted herself, "that's where it grew up. Who knows how it got to where you found it. Still, it's an unusual finding — trash grass, all the way from Mexico. Seems cost-ineffective to me — unless you can get some hayseed to pay top dollar for it, of course. Which is exactly what you told me happened."

"Did your brother find anything else?" Sammie asked.

"I'm sending you his report in an e-mail, which goes into more detail, but that's pretty much the punch line. He identifies the region in Mexico where your sample was grown, but unless your agency has the budget from heaven, I doubt you're going to do much about that. Call me crazy."

Sammie laughed. "Nope. Right on that count. Thanks for doing this, Chris — and make sure to tell your brother that there's a jug of maple syrup heading his way, assuming he likes the stuff."

"Kills for it," she said. "That's how I keep

him in line."

Sam disconnected the call and glanced at Willy. "What do you think?"

"The fact that bad weed is for sale up here just tells me the dealers are appealing to every level of the market," he said thoughtfully. "I was surprised to find Raffner owning any — given her fancy taste in other things. What is interesting," he added, "is that since we can prove it came from Mexico, it gives us a federal angle to exploit if we need it."

"You want to go to the feds with this?" she asked, surprised.

"Not necessarily. Maybe enlist them if we need to."

"That's refreshingly mature of you, Mr. Kunkle," she commented with raised eyebrows.

He scowled in return. "Hardly. It's just that when I called my Homeland Security contact, he said they'd help us out if we asked them. It's because of the whole Border Patrol and Immigration roots of their agency — any involvement by a foreign country definitely qualifies HSI to come on board."

"Well, we got that now," she said.

"Right," he agreed. "But there's more: If Manny is tied into this, and if he is exclusively into handling money, like Crawford claims, then HSI is the perfect partner for us if we need one — one of their specialties is confiscating other people's cash if they think it's dirty. I'm just saying we should keep them in mind."

"Meaning we'll have two triggers to pull against whoever's behind this — the dope and the money," Sam said.

Willy nodded. "It is nice to have options every once in a while."

Sammie, however, was thinking of the case in more specific terms. "Maybe, but unless all this is even remotely related to what got Susan Raffner killed," she said, "we'll be back to chasing our tails."

"Well then," Willy suggested, "we better just work the hell out of this lead." He punched her shoulder lightly and added cheerfully, "What can go wrong?"

Sammie grimaced in silence.

CHAPTER NINETEEN

Sergeant Tim Dugan was the Rutland police liaison assigned to the VBI. An eighteen-year veteran, he was a steady, quiet man, Joe thought as they settled down around a table on the top floor of the PD, and as such, a reflection of his chief's desire to be cooperative.

Also at the table were Sammie, Lester, Deputy Attorney General Brenda Weiss, Bob Crawford, and — equipped with a wireless keyboard to help him run an oversized computer screen in one corner of the room — Bruce Steinmetz.

"On behalf of Chief Quayles," Dugan began, "I'd like to welcome you all here. He wanted me to thank you, as well, for the way you approached us with this thing, instead of just marching in and taking over. This is maybe the biggest case — or at least the most high-profile one — to hit the state in a few years, and we appreciate what it must've taken to show your kind of courtesy."

Matching the man's form, Joe responded, "Tim, it's how we try to do business every time, but thanks all the same. I also thank you for not having grilled me too hard about what we're up to, until this meeting, so that Bruce and Brenda could be brought up to speed at the same time. Helps reduce the repetitiousness we go through so much in this business."

"No problem," Dugan replied.

"That being said," Joe continued, "we may end up going in circles. In the simplest terms, we're after whoever killed Senator Raffner. For that, we've got the biggest task force I've ever belonged to, combing through every scrap she left behind — physical and electronic — looking for anything relevant. But so far, both the sheer mass of it and the lack of real evidence have stymied us. That's why what Sam and her partner discovered struck us as possibly significant.

"It turns out that among the senator's enthusiasms, most of which were sociopolitical, she was also fond of a little recreational marijuana. In pursuit of restocking her supply, she had an intermediary buy her a large amount awhile back. This transaction occurred in Rutland and involved Buddy Ames and we think Stuey Nichols, to a degree we don't yet know. Problem was that when Raffner's representative delivered the product, it wasn't what had been expected or paid for. We believe that as a result of feeling ripped off, Raffner herself backtracked through the players that had been used to land the deal, and came to Rutland to confront Buddy Ames and force him to make good, one way or the other — as was her style. That past part is pure supposition by us."

"When was all this?" Brenda Weiss asked.

"Just before she was found hanging by her neck," Joe said bluntly. "That's what makes us think this lead has some meat on it."

"So we find Buddy Ames and we find her killer?" Weiss concluded.

"Only if you believe in miracles," Dugan told her. "Speaking as somebody who knows Buddy Ames, I have serious doubts he pulled this off on his own. He may have played a part, but the rest of it goes way beyond his brain wattage."

"How 'bout Stuey . . . What was his last name again?" she asked.

"Nichols," Sammie said.

"Stuey's as smart as your average jackal," Dugan allowed. "I don't think he's a natural

317

for this, but people sometimes stretch beyond what's expected of them."

"Implying a possible third player," Joe said. "Sam found out that the questionable marijuana originated in Mexico, which I gather Bob thinks is a little unusual."

"A little," Bob agreed. "But not unheard of in these more complicated times."

"I should add," Joe continued, "that we found heroin residue on the packaging. It, too, suggests a Mexican source."

"What're you referring to?" Bob asked.

"We received an analysis yesterday," Joe explained. "There wasn't much to work with — a dusting on the outside of the baggie — so it's not supersophisticated, but the telling detail turned out to be the adulterants used to cut the stuff. According to the lab, heroin out of New York is generally laced with fentanyl, Dilantin, and other higher-end pharmaceuticals, while Mexican smack is more often cut with much cheaper aspirin and the like. What was found on Raffner's bag of dope fits the latter. What we're hoping is that the similar sourcing of both drugs might help narrow down a suspect list and improve our chances of connecting this to Raffner's murder."

Crawford pulled on an earlobe. "Huh. Interesting. Most of the heroin hitting

Vermont right now is coming straight out of Brooklyn. But it used to be Holyoke." He glanced at Sammie. "Back when you were working your case, it was less heroin and more coke, but the source was heavily Mexican, involving cartels and organized crime and outfits like the Latin Kings and the Bloods. It might be that we're looking at a subgroup of old-fashioned dealers here."

"Like Manny Ruiz?" Sammie asked. "He would be smart enough to orchestrate Raffner's murder."

"He would fit, if he's who we get from Ames and/or Nichols when we find them. I have no clue why he would get involved in killing a state senator over a small deal gone bad, but that might be what's going to help us figure out who the real bad guy is. I mean, if all this does play out, and Manny is clean, he might even hand over who we're after, just so he can get back to business."

"Now you are dreaming," Lester groused.

"How're you doing finding those two, Bruce?" Dugan asked his colleague.

The screen in the corner came alive as Steinmetz spoke, making Joe think of the computer less as an extension of the young man's abilities, and more as his alter ego — blurring the distinctions between a hand

319

puppet and the hand.

"I started with those three names," he began, "Ames, Nichols, and Ruiz, and I applied the same process I did when you came by earlier and I got you Jackie Nunzio's information. I've split the screen into three panels, each acting independently, so I can pick up on any commonalities or overlays between and among them."

The people gathered around the table were watching one another as much as the ever-changing screen, perhaps wondering when the first of them might make a comment. Joe was nevertheless impressed by Bruce's command and enthusiasm. The man was a geek in his element, and confident enough that Joe doubted he would have cared if some wisecrack had been made.

"Ruiz," Bruce was still speaking, "is the hardest to track. Not too surprising, considering his climb up the food chain. Here, we can see his involvement with the case Detective Martens ran ten years ago — and his resulting fugitive warrant. After that, he only comes up when he's referred to by others — people saying that they work for him, or they're scared of crossing him, or whatever. That being said, you can see from this graph how those instances have increased to the present time, indicating his growing importance."

Joe found himself nodding, seeing precisely what Steinmetz was pointing out. He imagined how handy such graphics were at briefings with the patrol cops downstairs.

"Switching to Nichols," Bruce said, "we can see the enforced vacation he took as a result of attacking Detective Martens, followed by a few other infractions that then peter out into references by other people only — similar to in Ruiz's case. That tells me he started getting more cautious."

"Or he was told to keep a lid on it," Sam suggested.

"True." Bruce switched to his third subject. "Ames must be still in the trenches, if we follow that logic, because he's in plain view. Here he is getting arrested for disorderly, or DUI, or resisting arrest, or any number of minor offenses that get him little stretches of jail time or probation or hand slaps of that nature."

"He might be the one to lean on," Dugan ventured.

"He's also the one we have a definite eyewitness for," Sammie said. "Maggie Kinnison can put him there."

Joe asked Bruce, "We know that Ruiz and Nichols are lying low. But do we have a location on Buddy Ames, or an easy way to quietly grab hold of him? I'd like to have a chat about the company he's keeping, but without tipping anyone off that we're hovering overhead."

For the first time, Bruce looked away from the distant screen and smiled directly at Joe. "I think we might."

Tim Dugan was at the wheel. Joe had no problem ceding control to a man who was Rutland born. For some reason, although he'd been crisscrossing Vermont for his entire adult life, Joe had always found Rutland's streets to be a mazelike tangle. This was all the truer now that many of the familiar landmarks were hidden under a thick cover of fresh snow.

"We have the subject in sight, leaving the building," said a metallic-sounding voice.

Dugan spoke softly into his cell phone, which he'd put on speaker, for Joe's sake. "Ten-four."

"Amazing, those things," Joe commented.

Dugan hefted it in his hand. "Don't know how we functioned before. Damn things are a miracle — take pictures, download records, access data banks, and talk to each other securely without radio chatter. Who knew? And all in a couple of years."

"Except when they don't work," Joe couldn't resist saying.

Dugan chuckled. "Right. Well, that's *your* problem, traveling the whole state. Me? I'm stuck in an urban hole. It may not be much, but it's got good cell service."

"He's heading north, as discussed. Nothing hinky yet," the voice said.

Dugan stayed put, his engine running but his lights out. There were three teams out tonight — Sam and Willy in one vehicle, Lester and another Rutland cop named Robert Marshall in the other. It was this second unit that was tailing Buddy Ames at the moment, fresh from leaving his place of work at a pizza place on Route 7.

It was after midnight, in the middle of the week, during a time which — thanks to Bruce Steinmetz — they knew Rutland's population and traffic flow were in a traditional lull, a statistic only enhanced by the recent bad weather. By and large, Buddy and his police tail were almost alone on the streets.

This was the third night in a row that they'd had Buddy Ames under surveillance, establishing his habits. So far, he'd consistently left work, headed toward the Gut, dropped by a late-night bar for a few drinks, and then continued on — weaving slightly — to his humble home on the edge of town. It was the sort of routine they'd been hoping for, and which Bruce had suggested they might find. Buddy, he'd guessed, was a man of regular habits.

They left the neon glitter and open spaces of Rutland's most commercial area — Route 7 — Marshall swapping positions with Willy in order not to become too omnipresent in Buddy's rearview mirror. The snowbanks lining the streets thereafter acted as sound-absorbing walls, boxing in the cars and combining with the bitter cold and abrupt darkness to heighten a sense of isolation.

Winter in northern New England could sidle up to you that way — presenting as an eye-pleasing postcard while seeking out your vitality. Volcanic lava and ash were in-your-face threats to survival; snow and light-refracting ice — soft, seductive, rounded, and smooth — were subtler, slower, but no less lethal.

Joe and Dugan were waiting on the edge of the Gut, out of sight at the end of a still and somber block of darkened homes. In the past twenty minutes, they hadn't seen a single sign of life, and had heard only the two other teams exchanging details of their ever-changing locations.

"This might actually work," Dugan said softly, almost to himself.

"Happens, sometimes," Joe commented.

The last communication indicated that Sam and Willy were cutting around the block, in order to appear in front of Ames's car. The plan was for them to plant themselves in the middle of the street just below Joe and Tim — faking a breakdown, complete with Sammie acting the distressed motorist — so that the other two vehicles could then box in their quarry and grab him.

"We're in place," said Willy shortly, announcing the first step.

"He's heading down the street," Marshall reported from behind.

Tim instinctively moved the phone closer to his mouth as Buddy's beater slid by before them. "He just passed by us, going your way," he said, before turning on his headlights and entering the road in front of Spinney and Marshall's car.

From the passenger seat, Joe saw Buddy's dim headlights slowly revealing an SUV blocking the way ahead, flagrantly decorated by a young woman dressed in skintight jeans, her coat open to reveal her figure, waving at him for help.

Unconcerned about who might be behind

him, Buddy stopped and eagerly emerged into the night to approach her. She was babbling about how her car had quit, as Joe, Tim, and the two behind them all stepped into the street, fanned out to both sides, and quickly closed the distance. Buddy hadn't begun speaking before he was surrounded by powerful men who bundled him up, piled him into Sammie's car with Joe, Willy, and Lester, while Sam and the others redistributed themselves among the remaining three cars, including Buddy's.

In less than a minute, the street was as empty, quiet, and dark as before.

Chapter Twenty

"Who are you people?"

Joe smiled broadly and sat down. "We're in a police station, Buddy."

"You kidnapped me. Where's my car?"

Joe made a vague gesture. "You've been a bad boy, so we picked you up, which is when, by the way, you agreed to cooperate. Remember? Your car's in the lot outside, safely locked up. And you're not even under arrest, Buddy — yet. Do you want to leave now? You can if you want."

Ames didn't move from his chair. He looked around the small room suspiciously, taking in Joe, the half-open door near him, the mirrored window beside it, and the camera mounted high in the corner, its beady red light blinking steadily.

"What d'you want?"

"To discuss your options."

"What's that mean?"

"More than you might think. You're a local boy, aren't you?"

"So?"

"You've gotten used to the way things work here. Good guys, bad guys, the patsies in the middle. Kind of a comfortable routine."

"What's your point?"

"How many times've you been arrested, Buddy?"

"I don't know. Five or six."

"Maybe fifteen?"

"Maybe."

"You ever make a deal, to lighten your time, or reduce a charge?"

"I'm not a rat."

Joe feigned surprise. "Is that what I said?"

"It's what you meant."

"Totally wrong. I'm talking about the times you gave us something and we gave you a little less to worry about. No rats. Just common sense."

In the leading silence following, Buddy finally said, "Okay."

Joe rose just enough to hitch his chair slightly closer to Buddy's. The other man straightened, as if reacting to an odor.

Joe lowered his voice threateningly. "Well, this ain't one of those times."

Ames pursed his lips. "Why?"

"You may not know it, but you really

stepped in it this time."

Buddy's voice rose in protest. "I haven't done nuthin."

"Have you heard about the woman found hanging over the interstate?"

"Who hasn't? That's got nuthin to do with me."

Joe leaned forward, further closing the distance between them. "You see? That's the crazy thing. It really does — enough to cook you alive."

"I never met that lady. Wouldn't know her if she walked in the room." He pointed to the door.

"You know what a conspiracy is?" Joe asked him.

Buddy's eyes narrowed. "So?"

"So you know that when the *Titanic* went down, its innocent passengers went with it, even though they had nothing to do with hitting that iceberg."

Buddy hesitated, confused. "What?"

"You're not the least bit innocent, Buddy. You're *driving* your boat," Joe told him. "According to your record, you're a regular menace — even selling drugs."

"Yeah?"

"A lot of drugs, in fact. You're a connected man, with a source on one side and customers on the other. You're responsible for what you do."

Ames didn't respond.

"They call you The Indian," Joe said, pointing at Buddy's belt buckle. "Because of that. Which is why you were contacted by Brandon Younger awhile back and asked to sell some weed to a woman. She met you in her car on the street, when you were with Stuey Nichols. She really remembers that buckle. In fact, she remembers a bunch."

Buddy self-consciously touched his waist. "Lot of people have this."

Joe hitched his chair close enough that they were almost touching knees. "We're just talking about you. And so is she. Anyhow, that dope — that particular bag of marijuana, Buddy, the one you sold to that woman — it's been directly linked to Susan Raffner's death."

Ames opened his mouth slightly, as if preparing to comment, but then closed it.

"And here's the kicker," Joe said. "This is all about to go federal, and we local guys are going to disappear. That means no more people like me, willing to talk a deal. It means the death penalty gets put on the table."

Buddy looked pained. "For selling grass?"

Joe smiled. "You don't have to go down like those innocent passengers." He touched

Buddy's knee gently. "You could be maybe one of the lucky ones. But there's something I'm disappointed you didn't mention, right off the bat. Makes me think you're fucking me around, and that maybe you deserve to drown." His hand now squeezed Buddy's knee hard, making him flinch and try to move away.

"I don't know what you're talkin' about."

"A second woman came by to see you, after you sold that bag to the first one."

Buddy licked his lips and swallowed. "No," he barely whispered.

Joe was relieved by the reaction, since his statement had been a purely calculated gamble. "Oh, yes," he reassured him. "And that second woman was Susan Raffner, who ended up dead right after. You do understand what kind of jam that puts you in?"

Joe lessened his grip. "Nod if you understand."

Buddy Ames nodded.

Joe let go and sat back, if only slightly. "For the record, you also understand that you can still leave anytime you want? And that you're speaking to me now freely and willingly?"

"Yeah."

"Good man. That helps me think maybe

331

you didn't kill Susan Raffner — or at least that you didn't do it alone."

"I didn't do it at all," Ames protested. "I mean, sure. I sold her a bag — the other lady, I mean. But I didn't kill the next one — the older one. I barely had nuthin to do with her."

Joe was nodding throughout. "But you did meet her."

"Yeah. That stupid bastard Brandon put her onto me."

"Take me through it, Buddy. Describe what happened."

"He gave her my home address. Can you believe that? She came right up and pounded on the door. In the middle of the night. I didn't know what the fuck was happening — thought it was the cops. And it was that crazy bitch."

"You talked with her."

"She wasn't gonna take no for an answer. Sure I talked to her. She threatened to call you guys if I didn't. How weird is that?"

Joe leaned forward again, causing Ames to draw up nervously. "Tell me what happened clearly, Buddy, without the theatrics. Don't forget how important it is that you describe everything in order and accurately — down to the last detail. You have a lot riding on this."

"I'm trying," he whined.

"I know. So she came knocking on your door in the middle of the night. About what time?"

"I don't know. Maybe two? I was asleep, and I don't get home till after one, mostly."

"Did she know who you were when you opened the door?"

"Sort of. She called me by my name. 'Are you Buddy Ames?' is what she said."

"You live alone?"

"Yeah."

"Did you see her car out front? In your driveway, if you have one?"

Buddy looked thoughtful for the first time, becoming more at ease. "Yeah. It was one of those fancy eco-things, I think. I could barely see it. She'd left it near the street."

"All right. You let her in?"

"I didn't want to. I was telling her to fuck off. That's what got her worked up, threatening me like she did. After that, she just pushed her way in, like she owned the place and I was the trespasser. Unbelievable."

"What did she want?"

"Her money back," he said, his frustration rising. "Like I was Walmart."

"Okay," Joe soothed him. "Again, one step at a time. Give me details."

Buddy clamped his lips tightly for a moment, in a show of self-control, before letting out a breath and saying calmly, "She said she was the one who sent that first woman out, and what the hell was I thinking — that I could sell her bad dope for that much money? Those're her words. I'm not making nuthin up."

"What did you say?"

Buddy surprised him by actually looking embarrassed. "I told her I didn't have it anymore, but that maybe we could work something out."

"Really?" Joe asked, despite himself.

"She wasn't wrong about the weed," Buddy admitted. "It was crap. I knew we shouldn't've done it."

"You and Stuey?"

Buddy seemed surprised, as if caught out, although Joe had mentioned Stuey once already. "Yeah."

"So why did you?"

"She was no regular of ours — neither her or the one in the car earlier. From what I know, Brandon used to service one or the other, but he moved out of the pot business, like most people have. So Stuey didn't care, not from the get-go. He said he had some lousy stuff on hand, the customer was raring to go, so what the hell."

"And you didn't like it."

"I didn't like that he was gonna charge her full freight — hydro prices for Mexican cow shit. That's not good for business, you know?"

"What happened next? When you told her you no longer had her money?"

"She went ballistic. Said she didn't need this kind of hassle, today of all days."

Joe almost cut him off. "She explain that?"

"Nah, but she was pissed. I mean, she came in loaded for bear, and I didn't think it was about some stupid marijuana."

"Okay. Go ahead."

"So, like I said, I told her maybe we could work somethin' out. That's when she said that getting all her money back and keeping the stuff we sold her would be just fine. Well, that kinda got under my skin. You know — fair's fair — but screwin' us 'cause she got ripped off didn't seem right, neither. We coulda split the difference or somethin'."

"What happened?"

He shrugged. "I couldn't do nuthin. Stuey had the money. So I called him."

Joe tried to imagine the scene — the angry, entitled, self-righteous politician versus the pizza-slinging, street-level drug dealer, calling for arbitration from a sociopathic criminal. If the results hadn't already been made so dreadfully clear, it might have sounded like the makings of a TV soap opera.

"Did he come over?"

"No," Buddy told him. "He told me to give her the phone and they talked. After that, she left and that was it."

Joe hid his disappointment. "What did you overhear? Did he give her directions on where to meet him?"

"He coulda. I wouldn't know. When I gave her the phone, she stepped outside — I don't know why. All I heard her say was, 'Who's this?' as she was leaving. She was talking as she walked around — I could hear that — but I couldn't make out what she was saying."

"And then she left."

"Yeah. Handed me the phone back, through the door, and took off."

"You talk to Stuey after? To find out what happened?"

"I tried, but he's gone."

"Gone where?"

"Gone, gone. I don't know, man. Just disappeared. Nobody knows where he's at. I thought maybe you guys had him."

"Because you added up two-plus-two?" Joe asked him. "And figured the woman you saw that night was found dead the next day?"

Ames hesitated, unsure of his footing. "Maybe," he hedged.

"What was she wearing, Buddy?"

He stared at him a moment. "Wearing? You mean clothes?"

"Yeah."

Ames scratched his cheek. "Uh, a long coat. Dark. Maybe wool."

"Underneath?"

"Pants. Like fancy, though. Not jeans. They were dark, too. And a white shirt."

"Shoes?"

He paused. "I don't remember. They weren't like winter boots or anything. I woulda remembered that. I guess they were lady things. I dunno."

Joe nodded to himself. The description fit what he'd seen on Susan when they'd pulled her off the cliff — minus the long coat. At the time, they'd believed she'd been grabbed while indoors. Now, that was less clear.

"Talk to me about Stuey," Joe asked. "Where was the last place you know he was living?"

"Motel on Route Seven," Ames told him. "Some dump. Used to be called one thing, then it changed names, so now I don't know what to call it. Next to the Irving station, and the KFC."

"You remember what room?"

"It's on the second floor, about halfway along. He was living with a girl, like usual."

"She have a name?"

He thought a moment. "Jackie somebody. She's dead, though, so that's not gonna do much for you."

The news came out as if they'd been discussing an old car.

"Jackie Nunzio?" Joe asked, less for clarification and more to grant her a fragment of relevance.

He should have known better. "Yeah. That's it. Skanky bitch — real smack whore, complete with rug rats. I didn't see the appeal."

Joe couldn't find the appeal in any of this, and moved on. "Where else would Stuey go? He have family or contacts out of town? Or another place, like a hunting camp?"

Buddy laughed. "Right — Stuey hunting. There's a picture. I don't know what he'd use on a deer. Maybe a hammer. That would fit."

"So that's a no?"

The other man hitched his shoulders. "I don't know of any place. Doesn't mean there's not one. It's not like we're best pals."

"Could be a business associate," Joe suggested. "He's like mid-level, isn't he? You're the street guy, running the dope around town and collecting the cash, and Stuey passes it up the ladder to the higher-ups. Isn't that how it works?"

Buddy straightened in his chair, as if suddenly aware of his surroundings and his earlier concern about being a rat. "I wouldn't know."

Joe's expression darkened. "You and I aren't pals, either, you son of a bitch," he snarled, eager to keep Buddy defensive and off balance. "And that bullshit story about Stuey notwithstanding, you're still the one we got who's good for this murder. You understand that?"

"I told you. I had nuthin to do with that. I told you everything that happened. That fucking broad left my place alive."

Joe thrust his face inches from Buddy's and yelled, "Then where's Stuey?"

"I don't know," Buddy shouted back, his expression fearful.

Satisfied, Joe resumed his seat, as calm as if a switch had been thrown. "Tell me about his operation. Who's he work for?"

Ames was sweating now, his face pale. "A guy in Holyoke. I don't know names. I used to. We all did. But things've changed. The old gang's pretty much out, and new people've come in. But they're supercautious, probably 'cause of all the electronic snooping and the feds and drones and all the rest."

"They never come to Rutland to check things out?"

"They do. I hear about it. They get the VIP treatment, you know? Place to crash, one or two women to entertain 'em, all the fixin's. But like you said, us guys never get to play. We're the grunts — put up and shut up. That's us. I might meet one of them if I stepped outta line — first-time/last-time meeting, if you get what I'm sayin'. But that's it. So I'm not too eager to get that goin'."

Joe stood up. "All right. That's it for the moment. You have your cell on you?"

Ames reached into his pocket and laid a phone on the table. "Knock yourself out."

Joe got his meaning. "Drop phone?"

"Get a new one every few days."

"So there's nothing on this dating back to when you saw Raffner that night?"

"Nope," Buddy confirmed. "Can I get outta here now?"

"That what you want?"

"I didn't do nuthin."

Joe studied him for a moment. "Yeah. I heard that. Problem is, I'm not the one you have to convince anymore. Word'll get out how you spent the night with us, and got

340

off without a scratch. Those Holyoke folks probably won't like that much. What did you call it? A first-time/last-time meeting?"

Buddy was staring at him with his mouth open. "You bastards. What've you done to me?"

"Not a thing," Joe replied, and crossed to the door, where he turned and added, "But stay put. We're bound to come up with something."

CHAPTER TWENTY-ONE

"Great. Another fucking dead end."

Joe tilted his office chair back and crossed his ankles on his desk. "Damn, Willy. You *are* a good-news bear."

"How would you see this?" Willy asked him, making Sam and Lester look from one to the other like spectators at a tennis match. "We might as well be chasing the Invisible Man."

"That's who we've been chasing up to now," Joe countered patiently. "We didn't have a name and a history and a complete background. How likely do you think it is that Stuey Nichols'll be able to stay low, now that we have him in our sights? A BOL's been sent out across the Northeast. You really believe there's a hole deep enough to hide this loser? I don't."

The phone rang and Joe picked it up. "Gunther. VBI."

"Allard," said his boss. "We need to meet."

Joe took his feet down to better see the calendar on his computer screen. "Sure. When and where?"

"Now and downstairs, in the PD's detective unit. And keep this to yourself for right now."

Joe kept his voice light. "Nifty. Be there in a sec."

He hung up the phone and addressed his team. "I gotta go check on something, but to Willy's point earlier, we ought to recheck everything we've got to make sure it fits Stuey to a T."

"You want to cut back on going through all of Raffner's archives?" Sammie asked.

Joe pondered that a moment. "Not yet. Let's look at how we're using our resources. We might want to do that, but let's not get too carried away. Right now, we *think* we have a hot lead. We may be wrong. Be right back."

He took the old building's broad stairs down one flight and used the key he'd never returned to enter the locked office area he used to run, years before. Curious but not particularly concerned by being summoned, he greeted the two women in the front room with a wave and a smile, and passed through unchallenged to the conference room. There he was met by Allard, Ron Klesczewski —

the department's chief of detectives — and a man in a suit he'd never set eyes on before.

"Hey," he said, approaching the stranger with an outstretched hand. "Joe Gunther."

The man stood and shook hands. "Peter LaBelle, Homeland Security."

Joe shot Allard a quick glance as he sat down opposite LaBelle. "This should be interesting," he said.

Allard spoke first. "Peter contacted me as a result of some inquiries he learned about, surrounding the Raffner investigation."

"Okay," Joe said neutrally.

"We heard through the grapevine that you were looking for Allan Nichols," LaBelle explained.

"Stuey?" Joe replied, noting LaBelle's precise wording. "Yeah. You ever meet him?"

"Can't say I have. Why?"

"Just that his mother maybe called him Allan," Joe said. "The day he was born. It's been Stuey ever since. Made me think you'd never met him. How'd you hear we wanted him — specifically?"

"My God," Allard answered. "It's not like it's a secret. The man's name has been sent to every cop shop in the Northeast."

Joe kept his eyes on the newcomer. "I don't think that's what Peter meant. He said 'through the grapevine,' suggesting

344

something less official."

LaBelle smiled politely. "Very observant. Actually, it was one of your people — who, I don't know. He contacted someone in our Burlington office and asked about a couple of phone numbers that alerted us to your interest in Nichols."

"A couple of phone numbers . . ." Joe repeated, not finishing the sentence.

In the awkward silence that followed, La-Belle said, "Yeah."

Joe was thinking hard, trying to put together what had probably happened, while not revealing that he'd known nothing about it. He addressed Allard. "That would've been Kunkle."

He turned back to LaBelle. "What're you not telling us about how that inquiry went over at your end?"

For the first time, the man from HSI looked slightly uncomfortable. "Well, you know how these things work. People who know each other, keep in touch, sometimes help each other out on cases. Happens all the time. It's the old-boy network — your guy used it."

"And your guy ended up with his butt in a crack. You didn't answer the question."

LaBelle stopped tiptoeing. He lapsed into a smile, looking relieved. "Yeah — our boss read him the riot act. He's a by-the-book desk agent. Not super popular. When our man ran the numbers Kunkle . . . is that right?"

"Willy Kunkle. Yup."

". . . Kunkle gave him, he punched them into our system to see what came up. The catch is that those numbers — one of them, at least; the other went nowhere — once belonged to a person of interest in Holyoke. Nichols's name was connected to it as someone who'd dialed it a lot."

"So what happened? Willy didn't give me the blow-by-blow," Joe said casually.

"We gave him the owner of the phone number — Manuel Ruiz. That shouldn't have happened."

Joe worked to control his reaction. Ruiz was a loaded name in the short history of the VBI, given Sammie's history with him. He cast a look at Allard and said lightly, "There's a blast from the past."

Bill Allard didn't respond.

"He's moved up in the world," Joe commented vaguely to LaBelle, wondering what he'd learn next — that Ruiz was connected to Raffner's death?

"More importantly, so has Nichols," La-Belle countered. "He's the reason I'm here, and the answer to your question. Turns out that by helping Kunkle do an under-the-table favor, his HSI contact stirred up a wasp's nest, especially by referencing Nichols."

"Why?"

LaBelle paused, choosing his words. "Stuey Nichols is of particular use to us right now, something we don't want circulated."

Joe sat back as if pushed. "Of course he is. That slimy son of a bitch. You've turned him into an informant against Ruiz. You are dimly aware that Stuey put a cop in the hospital, and would've killed her if her partner hadn't stopped him?"

"We are," LaBelle answered evenly. "And that he served his time for doing so. We also know that he is now willing to help us bring down a major player. Ruiz is huge, especially in light of what's been happening with heroin in Vermont. He is organized, well-protected, heavily financed, and has a direct pipeline to some big operators south of the border, which is why he falls under our purview. You can see why we're already unhappy with Nichols's name floating around within law enforcement. We sure as hell don't want that to spread further, or for it to be associated with Ruiz."

He pointed at Joe. "If we can bring Manny

Ruiz down, it'll give the whole state a shot in the arm. And appealing to your own self-interest, that's something the governor should find very useful right now."

Joe studied him for a moment in silence, again struggling to not respond from feelings alone. It was a challenge. The reference to "the governor," coupled with the high probability that LaBelle knew of Joe's romantic past with her, implied a calculated and cynical gesture of monumental proportions.

One he might have used himself, had the tables been turned.

He therefore swallowed what Willy would have blurted out in his place, and asked instead, "With all that in mind — and I do wish you well, since we have no love for Mr. Ruiz, either — what happens if we establish that Stuey Nichols killed Susan Raffner and strung her up like a dead rabbit after mutilating her body with his pocketknife?"

His choice of words chilled the atmosphere, as intended. LaBelle, however, was not easily cowed. "Everyone in this room knows a murder charge trumps all, so your 'if you establish' becomes the operative phrase, doesn't it?" he countered. He shifted his glance to include the other two men in the room, and added, "What do you have that's solid against Nichols?"

Joe rapped his knuckles lightly on the table to regain his attention. "What I and my unit have is that just before she was murdered, Susan Raffner hung up the phone on Stuey and headed off to meet him, madder than a wet hen about having been ripped off in a dope deal." Joe shifted in his seat for emphasis. "You know Stuey, Peter — or at least his history — and we locals sure as hell knew the late Senator Raffner. How likely do you think it is that a nice, calm, rational business meeting took place between them?"

"And your source is good about this supposed phone call?"

"Immaculate," Joe said, his temper again rising.

Bill Allard weighed in diplomatically, "Surely it would be in everyone's best interest if Joe or someone of his choosing was allowed to have a sit-down with Nichols."

"It would certainly be in yours," LaBelle agreed.

"But not HSI's?" Allard asked. "You were the one who said you didn't want Nichols burned as a CI. How 'bout if he's charged in the most sensational murder in the state's history, and HSI is identified as having kept him under wraps?"

LaBelle avoided answering directly. "Ours is a large and complicated organization," he said unnecessarily. "I don't have the autonomy you do. I'll have to get back to you on that."

Joe controlled his frustration. "Can you give us a vague time frame?"

LaBelle glanced around the table and rose to his feet. "I'll move right on it." He began heading for the door.

"A phone call wouldn't do the trick?" Joe asked.

The HSI agent paused at the door. "Not in this instance, but we'll be fast. I promise."

He was gone with that, leaving the remaining three to look at one another silently.

Until Joe muttered, "I wish he hadn't said that last word."

"So," Willy challenged him as he reappeared in the VBI office upstairs a few minutes later. "What secret clubhouse did you just disappear into?"

Joe smiled grimly. "That obvious, huh?"

"We have *got* to play poker together sometime soon. You don't look happy, by the way, just in case you think you're keeping that to yourself, too."

Joe stood in the middle of the small room and addressed them all. "HSI just told me they have Stuey on board as a CI, and that they'll be getting back to us about how we can have a crack at him regarding the Raffner homicide."

"Wow," Lester said quietly.

"Fuck that," Willy added more succinctly.

Sammie was more directed. "Why're they laying claim to him?" she asked. "Don't they do border-related stuff?"

"It's Ruiz," Joe said. "And it is border-related, as we found out when we pegged the marijuana to its Mexican roots."

"They're using Stuey to get at Manny Ruiz?" Sam asked, almost incredulously.

"They're hoping to. They obviously weren't going to give me details, but they're clearly putting a lot of faith in the man."

"Have they met him?" Sam asked no one in particular.

"That's crazy," Willy stated. "They can't trump a murder investigation. One call to a paper would blow them right out of the water."

Joe gave him a severe look — and avoided repeating Allard's threat. "Don't even think about it. They're not saying we can't have access, or saying their case trumps ours — that much, they made clear. Right now, they're just claiming chain-of-command problems. The guy I talked to wants a boss on board."

"That's bogus and you know it."

"I don't disagree," Joe admitted. "And I'd love to know what they're really up to, but our hands are tied."

"It's not that complicated," Willy said bitterly. "They don't want to lose their case against Ruiz to our murder. It's a time and money thing, and I bet they've spent a ton of each chasing Manny."

Lester was shaking his head, his sense of fair play shaken. "I know the feds can play hardball, but I've never heard of them screwing anyone over that bad. She was a state senator, for Christ's sake."

"They don't give a rat's ass," Willy maintained.

"Okay, okay," Joe intervened. "None of that reflects what they said to me, but let me see what I can find out. In their defense, it is a top-down bureaucracy — not the nimblest of outfits. I think we're being a little paranoid."

"What do we do in the meantime?" Sam protested.

Joe addressed all three of them. "What I said earlier: We keep going on all cylinders, but we also make sure that Stuey fits the details of the crime. If we stick enough of the evidence to him, we won't need permission from HSI to talk to him. We'll get a judge to do that for us by issuing an arrest warrant. We owe it to the case to explore every possible avenue."

"You heard the man," Willy told her. "He said every possible avenue."

He and Sam were sitting together in his car in the municipal building's parking lot, masked from view by a thin layer of snow across the windshield. Not that discretion was key for the moment — the TV trucks and earlier hordes of reporters had tired of standing around hearing "no comment."

"You know that's not what he meant," Sammie responded. "Like he was really going to give you a license to kill. After all these years?"

"Whatever," Willy replied. "The point is: We know who we want, and we need to go get him. The feds're goin' to push this around for as long as they can — like hiding a pea under a shell." He stared at her to make his point. "This sorry fucker murdered somebody, Sam."

"I know, I know," she said. "Maybe."

Predictably, he ignored her qualifier. "So, let's track him down."

Joe copied the Burlington phone number

for HSI off his computer screen, in order to call and arrange a meeting with their head agent — a man he'd never met, but who he'd heard had been transferred to Vermont just recently.

For a man like Joe, who'd only worked for two outfits during his entire career — both of them in the same building — the idea of being shuttled among and between federal bureaucracies and across the map was foreign and disorienting. Joe came from the soil whose residents he policed; he shared a culture with the people he worked with, learned from, and occasionally arrested; and he used that inner, instinctive knowledge to help resolve many of the problems he confronted daily — from knowing who to call when he needed a saw blade sharpened, to who to consult when a mutual acquaintance had decided he didn't want to be found.

As a result, reaching out to a newly appointed outsider in order to gain access to a local felon felt counterintuitive. On the other hand, he'd seen the expression on Willy's face when he'd broken the news of HSI's involvement, and he knew that he didn't have much time before Kunkle — and probably Sam, who was visibly falling prey to Willy's independence — took the same kind of initiative that had resulted in Stuey's being identified in the first place. Those two — as they saw it — were on a roll.

CHAPTER TWENTY-TWO

Sam was not happy. Sitting alone in her car in the middle of the night, parked on a side street in downtown Holyoke, Massachusetts, she was adrift in her own misgivings.

Days ago, she'd been a happy mother and a respected cop, beset by no more than the usual self-doubts and challenges, and otherwise settled, well situated, and secure.

Now she was colluding in a rogue investigation, across state lines, in flagrant violation of her employer's wishes, all because she'd let an impulse born of an ancient embarrassment be hijacked by the one man who interpreted acting as a renegade as just thinking outside the box.

The cell phone in her lap spoke up, "You there?"

"Yeah," she said, almost regretfully.

"We got movement by the front door."

Willy was around the corner, crouching in

an abandoned apartment opposite Manuel Ruiz's stronghold. Willy's old sniper-school training — not to mention his inborn paranoia — had served him well in taking several hours to identify how best to approach Ruiz's address unnoticed. This had turned out to be a worthwhile caution, since he'd discovered that Ruiz had posted sentries around the neighborhood. Some had been predictable, assigned to a few surrounding rooftops; others had been more inspired, such as the bum Willy had spotted, seemingly passed out in a doorway at street level, but with well-cared-for fingernails, a military unit ring, and a strategically thought-out sprawl that favored his ability to quickly produce a concealed weapon.

In an urban environment, however, one can only place so many outposts. There are simply more nooks and crannies than manpower to control them. Willy had found himself such an overlooked crow's nest.

Still, he was impressed. Despite what movie directors tried to make their fans believe, most crooks in this country do not and cannot set up a fortress as had Manny Ruiz. It is generally too complex, too expensive, and too visible. In this case, though — and in this town — Ruiz's discretion and Holyoke's economic limitations had combined to make it possible.

"Is it him?" Sam asked.

Willy had night-vision binoculars trained on the building's entrance, which was now flanked by a group of casually menacing men, who'd formed a human corridor between the front door and a large, presumably armored SUV parked by the curb.

"If it isn't," Willy replied, "he's entertaining somebody with a serious hard-on for security."

Sam didn't respond, entering combat-ready mode herself.

"Wait for it . . ." Willy's voice announced like a game show's master of ceremonies. "Bingo. One Manuel Ruiz, stepping out for a little tour around his kingdom. You got your motor running?"

"Roger that."

"Pick me up at the corner in ninety seconds." The phone went dead.

Joe stood by the window of Beverly's bedroom, gazing out sightlessly at the cold gray water of Lake Champlain.

Beverly came up behind him and looped her arms around his waist. "In an old movie, I'd offer, 'Penny for your thoughts.' "

He chuckled despite himself and held her

wrists affectionately. "Doubt you'd get your money's worth."

"Seriously," she prompted. "Is it the case?"

"That's what everything is now," he admitted. "Although I won't deny that it's gotten a little more complicated with Homeland Security sticking their oar in the water."

She peered around to study his face. "Homeland Security? Really? Did the senator's death become a terrorist attack when I wasn't looking?"

He brought her up close to him, so they were facing the broad window side-by-side. "No — that's just what the title 'Homeland Security' does to people. Those guys chase after what the rest of us do. They just have a different jurisdiction — usually involving the border somehow, or at least what and who crosses it. Turns out the marijuana we found at Susan's was Mexican in origin."

"Ah," she said. "Ergo the border reference."

"Anyhow," he further explained, "it looks like they've already got some of the people we're interested in under a microscope, which means everybody's got to compare cards to see who's got the winning hand."

She scowled. "You have a murder."

"I know. Which is probably why this'll be

ironed out in our favor. But somebody's got to say it in so many words, and maybe put it in writing, and we've got to agree how to inflict the least possible damage to each other's investigation. And last but certainly not least, there's the unwritten rule about who's got the bird in hand, which in this case is them."

He gazed at her and waggled his eyebrows, adding, "I therefore called in for support — just before this morning's meeting."

"Oh?"

"I did unto her as she's done unto me in the past," he said. "I phoned the governor for a favor."

Beverly laughed and dug her fingers into his side. "You wheeler-dealer. Do tell."

"I owed her a call anyhow," he began disingenuously. "Both to find out how she was faring and to explain how and why we had issued a BOL for Stuey Nichols."

"How did she take it?" Beverly asked seriously.

"Better than I thought. She's actually sounding more like her old self. I think the coming out has helped, as has some of the advice she must be getting from outside experts. She told me she was no longer considering offers from people like Ellen DeGeneres and *The Daily Show,* so that

Vermonters won't think she's stepping out on them, taking advantage to attract national attention. Smart."

"Very," Beverly agreed, "since she also let it leak out that she turned those offers down. I heard about it on the news last night. So what's the favor you asked for?"

"Just to drop a line to the local boss of Homeland Security Investigations — the fellow I'm seeing in an hour. I'm letting her choose the wording, but I asked her to pass along how much VBI would appreciate their timely cooperation in solving Susan's murder."

Still smiling, Beverly was thoughtful as she said, "Just what you need to be worrying about. Politics. Why is that always such a factor in what we do? Still, it sounds like you're doing well." She reached up and touched his cheek. "So why do I think something else is chewing at you?"

Joe paused before replying, "It's not the feds that have me worried. I feel like there's something out of whack, somehow — something I'm not seeing. I just can't put my finger on it."

They'd opted for an underpowered rental, rather than anything smacking of police-issue. There were no high-speed chases anticipated, and, if any cropped up, he and Sam weren't going to join in. They were just another couple in the traffic heading toward Springfield.

"How many people're with him?" Sam asked, looking straight ahead.

"Three in the SUV, two more in the tail car."

"Heavy artillery?"

"Probably under their coats. That's what I'd do. They are clearly a cut above the usual street mopes."

He could tell she had more questions — where they were going, what they were about to do, why the hell she and Willy were doing this in the first place. But she didn't ask any of them, and he didn't make chitchat. He had his own coping mechanism during an operation, and it didn't involve getting increasingly wired. On the contrary, while he wouldn't have called it meditative, the end result was similar — Willy just became calmer as the action loomed nearer.

That helped her, as well, since she was no more capable of achieving Yogic tranquility under these circumstances than she might've been at suddenly speaking Chinese. As a result, his seeming calm was a good influence.

Of course, for her, the challenge wasn't

just wrestling with mounting excitement. She had her own issues as well — her past with Ruiz, her worries about what they were doing, and how much more was at stake, now that she had a child.

As Willy might have said, had he been consulted about any of it, "You should've thought of that sooner."

Which would have been correct, of course. All this fussing was a complete waste of effort. They were in it now.

"Where the fuck're they going?" she asked, essentially of herself. "This isn't how I'd go downtown."

Willy remained quiet, watching the cars ahead, instinctively doubtful, from what he'd seen so far, that they were headed anywhere important. The bodyguards had been careful, as expected, but not as they would have been gearing up for a fight.

They weren't going downtown.

"The mall?" Sammie asked herself incredulously a few minutes later. "You gotta be kidding."

"It's that time of year," Willy said, and checked his watch. "Good time for it, too."

"Why?"

"Twenty minutes before closing. Last of the stragglers are headin' out. They might even be telling people not to enter, except I bet these boys have one of their own on the door, allowing special access."

"That screws us, then," Sam said, part of her feeling a contradictory sense of relief.

But Willy was having none of it. "Nah. We want to use a different door anyhow. We just flash our badges and we're in, too."

Sam still couldn't believe it, and followed the small caravan thinking it would soon exit the enormous parking lot, having used it either as a shortcut or to check for tails, about which she'd been careful from the start.

But both the big SUV and its scout car pulled up near one of the mall's side entrances, and spilled out several passengers, who calmly, if tactically, prepared a phalanx for their boss.

Sam drove by without hesitation, aiming for the neighboring parking lot. There, she and Willy got out like any normal shoppers, pretending to be checking a list together as they headed toward a different entrance.

The mall's interior was as Willy had predicted — vaulting, blinding bright, echoing with canned music — but with no guard at the door.

As they approached the intersection of the entrance corridor and the mall's central atrium, Willy faded back, saying, "Let's split up. I'll have your back."

Sam paused. She never had a doubt of that, but she also had no clue about what was actually going on in here. Was Ruiz having a clandestine meeting in a public space? Was he about to make a move on some business outlet? How about a financial deposit as part of a money-laundering routine? She and Willy hadn't discussed a plan of action — opting instead to see what unfolded. The goal was for Sam to use her past relationship with Ruiz to see if he'd give her Stuey in exchange for not having a microscope trained on his enterprises. How to get that done was up to her.

She stepped cautiously out into the open and looked down the football field–length hallway toward where the SUV and escort car had unloaded their cargo. In the far distance, the incongruous, dark-clothed, all-male group filed up an escalator by the side of a sprinkling fountain. They looked like a bunch of hip bankers taking the day off at Disney World.

She bypassed her own escalator for the staircase beside it, taking two steps at a time. Willy was already lost to sight.

On the second level, feeling like she was on the lido deck of a near-abandoned cruise ship, she began working her way slowly toward where Ruiz's group had fanned out at the top of their escalator. She was still too far off to distinguish anyone's face, and so took advantage of that fact to pretend to be window shopping, glancing over every once in a while to see what they were doing.

They didn't waste time, but, once reassembled, marched as one toward a nearby store, whose identity she couldn't make out from her angle.

She started for the same spot, taking her time, checking to see if anything else might be developing — like another bunch from *Men in Black* arriving from yet another escalator. But aside from a handful of last-minute shoppers moving toward the exits, there appeared to be nothing.

Ten minutes passed. Announcements had been made about closing time. Now they were coming more often. Sam started to wonder if the people she was tailing had spotted her back in traffic, and had used all of this spy craft as a way to dump her. She drew close enough to the store they'd entered to recognize it as a high-end electronics outlet, and figured that if she had in fact been made, she had nothing to lose by being identified now. She therefore stopped some fifty feet away from the store's entrance and stood still, waiting — all pretense gone.

That, of course, was when they finally stepped out, the salesman behind them issuing multiple thanks and locking the door as the last of them emerged.

Like a well-trained pack of attack dogs, every man in the cluster turned to face her — the only potential threat among the few people still dawdling along the second level's vast expanse.

Sam didn't move, but stayed hands on hips, legs slightly apart, weight poised forward, ready to react.

For a moment, everyone froze, assessing the situation. Only one of them appeared relaxed — an attractive, well-dressed man carrying a small plastic shopping bag stamped with the store's logo. He tilted his head slightly to one side and pushed up an incongruous pair of dark glasses to see better.

"Greta?" he called out after a pause. "Is that you?"

In response, Sam raised her hand and wiggled her fingers.

Manuel Ruiz handed his bag to a bodyguard, saying something she couldn't hear, and stepped free of their midst, walking toward her, a smile spreading across his face.

"My God. Greta. Have you come back from the past to arrest me? You are still a police officer, no?"

She hadn't known what to expect, hadn't prepared for this to occur so spontaneously, and hadn't even fully considered meeting the man that she'd almost been intimate with ten years ago.

She shook the hand he proffered as he drew near. "Manny," she said, struggling to maintain an even voice.

He gave her an appraising look. "You are well. I can see it. You are happier than you were. I'm sure your name is not Greta, though, correct?"

"You don't know that?" she asked.

He shrugged. "We parted under hurried circumstances, as I recall. Your colleagues were almost through the front door when I headed out the back. Quite theatrical, actually."

"It's Samantha Martens. I work for the Vermont Bureau of Investigation."

He nodded, smiling. "So what do I call you?"

"Special Agent Martens."

He laughed, but shook his head. "I would guess they call you Sam."

She didn't answer. Overhead, the loudspeakers told them all to proceed to the nearest exit, the mall now being officially closed for business.

Ruiz raised his eyes briefly heavenward in response. "Shall we? I'm assuming you have something you'd like to discuss."

He turned on his heel and made a slight gesture with his hand, resulting in his men enveloping them without a word, and escorting them back down the escalator.

"I take it that you are not alone and that your company will not be joining us?" Ruiz asked.

"Right," she said, her thoughts in a jumble on how best to direct the conversation.

On the ground floor, with his escort more vigilant than before, Ruiz guided her, hand on her elbow, toward the exit and the parking lot beyond. Two of his men trotted ahead to check for security, their hands under their coats.

"You were a member of this Vermont Bureau when we were together?" he asked as they walked.

"Yes."

"I've heard of them, of course," he continued, his voice bringing her back to the intimacy of when they used to chat between transactions, as supposed fellow drug dealers. They'd operated out of a rented house in Rutland. Then, as now, he'd appeared deceptively soft-spoken, kind, and considerate.

"I thought, however," he continued, "that they only pursue major crimes. Is that what's brought us back together?"

She glanced at him. "You saying you're not involved in major crimes?"

He laughed, gesturing to her to precede him through a door being held open by one of his men, into the chilly night air. "I make a living as best I can, Sam. Just like everyone else."

She hadn't honestly expected much else. "How's your mom?" she asked instead. "Still cooking up wonders in the kitchen?"

Ruiz did a double take and smiled. "You remembered. She is, for a crowd of grandchildren these days, but in a much nicer place than where I grew up. To her, pots and pans are like instruments to a musician. A wonder to see."

The two vehicles were positioned right across from the glass doors. Ruiz looked around quickly. "I know you want to talk — at least that's what I'm assuming. I also assume that I'm not under arrest, or that would have already happened. It is freezing, though, and I'm not built for the cold. The best I can offer, unless you want to meet at a restaurant or come back to my home, is to talk alone in the car. It has a very good heater, and I'm sure that whatever listening device you're wearing will still work, despite the armor plating." He pointed invitingly at the SUV. "It's completely up to you, Sam."

She didn't hesitate, impressed by his grasp of the realities of their situation — which she found oddly comforting. "That suits me."

He gave a one-sentence command to his escort before motioning her into the dark, warm confines of the luxury car's rear seat, and closing the heavy door behind him. Through the tinted windows, she saw the bodyguards working out which four large, heavily armed men would cram themselves into a medium-sized sedan — and which one would be left in the cold to stand watch.

Ignoring their plight, Ruiz settled back against the leather cushions and crossed his legs. Back in the day, it had been sweats, jeans, and sneakers for him, albeit neat and tidy. Now, Sam noted, what he wore had to have set him back thousands — not to mention a gold and diamond-accented watch that probably rivaled the value of the car.

"I'd offer you a drink," he told her. "We

have a bar in here. But I doubt you'd accept."

"You're right," she said. "You've done okay for yourself, all this razzle-dazzle." She indicated their surroundings. "And we have good information telling us that Rutland's become a hard habit to break, even after all these years."

He waited patiently in silence.

"The problem with an outfit like yours, though," she went on, "is that it's tough to be too picky about your employees. You been paying attention to the headlines in Vermont lately?"

He frowned slightly. "The senator? I didn't have anything to do with that. I heard it was a hate crime — antigay or something."

Sam shook her head. "That was a dodge. It's coming home to you, Manny."

He pursed his lips, as if suddenly lost in thought, and then gave her a whimsical look. "You used to call me Manuel."

She smiled slightly. "Times change."

He nodded. "You implied that a business associate of mine may have stepped out of line."

Sam glanced out the window again, thinking hard. Sentimentality had prompted Ruiz to speak with her, which was unlikely to happen again. As had been the case a decade ago, she was finding herself in too deep, too fast with this man, and having to improvise. Was there a way to simultaneously get a location for Stuey Nichols and bring down Manuel Ruiz? Certainly not if she uttered Stuey's name now. Ruiz would simply have him killed. Similarly, telling Ruiz of the HSI investigation hanging over him wouldn't work — she was not a fed with powers to broker a deal, and it would just encourage him to thwart their efforts.

She considered her options realistically, rather than with high hopes. That, in part, was what had tangled her up last time — she'd sacrificed tactics for ambition and opportunity. She'd always been a cop to value the might of right, and considered it her mission to correct all ills. But Ruiz — despite the guilt she bore for having failed to bring him down — was no longer her problem. He was on Homeland Security's list of things to do.

Sam's concern had to be Stuey Nichols — alone — and not his welfare at his employer's hands. The truth was that word would be seeping out that Nichols was of interest to the cops. In Manny Ruiz's sanguinary view of the world, that alone was enough to make Stuey one of the earth's short-term residents. The only missing piece for Manny, therefore, was to hear from her directly how much of a liability his underling had become — along with the man's name. That, as she saw it, would conclude Stuey's career as a federal informant, force HSI to protect him, and encourage him to open up to VBI.

Having weighed her options, she cast her die, hoping to hell that HSI had a location on Stuey.

She gave Ruiz a level stare. "You want to know who I'm talking about, you have to let me out to make a phone call."

Ruiz smiled, his eyes betraying his own inner calculus. "Why would I do that?"

"You don't have a choice," she countered with false confidence. "I was just being polite."

He rolled down his window to speak rapidly to the bodyguard nearby, who crossed over to the escort car to inform his colleagues. Ruiz then resealed the window and nodded to Sam. "Please."

Sam stepped into the cold black air and walked some twenty feet into the middle of the parking lot, aware of the pale faces studying her from the smaller vehicle.

"You there?" she asked quietly. Her cell had been on from the start, on open mic so that Willy could hear everything.

He anticipated her request. "You want me to tell Joe to tell HSI they can either locate Stuey tonight and tie him down, or attend his funeral by tomorrow?"

"Something like that. This the right move?" she added, still doubtful.

He didn't hesitate. As he'd said earlier, he had her back. "Works for me."

"Thanks, Willy."

"Always, babe."

CHAPTER TWENTY-THREE

Joe took in the others around HSI's Burlington conference table. Peter LaBelle's was the only face he recognized of the five people there, although it wouldn't have mattered, had he been looking for a friend. Everyone in the room was visibly irritated with him. He wasn't surprised, nor was he all that happy himself — he'd been told of Sam's preemptive move on Manny Ruiz by Willy in the middle of the night. If nothing else, however, it had addressed what he'd mentioned earlier to Beverly, about something being in motion that he couldn't discern. Just in time.

"I'm John Beirne," said the man sitting at the head of the semicircle. "I'm the Resident Agent-in-Charge here."

That made Beirne the RAC, in their nomenclature, which put him roughly on a par with Joe.

Joe nodded.

"Normally, I would make introductions," Beirne continued, "and I might in a moment, but I wanted to start off by asking if what happened last night is typical of what you call interagency cooperation?"

"Is Nichols secure?" Joe asked instead.

"Of course he is. He was before your representative blew his cover."

"You chose not to tell us that when you could have," Joe said. "And we *didn't* blow his cover. We merely told Ruiz that Nichols was wanted for questioning in a homicide, as a way to shake the bushes and see what might break loose. His connection to you and your ongoing investigation was in no way compromised."

Beirne laughed derisively. "Until they find him and kill him for good measure, you mean? Just to keep things tidy?"

"Employees of Manuel Ruiz kill people all the time," Joe argued. "Nichols wouldn't be a standout on that score. Try looking at it this way: If we're right and Nichols murdered Raffner, then that's the end of his usefulness as a CI to you. If he didn't and we're wrong, you can get back into Ruiz's good graces by having Nichols do something spectacular, like hand over some crucial-sounding, bogus piece of intel. Right now, that latter option's looking unlikely to you only because Raffner was such a high-profile target and we haven't caught who killed her. We'll be remedying that either way. And in the unlikely case it wasn't Stuey, then the heat'll be off and you folks'll be back where you were."

Beirne's expression tightened. When he spoke, Joe could hear the effort of his self-control. "Special Agent Gunther, I've got to be perfectly honest: Your words right now sound all very tidy and levelheaded, but the actions of your organization last night in Holyoke smack of nothing less than blackmail."

"That wasn't their intention," Joe responded.

"Nevertheless," Beirne almost cut him off. "Only yesterday, Special Agent LaBelle" — he indicated the man on his right — "was in Brattleboro being briefed about your situation. Did he or did he not tell you at that time that he needed to confer with people up his chain of command in order to make everything happen that you were requesting?"

"Not to split hairs," Joe told him, "but no, he did not — not in so many words. With all due respect and knowing how these things can happen — since we're all human beings — he actually opted not to make a phone call as he might have, from our office, but to leave us hanging instead while he traveled back up here to do what he felt he had to do in person.

"That," he continued before anyone could cut him off, "left us high and dry exactly when we needed to move the fastest — since, to repeat, we had no idea you were keeping Stuey safe and sound. You can appreciate our lack of options."

He held up his hand as Beirne opened his mouth and added, "I'm not pointing fingers, either. I might've done the same thing if the roles had been reversed. Peter here was very clear that yours is a large, complex organization and that procedures have to be followed. But put yourselves in our shoes. The only person not breathing down our necks right now is the president of the United States, and he's probably just stuck behind a busy signal."

"That very argument," Beirne countered, "is part of our problem. We are fully supportive of your ambitions to solve this homicide, just as you say you're sensitive to our wanting to see a long and complicated investigation brought to a successful conclusion. The possible key to both is Mr. Nichols, although — as you pointed out — nothing is guaranteed in your case."

Here, Beirne could no longer control his agitation, and rose to stand by the window overlooking the Burlington cityscape. "Nevertheless, HSI will always do what it can to be a good partner, regardless of how it may be treated by others." His eyes narrowed as he emphasized, "Including high-pressure phone calls from the governor, which I found especially unnecessary.

"Our main objection to what's happened between our two agencies is the time element. You're in a rush because of the pressures you just mentioned; we're in just the opposite boat because of the care we've taken and the effort we've expended building a case against Ruiz and his suppliers in Mexico — of which Nichols is an important part."

He leaned on the table between them to make his point. "But is your cause really so pressing? Or is it — as I think it is — more driven by the need to get a headline that'll satisfy your governor's political ambitions during a reelection campaign?"

Joe had anticipated this. He kept his own voice calm, even slightly friendly, despite his reactive anger. "Entirely reasonable question, on the face of it. We've all been a little addled by the attention this has gotten. That being said, the fact remains that a homicide has occurred. Rule one of any murder investigation is that timing is crucial, and — politics or no — the victim in this case was intimately associated with the state's governor. My question to you, John, is: Given what I explained about how we've protected your investigation just in case Stuey proves innocent, do you really want to piss off this governor when in reality you're between a rock and a hard place, anyhow? I mean, it's not like you can actually deny us access to a key witness."

John Beirne was not happy, but he also didn't have much of a choice — something he confirmed with the slightest slump of his shoulders. He straightened back up and said, "Mr. Nichols will be made available to you on our terms, and at a place and time of our choosing. And with Special Agent LaBelle in attendance. Is that clear?"

"Today?" was Joe's only question, his heart beating as it might've following a bout in the ring.

Joe glanced around as he entered the cleanest, whitest, blandest interrogation room he'd ever used, admiring how even the floor's four corners looked as scrubbed and sterilized as an operating room's. By contrast, its sole occupant resembled a garbage bag with eyes.

Joe made the introductions. "Allan Steward Nichols, I am Special Agent Joe Gunther of the Vermont Bureau of Investigation." He stepped aside to reveal the man behind him. "This is Special Agent Peter LaBelle of Homeland Security Investigations. For the record, you should know that everything said in this room is being recorded and may be used as evidence. Is that clear?"

Nichols took them both in silently with a bored expression.

"For the record," Joe repeated. "Is that clear?"

"Yeah."

Joe sat near Nichols, at the corner of a small table bolted to the wall. LaBelle took the third chair and moved it toward one of the corners, well within the camera's view.

"How would you prefer to be called?" Joe asked Nichols as he settled in, spreading several sheets of paper before him.

"What?" Nichols asked, his brow knitted in confusion.

"What do they call you?"

"Stuey."

"Okay, Stuey. Have you been read your rights?"

"Yeah."

"Did you fully understand those rights?"

"Sure."

"Did you sign a document attesting to that fact?"

"Yeah. A few minutes ago."

"Right. And are you now willing to speak to me without a lawyer present?"

"Don't need one."

"Okay. That's fine. If at any time you change your mind, just state as much and this interview will stop. Do you also understand that?"

"I'm not dumb."

"I know that. For the record, do you understand that?"

"Yeah, yeah, yeah."

"All right. Let's begin. On the night when Buddy Ames sold some marijuana to Maggie Kinnison on or near South Street in Rutland, were you or were you not right there?"

"I had nuthin to do with that senator dyin'."

"Why do you say that, Stuey?"

" 'Cause that's what this is all about. You think I killed her, and I didn't."

Joe crossed his legs and studied him a moment. "You're partly right — I do think you had something to do with it. Maybe even that you killed her. But I'm not sure yet.

383

Some of that depends on what you tell me. Some of it depends on what I already know."

"What's that?"

Joe shook his head. "That's not how it works, Stuey. See, this is like a test you have to pass before you can get back to your cushy deal with the feds. And you probably remember how it works with tests — you have to take the whole thing in order to pass or fail."

"I don't have to do squat. I didn't do anything wrong."

"A lot of guys take that approach," Joe told him. "If you convince yourself that something's true, it makes you more believable to the people you're telling it to. But here's the crucial catch: The very people you want to go back to — the feds — are the same ones that'll do you the most harm if you dick me around."

Stuey seemed confused by the statement, and watched Joe's face for an explanation.

"It's simple, really," Joe went on. "When you carve the word 'dyke' on someone's chest as you kill them, it makes it a hate crime. That's a federal offense, and the feds, as you know, still have the death penalty. Vermont doesn't. Does that help you see how important it is that you tell me the whole truth?"

Stuey processed that information thoughtfully. "Okay."

Joe smiled encouragingly. "Good. So let's try this again. Were you a witness to the sale of marijuana by Buddy Ames to Maggie Kinnison?"

"I don't know her name, but yeah, I saw Buddy do a sale to some woman."

"Describe the circumstances."

Stuey's eyes narrowed. "I got immunity on all this drug stuff. You know that, right?"

"This has nothing to do with that, Stuey. Answer the question."

"What's to describe? He did the deal and she took off. End of story."

"Except that it wasn't the end, and nor was it the beginning. Who made the decision to sell her low-quality product when she'd made it clear the transaction was supposed to be for high-grade stuff?"

Stuey's face hardened. "These're dope-related questions. I got a deal."

Joe gathered his paperwork and stood up. "You know what? I think maybe you are as stupid as you look. You deserve a lethal injection. We're done here."

Nichols's mouth fell open. "Whad'ya mean? I'm talkin' to you."

Joe leaned over him. "I'm sorry? You're doing what? All I'm hearing is crap, Stuey.

385

You're wasting my time and committing suicide at the same time. You are the idiot poster child." He headed for the door as LaBelle rose to join him.

"How're you gonna make your case without me?" Stuey shouted.

Joe turned to face him. "You *are* my case, dipwad. Your two choices, unless you convince me otherwise, are to die in a federal prison or spend a few decades in a Vermont country club jail. Do you think I'd have wrestled with the feds to get you into this room if I didn't have a solid case against you? I made you a one-time offer, and now it's off the table. Good-bye." He placed his hand on the doorknob, praying that this string of clichés would work.

Fortunately, they aren't clichés for nothing. More often than not, they do work.

"Fine," Stuey complained. "Have it your way. You wanna talk drugs with me who has total immunity, knock yourself out. I mean, what the fuck, right?"

Joe pretended to think it over, painfully aware of how little evidence he had in fact against this man, and of how he'd nevertheless used it twice as a crowbar against the HSI and now against Stuey.

"You going to tell me the truth from now on?" he asked.

"Sure. Whatever."

Joe returned to his chair and laid out his paperwork once more. LaBelle leaned against the wall. "All right, for the third time, tell me about the deal Buddy did with Maggie Kinnison, including the before and after parts."

Stuey scratched his head. "Buddy called me a couple of days before, said he'd gotten a call from Brandon Younger in Hartford about a regular — this Maggie Kinnison — who was looking for a bunch of weed. He didn't have it, so he was reaching out to Buddy. It was no big whoop — kinda stuff happens all the time. You pass people around, sometimes share product. It's good for business, you know?"

"Until you shortchange the customer."

Stuey made a face. "Yeah, well . . . So, here's the thing. It was a special circumstance, you know?"

"I don't. Tell me."

Stuey sighed, in fact looking slightly embarrassed. "It was a typical feast-or-famine situation, or whatever they call it. The broad had a ton of money, cash flow for me was a little tight right then, weed — believe it or not in this crazy state — was in short supply. It was like the perfect shit storm — nuthin was clickin' right."

"Spell it out for me."

Stuey spread his hands wide, palms up. "I'm a little guy. I mean, I got worker bees like Buddy, but I'm strictly in the middle. I piss off the boss, he kicks my ass. Except in this business, when those people're done with you, you got no ass left, you know what I'm sayin'?"

"Don't be shy, Stuey. You said you have immunity."

"Okay, okay. So it's Ruiz and his people. Real hard-assed. They want a lot of business all the time, they don't want excuses, they don't want problems, and they don't take prisoners. And me? I'm looking at the Rutland cops clampin' down, the neighborhood turning into a bunch of squealers, and, on top of it, an interruption in my supply line of Canadian high-class hydro. Fuckin' nightmare. No surprise I freelance for the feds, huh?" he added with a grin.

Joe kept on message. "Until Kinnison saves the day by knocking on your door with a bag full of cash."

Stuey laughed. "Bingo. Like the answer to a prayer. I mean, who cares about customer relations with somebody you never met? A referral, no less. It was Brandon that would catch hell later. What did I care?"

"Okay," Joe reiterated. "Again, so we've

got it for the record: You sold low-grade marijuana to Kinnison without telling her because you needed the money, had nothing better to sell, and had to stay on Manuel Ruiz's good side. Is that a fair summary of what you just told me?"

"Yeah — like I said."

"Throughout any of this, did the name Susan Raffner ever come up?"

"Nope. When Buddy was closing the deal with the lady in the car, she said something like how this would get her boss off her back, but that was it. I didn't know anything about that crazy bitch senator till afterward."

"All right, let's get into that. What happened after the sale to Kinnison?"

"Nothing at first, then — outta the blue — I got a call from Buddy saying the bitch was tearin' his head off and wanted her money back and was gonna call the cops, and stuff like that. It was insane. Call you guys on a drug deal? Are you kidding me? And she's a state senator? Jesus, I mean, I knew right then *why* she took weed — no doubt about it. Musta barely scratched the surface. No wonder she wanted high-grade stuff."

Joe waited for him to finish before gently prodding, "Details, Stuey. One after the other. For example, what time was it?"

"When I got the call from Buddy? I don't know. Middle of the night. I don't log in phone calls — not my style."

"What did he say?"

"What I told you — he had this woman demanding satisfaction."

"Demanding satisfaction?" Joe asked. "Whose phrase was that? She actually say that?"

"After she took the phone from Buddy and talked to me direct, yeah."

"Did you ask to speak with her or did Buddy want you two to talk directly?"

"I told him to put her on. I was sick of him being in the middle."

"What happened then?"

"Me and her talked. I already told you this, for Christ's sake."

"What did you say?" Joe prodded him patiently.

"She demanded we meet. I said sure and told her where."

"Which was?"

"A friend's house."

Joe stared at him silently, encouraging Stuey to volunteer the address — a trailer park outside of Rutland.

"Go on."

"I didn't kill her."

Joe was silent for a slow count, watching

Stuey's face like a scientist studying a bug. "Why would you say that, all of a sudden?"

Stuey had become anxious. " 'Cause you fuckers're trying to pin it on me. You think I don't know? You got zip and you're pissin' on my shoes 'cause of what I did to that bitch cop way back, and now it's payback. Don't have to be a genius."

"Tell me about Raffner getting to the trailer park."

Nichols looked from one to the other of them. "You gonna let him treat me like this?" he asked LaBelle. "I work for you."

"I want to hear the answer, too," LaBelle said mildly.

"She drove up, I told her to fuck off, and she left," he said, virtually in one word.

Joe made an expression as if he'd swallowed something sour. "Right. All of a sudden, I'm gonna be happy with that. Get it over, Stuey. If you're clear of this, you have nothing to worry about."

But as soon as the words had left his mouth, he sensed why Nichols was so concerned. Joe recalled Beverly's findings during Raffner's autopsy.

"You should know something, Stuey, in case it helps," he said. "If you roughed her up a bit — maybe pushed her around — we're not gonna jam you up over it. We've

391

got bigger fish on the line than an assault charge."

That reached home. The fear left Stuey's eyes. "Okay," he said.

"Now, tell me what happened after she drove up. First of all, what was she driving and how was she dressed?"

"Hard to tell about the car. Dark sedan, ugly. New. Mighta been one of those half-battery, half-motor things that cost a fortune. Prius?"

"And the clothes?"

"Long, dark coat, sweater, white shirt, pants."

"Did you see her drive up or did she knock at the door?"

"Oh, I was waitin' for her. What d'ya think? Having a fucking hissy fit in the middle of the night, waking me up? I was pissed."

"So you met her in the driveway?"

Stuey opened his mouth to answer and then paused a split second to think before saying, "No. I was standing in the doorway."

"You made her come to you," Joe suggested.

"Damn straight."

"You invite her inside?"

"Fuck no, I did not. We weren't gonna talk that long."

"All right. And then?"

"She walked up, poking her finger at me and sayin', 'I want my money back or you're gonna wish you'd never been born,' or some crap like that, and I told her to go fuck herself. I even said that if she hadn't been such a douche about it, I mighta been willing to work something out, but that she'd burned that bridge a long time ago."

"How did she react?"

Stuey was getting upset again, shifting in his chair and motioning excitedly with his hands. "The bitch came at me. I thought she was goin' to slug me. I couldn't believe it. I mean, the balls on her. I had a gun on me. I coulda killed her." He wiped his mouth with the back of his hand and quickly added, "I didn't, though, and I didn't show the piece."

His eyes betrayed that he'd gotten carried away, glancing nervously from one cop to the other. All three of them knew that he wasn't supposed to be near a gun, given his record.

Joe ignored the issue. "Go on."

"Well," Nichols said more carefully, "that's when it happened — to protect myself — I had to kind of hold her off."

"You were standing in the doorway of the trailer?"

"Yeah," he said slowly.

"At the top of the steps?"

"Yeah."

Joe shook his head. "Don't mess this up, Stuey. Not now. You can't hold off anyone from there — you're like three feet higher than anyone coming at you. What exactly did you do?"

Stuey's voice fell. "I came off the stairs and I let her have it. She was askin' for it, man."

"You hit her?"

"Yeah."

"Where?"

"I slapped her across the face. That just got her goin' more, so I hit her a couple of times in the ribs. That put an end to it."

"She fall?"

"Yeah, she fell. I put some muscle into it. Then I grabbed her by the scruff of her neck and yanked her up and sent her flyin' toward her car. That's when her coat came off. Guess she hadn't buttoned it. I got rid of it later, after what happened to her hit the papers."

He hesitated, looking shamefaced, or perhaps just embarrassed, and said, "Look, I was really angry. She was so over the top. I know she was pissed, and I know we . . . okay, *I* screwed her on the dope. But it was like she was on fire, you know? It was a little crazy. She just ticked me off."

Joe eyed him in silence, recalling what Stuey had done to Sam ten years earlier. Over the decades that Joe had been doing this job, over the thousands of interviews he'd conducted, he'd grown used to witnessing this level of sociopathy — indeed, he'd had to struggle against concluding that it defined the human norm. But the level of disgust that Stuey Nichols stirred in him was a thick, penetrating ooze that was hard to take in stride.

"What did you use to smack her in the back of the head?" he asked, again referring to the autopsy. "That pistol come in handy after all?"

Stuey reacted immediately. "That's a crock. I did nuthin like that. Didn't have to."

"You didn't hit her in the head at all?"

"Just the slap."

Joe acknowledged the precision of the answer, which he thought added to its credibility. "What happened next?" he asked without affect.

"It took the fight right outta her," Stuey said, a touch of pride returning. "She fell against the hood of her fancy car, gasping and holding herself like some old cow.

Served her right. I told her if she wanted to call the Better Business Bureau, that was fine with me. Otherwise, she could screw off."

"She say anything?" Joe wanted to know.

"Nuthin to say. And I wasn't interested. Her friend was comin' outta the car to help her anyhow, so I just went back inside and slammed the door. That was the last I saw her." He pointed at Joe. "And I'm not shittin' you. She was fine. A little winded, is all."

Joe kept his demeanor neutral, despite the jolt he'd received. "Describe the friend."

"I don't know. There wasn't any light. Once I saw they didn't have a gun and weren't coming for me, I didn't care."

"Man? Woman?"

Nichols looked frustrated. "I don't know. I told you. Dark clothes, wearing a hat. Moved like a guy — sort of fast and smooth, and tall enough. I couldn't tell and I didn't ask."

"You must've made sure they left."

"Yeah. A few minutes later. I saw 'em go."

"Who was driving?"

Stuey shrugged. "Dunno."

"And you went back to your life, no questions asked?"

"Yup."

"You didn't get in touch with either Buddy or Brandon Younger to either bitch 'em out or compare notes?"

"Nope. Life goes on. You let it go."

"Very Zen," Joe commented.

Nichols smiled. "Yeah. She coulda learned from that."

For once, Joe couldn't argue with him. The comment did, however, trigger another question. "Stuey, you said that when Raffner came out of her car, she seemed 'on fire,' implying she might've been mad about something else, as well. What did you mean?"

"You know how it is when everything goes wrong some days? It was like that — she made me think of me sometimes, when everything I touch turns to crap."

Joe sympathized in principle, but it wasn't how he was feeling now.

CHAPTER TWENTY-FOUR

"Where's Willy?" Joe asked, adjusting the car's heater.

Sammie watched him carefully. "Inside, reading Emma to sleep."

"He ask why you stepped outside?"

"He doesn't know. I was in the kitchen washing dishes when you called. I didn't want to disturb them." She placed a hand on the door handle. "I can tell him, if we're going somewhere."

"No. This won't take long." Joe stayed looking out the front window, his hands in his lap. He'd killed the headlights, but the engine was still running. It was quiet and peaceful and comfortable.

Except that Sam wasn't feeling that way. Her boss had something to get off his chest, and she was painfully aware that it probably involved her field trip to Holyoke.

"Susan Raffner wasn't alone, the night she met Stuey."

"Who was with her?" she asked, caught off guard.

"I don't know. He couldn't make it out — too dark. But it kicks the investigation wide-open, at long last. And in my gut, I feel we finally got where we've been going. The timeline is too tight for anyone else to have killed her."

For the first time since she'd slid into his passenger seat, he turned and looked at her, his face barely visible in the green glow from the instrument panel before him. "It's the breakthrough we've been looking for, Sam, and you and Willy bagged it."

She heard the ambiguity in his voice. "I'm sorry we did it the way we did, Joe."

He went back to staring forward. "Yeah. So am I."

"It was just so frustrating hearing that HSI had put Stuey off-limits," she said, instantly regretting the comment.

"Which therefore justified you two running the risk of making Emma an orphan." It was a statement, not a question.

Sam was silent.

"Willy was responding to pure instinct," Joe continued. "He's built that way. He meets a barrier and he kicks it down, almost without thought."

Again, he faced her. "But you? I think you

put pride before responsibility, Sam, and you were careless of everything and everyone in the process. When you and I started out, I thought you'd increasingly find your footing, including when you hooked up with Willy, and that I'd have to worry less and less. But there's something about Rutland and Stuey and Manuel Ruiz that makes you stupid."

He paused. She sensed it wasn't to allow her to respond.

"Ten years ago," he resumed, "you acted impulsively, went undercover, and made it out intact. It wasn't pretty, but it worked for the most part, and everybody survived. Ironically, this time wasn't as bad, and you came up undamaged and with the goods. But I'm twice as disappointed with you. I gotta be honest: If you want to stay being a cop, and sure as hell if you want to stay working with me, you're going to have to stop pretending that the ends justify the means. They don't.

"I know this sounds unfair," he went on, "because it's you in this car and not the both of you. But I think you know what I mean when I say that Willy's beyond your kind of salvation. He's better because of you, but he'll always be damaged goods. You, on the other hand, can actually affect

400

your own destiny. You have that much intelligence and strength of character. At least, I hope so."

He stopped speaking, but remained motionless. She was overtaken by emotion, and her head flooded with paradoxical images of Emma, Manny Ruiz as a younger man, Willy, and — always — Joe, her surrogate father.

"I'm really sorry," she managed to whisper.

"I'm glad for that, but what I want to hear is that this is going to stop," he said calmly. "One Willy Kunkle is all I can handle. I need to have back the woman who provides him with a centerboard and gives me someone I can trust with my life — like I always have."

She waited for more, but that was not his style. He was inclined to utter a few words, with the expectation that his listener would absorb their full dose.

To drive the point home, he reached out, briefly laid his hand atop hers, and said, "Go back to your family. I'll see you in the morning."

"Hey," Willy addressed Joe before the latter had even taken off his coat the next day. "We're actually going on Stuey's say-so that

Raffner had a phantom passenger? That lying sack of shit killed that woman, sure as hell, and now he's blowing smoke up your skirt just for fun."

Joe shook his head, removed the coat, and crossed to the coffeemaker. "Don't think so. The whole interview is recorded." He reached into his pocket and tossed a thumb drive to Lester. "Check it out and let me know what you think. It won't take long and it's worth every second."

He and Sam set it up while Joe continued preparing his usual concoction of cream and maple syrup in his coffee.

Thirty minutes later, he'd finished catching up on his e-mails and the statewide dailies from the other VBI offices, and his squad had returned to their respective desks.

Joe looked directly at Willy. "So?"

The response was pure Kunkle — completely at odds with his earlier outburst. "I'm not a hundred percent, but I see what you mean."

"And what he says he did to Susan matches what Hillstrom found at the autopsy," Sam added.

"Except for the two sequential blows to the head," Joe partially agreed. "One of which — to the occiput — preceded death and might have been intended to knock her out. Also, the horizontal marks across her back don't fit Stuey's narrative."

"They would if she was bludgeoned and shoved into the back of the car," Lester said. "Like we were thinking."

Joe put his feet up on his desk. "Which is probably what happened right after. As I was telling Sam earlier, this is the missing piece we've been looking for. Let's talk it through. What d'we got?"

"Both Stuey and Buddy Ames said she was hotter'n hell," Sammie said. "Madder than she should've been over a bad business deal and a few bucks."

"She coulda been arguing with her passenger," Willy suggested.

"A passenger who then immediately took advantage of her weakened state," Joe continued, "further rendered her harmless, and then cobbled together a plan to throw us off the trail."

"Why not just frame Stuey?" Lester asked.

"Too direct," Sammie said, "and too easily proven wrong."

Joe agreed. "Even Stuey could pass a lie detector test. Plus, he told me after the interview that he had a girlfriend in the trailer. I sent someone to talk with her and she backed him up — saw everything through the window. And, no, she couldn't identify the passenger, either."

"I agree," Willy said. "It's looking like Stuey punching Raffner in the ribs was manna from heaven for our mystery player — an inspiration that set him off on his own plan."

"An almost unbelievably complicated plan," Lester commented. "For something made up on the go."

"How so?" Sammie asked.

"Look at it. The hanging, the mutilation, the ditching of the car in exchange for a pickup truck. Like Willy was saying — way beyond Stuey's capability. Most people's, for that matter."

"And knowing just where to hang the body, too," Joe said thoughtfully. "We considered that earlier, but we never really chased it down."

"No one we've looked at lives in that area," Sam said.

"Doesn't mean they might not've been born there," Willy countered. "Or have a camp nearby."

"Or that he travels the state a lot," Joe said. "Maybe with a specific purpose."

Sam heard something in his voice. "What're you thinking, boss?"

"There's symbolism in all this, or at least attention-getting posturing. It could've been so much simpler, and still've left us in the dark. But it was flashy — a look-at-me kind of thing."

"Small kid on the block getting back at the world?" Lester said.

"More like someone used to influencing people, and who knows the state," Joe expanded. "Most crimes are localized to a pretty small area. This one's all over the place."

"You make him sound like a traveling circus performer," Sam commented incredulously.

Willy laughed, looking at Joe. "That's not what he's saying. He's thinking of a Raffner type, aren't you, boss? The kind of person she'd have riding around with her in a car in the first place. You're saying politics."

Joe took them in as a group. "It does have a ring to it. You gotta admit."

"A politician?" Sammie asked, only slightly less doubtful.

"Someone *in* politics," Joe emphasized. "Certainly someone trained to suddenly changing situations, redirecting people's focus, and staging sensationalist events."

"That doesn't help us much," Lester said. "Raffner was in politics for most of her life, so we're still looking at roughly the same pool of people."

"Maybe, maybe not," Joe argued. "Let's take this from the top without the distractions."

"From where Mystery Man sees Raffner get pushed around by Stuey?" Sam asked.

"How 'bout what put him in her car to begin with?" Lester suggested.

"Not yet," Willy replied. "Boss is right. We'll get to that later. Right now, Mystery Man — MM — gets a situation handed to him — *bam*. Stuey acts out, Raffner's on the ropes, and MM's suddenly got his opportunity. Whatever it was that got him in the car with Raffner in the first place, now it's time to *carpe diem*."

Sammie picked it up. "But first things first, MM severs all connection to Stuey by leaving."

"We don't know who was driving," Lester pointed out.

"Doesn't matter," Sam continued. "Either MM grabs the wheel because Susan's too woozy, or he tells her where to drive in order to get out of danger so that he can take a closer look at her."

" 'Cept he does a little more than that," Lester picked up.

"Right. He smacks her a good one."

"The first injury to the head," Joe suggested, "rendering her unconscious."

"They might've been simultaneous," Willy argued. "A blow to the back of the head followed by the fatal follow-up to the temple. Could Hillstrom tell if there was any time-lapse between them?"

Joe shook his head. "Not with one hundred percent accuracy. But, if the two blows came at once, how do you explain the bruising across her lumbar, presumably from tipping her into the rear of the car? There wouldn't've been bruising if she'd been dead. And don't forget that David Hawke found her nail back there, which Raffner's bloody fingertip tells us was ripped off as she was trying to get out."

"The point is," Sammie almost interrupted, wanting to keep the momentum going, "MM gets the upper hand one way or the other, and then without a doubt takes the wheel."

"So he can swap vehicles for a pickup," Lester finished, adding, "But why? It's not like he went seriously off-road to hang her from the cliff."

"You sure about that?" Willy asked. "You know you're gonna be driving in the snow, and nothing sucks worse in the snow than a Prius. Seems like a smart trade to me."

"Plus, it's not just the truck you need," Sammie threw in. "You need rope, boots, whatever else . . ."

"Maybe do the chest carving then, too, since she's dead by now," Willy said.

"Then off to the cliff for the grand finale?" Lester said tentatively.

"Not yet," Joe replied. They looked at him as he explained, "He has to set up his frame — or his misdirection. The fake letter from Nate Fellows, found in Susan's Montpelier apartment — with the conveniently missing canceled stamp — to go along with the carving. This is his only opportunity to do that."

"Which means Montpelier."

"Which means that crazy old bat," Willy said.

Sam stared at him. "Regina Rockefeller," he clarified. "Raffner's landlady. What do the case notes say about what she saw? It would've had to've been in the middle of the night."

Silence.

"Damn," Lester half whispered.

"Good," Joe said. "Then she needs to be interviewed more in depth. Don't know how those questions were missed."

"I do," Sammie said. "I remember talking to Parker on the phone about her. He said she wouldn't shut up — ran her mouth from the moment they walked in to the time they left."

"She talked so much they didn't get what they should've," Joe finished. "We've all been there. So, let's hit her again, and keep our fingers crossed that she was in when MM dropped by — 'cause he had to have been on his own, which might've made him stand out. What else?"

"Why Nate Fellows?" Willy asked. "Of all the screwballs in the world? And MM knew exactly where Raffner lived, and that she had an office with a recycle box? Those're two questions I'd like answered."

"Did he know where and how to access the cliff?" Lester asked. "That's a third."

"And a fourth," Sammie contributed. "The salvage yard where the Prius was left. That didn't happen without prior knowledge."

Lester was shaking his head. "We still have hundreds — maybe a thousand — names to go through."

"Not really," Joe argued. "We've had dozens of people combing through Susan's files from the beginning. *They're* the ones we should ask to see if any of these details rings a bell. And let's dig into each area more thoroughly — like interviewing Rockefeller — to see if a single name doesn't begin to repeat."

Sam suggested, "There's a fifth item we haven't mentioned, and that's Raffner's Prius. If we're right, MM and Raffner spent a lot of shared time riding around in it."

"It's still in Waterbury," Lester said. "They finished processing it. There were several prints they couldn't match to anyone, mostly from the passenger seat, but nothing that stood out. Might be worth one of us going by to at least take a look at what they pulled out of it."

"David Hawke and I are old friends," Joe commented. "I don't mind doing that."

"I'll take Rockefeller," Sam said. "Might be different if it's woman-to-woman this time."

"What about all that riding around together with MM and Raffner that Sam brought up?" Willy asked. "Can we explain what that was all about?"

Nobody answered.

Willy smiled. "Right. One piece of fantasy at a time."

"Hey," Joe countered hopefully, "we get lucky with this other stuff, that may just come gift-wrapped at the end."

Sammie was pleased with the Regina Rockefeller assignment. It wasn't that she was holding out hope that the old woman had actually witnessed someone creeping into her house to plant evidence — that probably would've come up by now. Mostly, Sam was just happy to still be employed.

She hadn't told Willy of Joe's visit until early the next morning, and then only that he'd dropped by to tell her that their pursuit of Manny Ruiz had paid off. Willy, naturally, hadn't completely missed the point. He'd responded, "I bet he wasn't thrilled." She hadn't said he was wrong.

But she'd also understood why Joe had made their conversation private. Willy hadn't let Joe down — from the start of this investigation, Joe had made Willy's job open-ended and nonspecific. Joe knew his man. He had hoped he'd known her, and that's where she had dropped the ball.

What troubled her, however, was less the actual transgression — Joe had dealt with that last night. It was more what had led up to it, which was more deep-seated in Sammie's personal psychology. All her life, she'd had a self-destructive trait — in her willfulness as a child, her careless choice of men later, her volunteering for dangerous tasks in the military, and even in her decision to link her future with Willy Kunkle's and have a child with him. Joe's more hopeful view of her notwithstanding, her actions of a decade ago had been a typically rash example, and one she'd hoped had marked a turn toward more rational thinking.

But what she'd just done — despite its successful conclusion, and Willy's active role in it — raised doubts in her mind that she could rid herself of her own corrosive impulsiveness. Joe's response had been thoughtful, supportive, and unequivocal, all at the same time. It had also made clear that she was no longer an irresponsible kid, and that he wasn't the only person that she needed to impress and respect.

When Sam drove up, Regina Rockefeller was in front of her battered Victorian, stabbing erratically at the snow on her top step with a rickety shovel. She was dressed in an odd assortment of clothes — clearly grabbed on the way out with no thought as to their originally intended use. She looked like a deranged stage actor impersonating a bag lady.

"Welcome, welcome," she called out cheerily as Sam picked her way carefully up the roughly hewn path. "You'll have to excuse the minefield. I tell all my guests to make sure they're wearing climbing gear when they visit. Not that they pay attention, of course, although if you think about it, most people around here tend to wear pretty practical foot gear, just out of habit. I notice you're doing just that yourself, young lady, which I can only applaud."

Sam had gotten close enough by now to reach out and take the shovel. "Can I help? I'm pretty handy with one of these."

Looking up from her crooked stance, Regina flashed her a broad smile. "Well, I'm not going to say no. Generosity and good manners are a rare thing nowadays, and I won't turn either one of them down. Not that I'm complaining, mind you. Young people these days seem to have much more on their minds than we did when I was their age. Back then, we were more concerned about society and parties and who was who on the social register. When I think back, I'm staggered by how much energy we wasted on snobbery and prejudice."

Through this and much, much more, Sammie merely applied her shoveling skills to the walkway, working her way slowly toward the street, Regina dogging her heels and talking nonstop. Given the inner dialog Sam had been suffering during the ninety-minute drive here, she was in fact relieved to coast along on the hard work and endless patter, finding both refreshingly therapeutic. By the time she'd heaved the last load of snow onto the buried lawn, she was feeling pretty much like her old self: employed, engaged, and forwardly mobile, her nagging self-doubts strung out behind her like cans trailing a newlywed couple's escape car.

Thoroughly warmed by her exercise, she leaned on the shovel and smiled down at the old lady, interrupting her in mid-sentence. "Ms. Rockefeller, I'm from the police. I was wondering if I could ask you a couple of questions."

Rockefeller laughed outright and seized the shovel to bring it back to the porch. "Good luck with that, young woman, I'm well known for not letting most people get a word in edgewise. I can't understand that myself, since my mother used to say I was a good listener. As you can imagine, a compliment like that wouldn't have been given to a blabber-mouth. I personally can't bear people who won't shut up. That was one reason I so enjoyed having Susan as a renter. She was as quiet as a mouse."

And on it went, Rockefeller in the lead, bent over and shuffling in a pair of basketball sneakers, using the shovel as a cane, and Sammie behind her, taking in the bright blue sky and radiant if ineffectual sunshine, listening with the not-quite total inattention of a long-suffering sitcom spouse.

Once inside, Sam began to overtalk Regina as she struggled to remove a few of the odds and ends she'd been wearing. Sam's earlier hope that she might have better luck conducting this interview woman-to-woman had effectively been vaporized. "Ms. Rockefeller, as you know, we're investigating Susan's murder, and I wanted to let you know, first and foremost, how grateful we are for your help and cooperation so far."

By then, Regina's patter had faded away as she'd realized Sammie was speaking. She dropped a shawl on the back of a nearby chair in the entrance to the ornate living room, and twisted her head around to fix her guest with an appraising look, revealing the intelligence lurking beneath her caricatured manner.

"But you'd like to know something more," she suggested.

Sam smiled, impressed by the brevity. "Yes, we would. About the night this all happened — before Susan was found the following day."

Rockefeller blinked at her twice before saying, "Would you like some tea?"

"No."

The terseness of Sam's response stilled

her for a moment. She then indicated one of the elaborately upholstered but worn armchairs near the darkened fireplace. "I'm sensing that the little-old-lady routine isn't working with you. Have a seat."

Sam hesitated, her mouth half open. "It's an act? Why, in God's name?"

Rockefeller walked to a chair and settled down with a sigh. It was evident only then that the curved back and hunched-over posture took a daily toll in discomfort. "Not an act; not really. I do like to talk, but it's also a bit of a wall I put up. People see me — at my age, in this huge old house, renting out rooms — and they take liberties with their advice. My talking them half to death keeps them at bay." She smiled impishly. "And I get to say almost anything I wish and get away with it." She tapped her temple with a gnarled finger. "Only the polite ones think I'm eccentric. The rest consider me quite nutty."

Sammie sat opposite her. "Well, for what it's worth, it's working. One of the reasons I'm talking to you now is because nobody else felt up to it."

"Ah, yes." She nodded enthusiastically. "The two young men. I thought I might have scared them off. Not that I have much to say. You do realize that, don't you? I never would have been playful at the expense of finding Susan's killer."

"Okay," Sam asked her. "To that point, then: What did you see or hear that night, let's say from dinnertime on?"

Rockefeller looked mournful. "Not much. I assumed Susan was out of town, since I didn't hear her usual back-and-forth. I don't know if I mentioned it, but she and I share that front entrance you just shoveled out. Anne — the back renter — has her own door. That means I'm generally more aware of Susan's comings and goings."

"But there was nothing that night?"

The old woman hesitated. "Not nothing, exactly. In the middle of the night, there was some activity. I only heard it because at my age, I'm up every two hours to go pee, and I was sitting on the pot when someone came in, climbed the stairs, and went out again. I assumed it was Susan because only she and I have keys, and she was being very quiet, no doubt thinking I was asleep. At least, that's what I thought. Do you think it was someone else?"

Sam avoided answering. "Are you sure that Susan never had the key duplicated?" she asked. "Maybe for a close friend?"

"Oh, no. We discussed that. I asked her specifically to let me know if she ever wanted another one made, and I also stressed that I didn't give two hoots who she brought in to share her bed." She glanced around. "Anything to give a little life to the old place."

"Did she have friends over?"

Regina Rockefeller chuckled knowingly. "Lady friends, you mean? What we used to call bosom buddies?"

"You knew she was gay?"

"I wasn't always the bag of bones you see now," she countered, if a little obliquely.

"Any men at all?"

Rockefeller shook her head. "No — not that I ever saw. And not that many women, either."

"Did you know any of them?"

Surprising Sam, Rockefeller's face colored slightly. "Oh. Well, I guess it's all right, considering what's been in the papers. Still . . ."

"The governor?" Sam prompted her.

She looked relieved. "Thank you. It was so awkward, seeing her here that one time. She was obviously uncomfortable. I felt for her."

"Fair to say that's all in the past now," Sam commented. "Who else besides the governor?"

"There were maybe a couple of others —

only one I met, but she was quite awhile ago."

"Can you describe her?"

"Oh, goodness, no. I doubt I could describe you five minutes from now. I'm terrible with faces. I'm always asking people I know quite well what their names are."

"How 'bout how she struck you?" Sam asked. "Something about her that stayed in your mind?"

"Just that they seemed to know each other well. They were laughing and joking like very good friends."

"Did they arrive in the woman's car that you might've seen outside the window?"

"No," Regina said apologetically. "I'm afraid I took no notice. I'm feeling very useless to you with all this. I wish I could be more helpful."

"You're doing fine, Ms. Rockefeller. It's hard. Let's go back to the night you heard someone come and go. Was Susan inclined to do that, ever? In the middle of the night?"

"Oh, yes. It would happen now and then, especially when the legislature was in session. They work all hours sometimes, and I would hear her come in and out, I suppose to get some paperwork or something. I never asked."

"So you thought it was the same thing on

the night we're discussing?"

But here Regina reflected before answering, "I did *think* so, but there was something . . ."

"What?"

"It's hard to explain. As I said, I was in the bathroom when she climbed the stairs, but I'd finished when I heard her coming back down, so I walked over to the hallway door. . . ." She interrupted herself to point out a door opening onto the central hall. "I called her name just as I saw her back — or someone's back — disappear into the front lobby, but she didn't answer, and I heard the door slam instead."

"It didn't look like her?" Sammie asked.

Regina shook her head. "No, no. That's not it. I couldn't tell who it looked like, since it was too dark and too fast. No, what I mean is that Susan would have stopped and answered. You've heard my voice. It's not the most delicate instrument in the whole world. But the other thing is that the door actually slammed. Susan would never do that. Remember what I said about her? Quiet as a mouse. That included how she shut the door."

"What did you make of it?" Sam wanted to know.

"I just assumed she'd been upset by

something — probably the reason she'd come back home in the middle of the night — and that she was angry enough to ignore me and slam the door. I was going to ask her if everything was all right, the next time I saw her, because I was concerned."

She sighed deeply and slumped in her seat. When she spoke again, Sam could hear the emotion in her voice. "Poor girl," she said quietly. "I had no idea I would never see her again. What a terrible world it's become."

Amen, Sammie thought.

CHAPTER TWENTY-FIVE

Joe was signing in at the reception desk of the forensic lab when the side door to the lobby opened and David Hawke stuck his head out. "We ought to get you an office here," he said cheerfully. "Cut down on the commute."

Joe hung his visitor's badge around his neck and crossed to shake hands. Hawke escorted him into the building's inner sanctum, still speaking. "How goes the battle? Seems almost lucky to me that the governor made her announcement when she did. That must've taken some heat off you, no?"

"I suppose," Joe answered vaguely. But in fact, he'd been saddened that the sexual preferences of a head of state had proven more interesting to the media than someone's killing — even a prominent someone. On a personal note, however, Joe had been happy to see that Gail's revelation had done her some good, as well. Her precampaign numbers were on the upswing, and she seemed more determined and more comfortable than ever in her public appearances — a self-confidence he'd noticed as well when he'd talked to her about putting pressure on HSI.

"You said on the phone that you wanted to see everything we had," David said. "As I mentioned, it's not a huge amount, and we already passed along the interesting stuff. What do you think you're looking for?"

"Hard to say, David. You know how it is, sometimes. You've got to return to the scene and stand there for a while, look at it with fresh eyes, I guess."

"Meaning you're stumped."

"We're not flush with ideas," Joe answered cautiously, at once coy and yet trusting that none of this would go beyond the two of them. His reluctance was mostly instinctual — no cop of experience reveals much, even to a colleague of Hawke's standing — but it had a touch of the superstitious, as well. Joe's instincts told him he was close to a solution, but he had yet to locate the keystone that would lock it all into place.

Hawke escorted him to a secure room, where an array of objects, photographs, computer printouts, and fingerprint cards had been laid out across a long table for display and analysis.

"There are naturally more avenues to pursue," David said as he closed the door. Joe cast an eye over the collection. "There always are, assuming there's cause and money enough to justify it. Like that time you drove down to Brookhaven National Laboratory to get that blood examined. Wild guess is that you don't have anything like that up your sleeve this time, though."

"No," Joe answered him. "You're right. On the other hand, I don't think I'm facing quite the brick wall I was then. Whoever did this acted spontaneously. It wasn't planned. At least that's the theory. So, if we're right, that means he had to have made mistakes, or made compromises, while he was working under the gun and against the clock."

He was traveling the length of the table, scrutinizing Hawke's findings as he spoke. He came to a row of fingerprint cards. "I take it these were all from the passenger seat position?"

"Mostly. Your colleagues have been collecting comparison prints right and left, which has been a huge help. But passenger seats are historically tough. Prints overlie one another, get smudged, or they're just too random to discover within the general population. I mean — I know it doesn't apply in this case — but think of a carpooling situation, or a mom using her vehicle as a virtual school bus. There can be hundreds of prints left behind. Raffner was single, had no kids, and the car was relatively new, but still . . ."

Joe came to a neat arrangement of pennies, quarters, sales slips, paper clips, a Black Jack gum wrapper, a movie ticket stub, two pencils — one broken — even a pair of shoes, and several wadded-up, dirty tissues, among other random jetsam.

He pointed to the entire section. "Under the seats, I'm assuming?" he asked.

"Right. She was actually neater than most, or had recently cleaned her car. Lucky, considering what I heard about her two residences. Word is she was a real pack rat."

"That she was," Joe replied distractedly, still moving down the line. He came to the clothing he'd seen Beverly's diener remove at the autopsy. "I'm guessing you got nothing from these?"

David had been walking along behind him, looking over his shoulder. "Nothing tangible. The cuts in the clothing appear consistent with the type of instrument used on her chest, but that's not saying much. Beverly sent us microscopic swabs from the inner aspects of the incised letters, thinking we might pick up some transfer from the blade, but there again — shy of the kind of equipment the super labs have — we found nothing."

After another fifteen minutes, Joe finally straightened and shook David's hand in thanks.

"This do you any good?" Hawke asked him, opening the door to the hallway.

"Not obviously," Joe conceded. "But it was helpful to see it all. After a while, with the e-mails and faxes and phone calls and teleconferences, you sort of lose touch with the reality of the thing. It's nice to return to square one every once in a while. Thanks for that, David."

"Sure thing, Joe. Happy hunting."

Montpelier being two exits away from the lab — and on the way back to Brattleboro — Joe stopped by Gail's office in the Pavilion, which was attached to the rear of the Vermont History Museum. A mundane brick structure, it housed a variety of governmental agencies and was overseen by a single guard in the lobby. However, even with the paranoid times and how most other states protected their upper management personnel, the Pavilion was just a fraction more secure than the wide-open, neighboring capitol building. Ironically, given his job and sense of privacy, Joe rather liked the pragmatism of Vermont's minimal safeguards. If it wasn't broke, there was no special need to fix it.

Upstairs, in the waiting room outside the governor's combined office and apartment suite, Joe found John Carter, Gail's head of security, sitting on the visitor's couch, working his smartphone.

Joe sat beside him and shook his hand. "John, how've you been? Things crazy enough for you?"

John pocketed his phone and shook his head. "We've been earning our pay. I can tell you that. How's the investigation going?"

"We're making inroads," Joe said. "You just hanging around, waiting for more media to storm the door?"

Carter chuckled. "Not at the moment. Things have quieted down a bit. The one-minute-one-mile attention span of most of those people is helping us out there. I'm just waiting for the governor. She's due to head out soon."

Joe got back up. "I better drop in now, then," he said. "Don't want to make her late — or miss her altogether."

Carter stayed put, but held up a hand. "I've been meaning to call you about Nate Fellows."

Joe paused. "Oh?"

"It's no big deal, but I know your unit's been looking under every rock. Did you know that he'd written threats to the governor, as well?"

"I knew her name was on a hate list he'd made. What was the nature of the threats?"

"Nothing specific. It was more crank than hate. You read the same sort of crap in letters to the editor. But he went on about how she was a disgrace and a traitor to Vermont and should stay in the kitchen and all the rest. You get the idea. We checked it out at the time, but found nothing to move on. He never crossed the line. You know: letter of the law and all that. Freedom of speech."

"When was this?"

Carter shrugged. "Months ago. I just wanted to make sure you knew he hadn't just targeted Raffner. It seemed like a general kind of thing." He quickly glanced at his watch. "You better get going. She's already running late."

"Thanks, John. I appreciate it. Good seeing you," Joe said, thinking that their Mystery Man's selection of Nate Fellows as a patsy might not have been as random as they'd thought. Within the right circles, it seemed that Fellows had been a known entity.

Alice Drim looked up from the copy machine in the office's front room and greeted Joe with a bright smile. "You here to see the governor?" she asked.

"I am, but I hear she's already running late."

"Another event to raise money. Things've heated up, what with one thing and the other. We won't all be looking for jobs next year, but she's got her work cut out for her."

Joe knew that Alice was also the campaign's volunteer fund-raising coordinator. "How's the money holding up? If that's not too indiscreet?"

She laughed. "For you? I don't think so. There was like a big theatrical pause when we were holding our breath, but the governor played it like a pro and the coffers opened back up. So we're looking good. A big break in your case wouldn't hurt."

He returned the smile as he passed into the office's inner sanctum. "I hear you, Alice. We're working on it."

He met Gail and her entourage of Rob Perkins, Kayla Robinson, Joan Renaud, and a couple of others coming down the short hallway. Gail's face brightened at the sight of him and she gave him a warm embrace. "God, it's good to see you. Did you need something? I'm afraid I'm running out the door."

"I know. I heard," he told her, walking alongside. "I was just in the neighborhood, as they say — at the lab seeing David Hawke — and I thought I'd say hi."

"Damn. Let me call you later. Things've become pretty nuts, mostly due to my rabbit-out-of-the-hat trick. But the campaign's building steam, too, as a result. This place has been crawling with people all day."

"It's helped you regain your focus, from what I've been seeing," Joe said.

She stopped at the front door to the suite and took his arm, looking into his eyes as she'd once used to. "You know that's true, don't you, Joe? Especially now."

Very briefly, he saw her eyes dampen with the thought. He quickly kissed her cheek and murmured, "You're doing well. Knock 'em dead."

He stepped aside in the front office, where John Carter and a couple of others were waiting, including a woman who stared at Gail as at a store mannequin, quickly and professionally swapping out her earrings and altering the lay of her collar. She also muttered something to her, which caused Gail to forage through her pockets at speed and empty them of accumulated trash into the receptacle by the door — to smooth out the lines of her long coat. With a false smile and a nod of the head, the handler faded back and let the cortege file out. They moved fast, murmuring urgently — like water released from a sluice gate — most of them with their smartphones out, which were glowing for attention. Joe stayed inside the doorframe, watching them head for the elevator. With their departure, and the absence of Alice as well as the receptionist, who'd vanished into the office's nether regions, Joe suddenly found himself alone and surrounded by silence, as if in the aftermath of a tornado.

His foot bumped against the half-full trash can Gail had used, which had been jostled slightly from its place near the wall. He stared at its contents a moment as he pushed it back, his memory abruptly jarred, and his heart falling. He crouched to take a closer look.

Checking over his shoulder to make sure he was still alone, he retrieved an envelope from his inner pocket and used it to carefully lift a gum wrapper from the trash. It was labeled Black Jack, written on a black oval against a pale blue background. It was a perfect match for a similar wrapper he'd just seen laid out on David Hawke's lab table.

CHAPTER TWENTY-SIX

"What did Hawke say?" Sam asked.

Joe shifted the cell phone to his other ear. He was parked outside the forensic lab, to which he'd returned in a fog of mixed emotions after finding the Black Jack wrapper Gail had dropped into the trash can.

"They match. Same fingerprint on each wrapper, but nothing's on file, so we have nothing to go on."

"But it's the governor's office," Sam protested. "How many people can that mean?"

Joe's eyes were sightlessly fixed on the snow directly before his bumper. He was reflecting on the possibility of a near lifelong friendship gone lethally sour, and on one woman turning on her lover with a viciousness Joe would never have imagined.

"It's like a beehive," he replied, doggedly forcing himself to heed the literal truth, in place of his worst fears. He hadn't actually seen the contents of Gail's pockets hitting the trash — he'd merely retrieved what he'd found on top of the pile. He wasn't an eyewitness. "The trash can was by the front door. The wrapper doesn't necessarily belong to a staffer. We can't jump too fast here — not now."

"But we could ask around," Sam protested. "Black Jack? That's what you called it? Who the hell's ever heard of that? It's gotta be super rare."

"That's exactly what I mean," Joe countered, struggling not to sound testy. "If we show an undue interest, then we've revealed our hand. Assume it is someone in Gail's office. Right now, he — or she — is probably feeling safe. We need to take a careful, under-the-radar look at each of them — backgrounds, lifestyles, whereabouts on the night of the murder, fingerprints, the whole ball of wax — and see if we can find something that ties one of them into this. Speaking of which, what did you get out of Regina Rockefeller?"

"She was better than I thought she'd be," Sam said, immediately falling into line with Joe's marching orders, which only fueled his guilt about keeping his suspicions from her — his most loyal and trusting of colleagues. "Turns out the chatty crazy lady imitation is partly camouflage, which is maybe a little crazy in itself. But she still didn't have much to offer. She heard what she thought was Susan coming and going that night, but when she called out just as the supposed Susan was leaving the house, there was no answer and the person slammed the door, which was something Raffner apparently never, ever did. Regina wrote it off to Raffner being pissed off for some reason, and said that Raffner came and went all the time in the middle of the night when the legislature was running. It was only later that she wondered if it might've been somebody else. *Oh.* And before you ask, there was no extra key that Regina knew anything about."

There was a pause — Joe lost in his thoughts, Sam reviewing what she'd just said. "About the background checks," she then followed. "Does that include the governor? I mean, that's a little offbeat, isn't it?"

The nature of the question allowed him to display some remnants of responsibility. "Of course it does. We can't play favorites. And I shouldn't be anywhere near it. I probably shouldn't even be briefed on it. You handle the details of this and don't tell me of your progress."

She hesitated before replying, "Got it. You okay? You sound a little off."

"I've had better days," he answered, his memory fruitlessly stretching back over the years to any outbursts of anger that he'd witnessed in Gail, searching in vain for demonstrations of real violence.

"You ready to throw away more of the taxpayer's hard-earned cash?" Willy asked. "We ought to head out and do some street work — check out the salvage yard again, maybe, and establish if someone on our lists knew about it."

Lester was hunched over his desk, studying line after line of what looked like a bill. He didn't stop as he spoke, "I thought of something that might be more useful. Raffner got a piece of mail this morning that got me thinking."

Willy was intrigued. "What d'ya got?"

Lester kept reading. "Well, if it's nothing, we'll both get called on the carpet for wasting time, so beware the company you keep, but it occurred to me that there may have been one aspect of Raffner's Prius that no one's looked into."

"Do tell." Willy leaned over and saw that Lester was looking at automotive gas receipts.

436

"The Prius had a relatively full tank," he explained. "Made me think about her buying gas. Most of us are creatures of habit, especially when it comes to our cars. We go to the same mechanic, use our favorite gas stations, and most of us stick to a regular commuter route, at least to and from work."

"Tell me what I don't know, Grasshopper."

Lester continued, unfazed. "Well, up until the trip she took with her mystery passenger, from Brandon in Hartford to Buddy in Rutland, Raffner was boringly predictable, back and forth between Montpelier and Bratt. But according to her most recent credit card bill, and the mileage accrued by this routine, I calculated that she was due for a refill, which she had to have gotten near the end of her last trip."

"Maybe around Rutland?" Willy proposed. "Buncha all-night gas stations there, 'cause it woulda been late. How full is relatively full?"

Lester looked up at him. "That's another habitual thing, right? At least among people who can afford it — filling up the tank when you need gas. I asked for the lab to give me an estimate on the amount of spent fuel, and you're right — it's looking like she burned off enough to get from Rutland to where the car was found in that salvage yard."

Willy straightened and returned to his desk to grab his gloves. "I think I know where you're heading, but why do we give a rat's ass where she filled up last?"

Lester grinned at him. "We don't. But if we find the station" — here he tapped the receipts before him — "like I just did — maybe — if we're lucky . . ."

"We find video footage," Willy finished for him.

The Rutland gas station Les and Willy pulled into an hour and a half later was big, busy, and — Willy noticed before the car rolled to a stop — equipped with surveillance cameras.

"There's no time stamp on that bill, is there?" he asked his colleague.

"Just the date," Lester answered, killing the engine. "But I'm going with the theory that she filled up before she started pounding on doors."

Willy was derisive as he opened his door to get out. "You don't think whoever whacked her and stuffed her into the back then stopped here for gas and a quick latte? You're hard."

The store manager was an accommodating sort — or his unseen boss was, somewhere up the corporate ladder. Upon being shown two badges, he didn't hesitate allowing them access to his video console in the store's back room. Additionally, he administered a crash course on how to run the equipment — including operating the DVD burner — and left both men to their own devices.

That last courtesy, along with two chairs, turned out to be important, as neither Les nor Willy had any idea when the Prius had pulled in, nor could they fast-forward through any dormant stretches, since the station was so busy that there weren't any.

They settled for watching the tape at twice its recording speed. Nevertheless, they sat there for two hours before finally saying in unison, "There."

Spinney froze the picture of Raffner's car — complete with legible front license plate — coming to a stop at pump number seven.

He began advancing the footage frame-by-frame, revealing a jerkily moving Susan Raffner getting out of the car and swiping her credit card at the pump. The video was not a seamless film, but a series of closely spaced still photos, taken seconds apart. That made it easier to analyze each frame;

it also meant they couldn't see between the gaps.

"You make out the passenger?" Lester asked nervously.

"Yeah," Willy replied. "I been holding off telling you, just to drive you nuts."

Les ignored him. "I can't tell if it's a man or a woman. Goddamn it."

"Here you go," Willy then said, his own eagerness showing through. "Door's opening."

But they were disappointed yet again. The pause in the footage fell precisely between when the passenger emerged and when he or she headed toward the rear of the car. All they could get, switching back and forth between images, were the departing lower body of someone walking away.

"Jesus H. Christ," Willy swore. "I guess it's a latte, after all. We got interior footage somewhere?"

They scanned the computerized library that the manager had explained and found what they were looking for. Moments later, the screen lit up with the garishly lighted store, as seen from behind and above the clerk's position at the cash register. Right on cue, a person entered through the double glass doors, wearing a long coat and a dark hat — and holding a hand alongside his or her cheek, blocking all facial features.

"For God's sake," Lester said. "Give me a break."

The next shot showed their subject's back, heading toward the ladies' restroom.

"At least that's settled," Willy said. "Can't say I saw that coming."

Frame by frame, they clicked through the series, waiting for the woman's re-appearance.

"Who'd she look like to you?" Lester couldn't resist asking.

"Spare me," Willy shot back, adding more thoughtfully, "I can see why there was some confusion about her gender, though. She's kinda built like a guy."

Finally, the door to the restroom opened, the woman stepped out, and — at last — stared directly at the camera.

"Gotcha," Willy said as Lester froze the video one last time.

"Who is she?" he asked.

Willy stared at him, outraged. "You asking me? You been looking at suspect photos for days, for cryin' out loud. You're the human computer. What the fuck, Lester?"

But Spinney was already working on a solution. "I got it," he said, pushing buttons on his smartphone. He held it up to the screen and took a picture, which he turned into an e-mail.

"Who're you sending it to?"

"Why screw around?" Lester asked. "The boss. We gotta tell him what we been up to anyhow. Might as well be with the evidence hot in our hands."

He hit Send and sat back.

"You know," Willy cautioned him, "Joe may be many things to many people, but a fan of cell phones, he is not. He's probably got the damned thing turned off."

"Be patient," Les counseled, his own phone cradled in the palm of his hand, its small display glowing up at them.

The screen flickered briefly as the response appeared, consisting of a single sentence.

"Wow," Lester said in a half whisper. "I wouldn't've guessed her."

Willy remained silent. On the phone was, "Get everyone going on background NOW — that's Alice Drim."

CHAPTER TWENTY-SEVEN

Joe stared at the cell phone in his hand for a moment after disconnecting with Lester, still stunned by the news that he and Willy had just uncovered.

It wasn't jarring logically, of course. Alice had once worked for Susan, was tall and muscular, and had reportedly been in the doldrums. He knew nothing yet about the details they would undoubtedly soon uncover — motivation, opportunity, all the rest — although he had little doubt that it would be surfacing soon, now that they knew what to focus on.

But it remained as startling to him as it so often did, when an erstwhile innocent stood suddenly revealed as something else. He could never stop himself from reaching back in time and memory, faulting himself for not having seen the signs sooner.

Shaking his head, he dialed John Carter.

"Joe?" Carter answered. "You forget

something in Montpelier? We did head out the door pretty fast."

"It's not that, John. You in a place where no one can listen in?"

"Hang on."

Joe could hear the usual background noises that cell phones had made so common in modern times — of people shifting about to catch a little quiet, or a better signal, or to disengage from whatever they might've been doing before being interrupted. It seemed to Joe that cells had been invented to catch you always at precisely the wrong time.

"Okay," Carter finally reported. "I'm good. Shoot."

"This is strictly between us," Joe warned him. "Related to the case."

"Got it," was the immediate response.

"What've you noticed about Alice Drim lately? Moods, habits, any odd behavior. You're the one cop I know and trust who sees her more than anyone else I can think of."

Carter had been at the job far too long to ask questions. Instead, he paused before reporting succinctly, "Her love life's a mess, and she's had a brother at death's door till recently. Whatever I've seen out of whack, I've written off to that."

Joe's interest was heightened nevertheless. "Why 'till recently' with the brother? He die?"

"Just the opposite. Supposedly, the family was scratching for the money needed for some procedure — over fifty thousand — and it finally came through. He's not out of the woods, but things're looking up. That's all water cooler stuff, of course. You want me to check anything out?"

"No," Joe answered quickly. "Right now, it's just a puzzle piece I needed clarified. Keep it under your hat for now. And thanks."

"You bet, Joe. Happy to help."

Joe was about to sign off when he suddenly blurted, "John? Hang on. You still there?"

"Yeah. What's up?"

"This is gonna sound out of left field — totally — but does Alice chew gum?"

Carter laughed. "No shit? You kidding me? Yeah, she does. It's the talk of the office. It's called Black Jack. Nobody else can stand it. I'm not a gum chewer — not my thing — but I tried it a few months ago, basically on a dare. Horrible."

"That explains the wrapper I found in the trash, then," Joe explained. "I thought it might've been from the governor."

"Nah. Not a chance. The governor never does gum anyhow, and I doubt she'd have a taste for it. Too bitter. It's got a licorice base, or something. Anyhow, it's a bit of a joke around here — if you see those wrappers, you know Alice is nearby."

"Thanks, John. That's what I was after."

In more ways than one, Joe thought after hanging up.

It was long after dark when they all convened in the Brattleboro office, Sammie carrying her sleeping child since she'd had no time to find a babysitter.

The general conversation was conducted in hushed tones.

To Sam's relief, Joe seemed to have shaken off his odd mood of before. He put his hands together in a mock salute of respect and bowed slightly to Les and Willy. "Gentlemen, congratulations on following your own initiative. You did good work."

"There a pay increase in that?" Willy asked, his satisfaction showing through.

Joe laughed. "Only in your dreams. Okay. Sam, you've been coordinating this break — what've we got on Drim?"

She quickly checked on Emma in her portable crib, finding her still contentedly working on her pacifier, before moving to the computer to consult her notes. "It's looking solid. I told people to be on the Q.T., so I don't think she's been spooked by our nosing around.

"That being said, our biggest lead is a geographical one, connecting the cliff site with Drim's past. By putting our small army of diggers to work, like you suggested, I found out that she has a cousin who lives a few miles from there. They were tight as kids, and she used to hang out at his farm a lot. I had someone discreetly check the place out, and he took this photo, among others."

She swiveled the computer to allow them a view of the screen, which showed a close-up picture of a truck tire's tread.

"I ran this by the lab for comparison, but as soon as I saw it, I knew it matched the tread marks at the top of the cliff."

"So that's where she swapped vehicles," Lester said.

Joe shook his head, recalling an earlier conversation with Beverly. "Maybe, but if so, then the cousin also drove her to the junkyard, which makes him a possible coconspirator and the whole spontaneous nature of this setup more complicated."

"So, she asked him to leave the truck at Dana's with everything she needed, based on some cover story," Sam countered. "We'll grab him later and sort out what's what, but I like what you're saying. For that matter, she could've used him as a kind of one-stop-shopping source, for the rope, the knife, a hammer for that final kill shot to the head, and whatever else."

"Including a pair of boots," Willy suggested. "That might explain why the footprints at the scene looked so out of whack, like the owner had a limp or palsy or something. They were probably too big, and slopped around on her feet. Either lucky for her, or crafty as hell."

"You think the rope came from the same source?" Joe asked.

"So she drove to the junkyard right after the blowup at Stuey's?" Lester asked.

Joe interjected, "Not right after — first, she had to stuff Susan into the back — probably after knocking her unconscious outside of Rutland someplace. Then she would've gone to Montpelier to plant the letter framing Nate Fellows."

"Proving premeditation," Willy stated. "There goes your spontaneity."

"Not necessarily. Premeditated, for sure, but she could have prepared the letter and kept it and its bogus, stamp-free envelope with her until the right opportunity."

"Which came up when Raffner reached out and suggested a drive in the car."

"Hold on," Willy said. "Back up. She just pulled Nate's name out of the air? The perfect patsy?"

"They knew each other," Sammie told them. "That's another thing I had the diggers come up with."

She looked at Joe as she continued. "After you got conked out in Newport, we all sort of forgot why you'd gone up there in the first place, which was to find out more about Nate. With Alice popping out of the woodwork like this, I suddenly remembered that, and had the guys run Nate under the microscope as well.

"They went to the same high school," she continued, by now enjoying her moment in the limelight — a pleasant change from her recent self-recrimination. "They were in different grades, and Nate got thrown out before graduating — surprise, surprise. But rumor was they may've even dated briefly."

"Damn," Lester chimed in, "I can just imagine the effect of Alice seeing Nate's name on the threat list Carter was telling Joe about. Must've been like a gift from God. I bet we'll find out she got Nate all worked up before that shoot-out — maybe with a phone call or a visit. We always

449

wondered why he reacted the way he did."

"Okay," Willy conceded. "So how did the two women end up in the car together?"

But Joe held up a hand. "We'll get to that in a second — or at least take a stab at it. Sam, I want to know first about Alice's connection to Susan. Maybe she rifled through Susan's purse for the key to her Montpelier apartment, but how did she know exactly where to plant the Nate letter, in the recycle box? That shows familiarity with the place."

"Regina Rockefeller said Susan had more than one guest," Sammie explained. "My bet is that when we show her a photo of Alice, a lightbulb'll go on."

"They were girlfriends, too?" Willy asked.

"Not necessarily," Joe cautioned. "Don't forget that Alice got her job in Gail's office through Susan. It could've been job-related."

"After we have Alice under lock and key," Sam suggested, "I doubt it'll be hard to get Susan's old Brattleboro gang to open up about how Alice fit in."

"There is one big question still floating out there," Lester said. "What the hell was her motivation?"

"I think I know," Joe told them, and explained what he'd learned about Alice's brother from John Carter.

Willy chuckled as a result. "And there's Alice as the volunteer in charge of the governor's reelection fund-raising."

Sam nodded approvingly. "Bingo."

"And Susan was Gail's campaign chair," Lester followed up. "Usually that's a window dressing job — for show only — but being the mongoose she was, she must've tumbled to something hinky and decided to chase it down. 'Cept, she didn't want to tell the governor and blow any covers off prematurely."

"She therefore reached out to Alice on her own," Joe concluded. "Which would explain why the two of them ended up in the same car in the middle of the night. Susan had an errand to run — which was to confront whoever had sold her bad weed — and probably figured on killing two birds with one stone, by bringing Alice along to ask her about the money."

"Wasn't that a little risky on Susan's part?" Lester argued.

Joe shrugged. "Sounds like it now. But let's say she only noticed a financial discrepancy. Wouldn't she want to ask her protégée about it first? Before she started making accusations? It might've been some sticky-fingered accountant Alice knew nothing about, after all. Susan was a Don Quixote type — always rallying to the disadvantaged. She would've started by thinking Alice was either ignorant or had a good explanation — they were old friends, colleagues, and maybe even lovers, for all we know."

"Still," Lester persisted. "Beating her brains in and carving on her chest? That is so over the top, especially for such a small amount of money."

Willy's familiarity with the darker shades of humanity prompted him to say, "We know diddly about this woman or what made her tick."

Joe took advantage of the observation to comment, "Which means we need to bust our butts tomorrow, turn all this theorizing into solid evidence. In other words, search warrants, taped interviews, an expansion on Sammie's outstanding homework — the works. Including — last but not least — an arrest warrant for Alice Drim."

He pointed to the quietly sleeping Emma. "In the meantime, go home, get some sleep, and I'll see you here tomorrow morning. Outstanding job — everyone."

"Chicken ain't hatched yet, boss," Willy said predictably, picking up his daughter.

It had rained the night before Joe and his

team met up in Montpelier two days later. In the dawn sun of a chilly Sunday, the entire town glittered under a thin sheen of ice, lending a paradoxical sparkle to the reason they were assembled.

Joining them were the inseparable Parker Murray and Perry Craver, several tactical members of the state police — as usual outfitted in combat gear — and the city's police chief. They were grouped around a VSP command vehicle, a block-and-a-half from Alice Drim's address. The hour had been chosen from long experience — it was usually safer to approach someone's residence when they were still in bed, or at least groggy from sleep.

The circumstances, however, were not ideal, though picturesque.

"Fuckin' ice," as Willy put it succinctly, sliding the toe of his boot across the slippery pavement. "She better not make a run for it."

The idea, of course, was to prevent just that, not only by choosing the early hour, but by surrounding Drim's apartment building and closing off all possible escape routes.

Driving the point home, the tactical team's commander announced, "We do this right, we do it fast, and we don't screw up.

453

Everyone clear?"

There was a small chorus of affirmative grunts, followed by his ordering, "Okay — everyone in position. Radio when you're set."

The group divided according to the plan set up the night before. Joe and Sammie tailed the commander as he led the heavily armed entry team quietly and gingerly down the block, up the building's ice-slick wooden steps, and into the front lobby.

The building was yet another old New England triple-decker, this one dating back to Montpelier's iron industry and railroading heyday, and equipped with the usual zigzagging exterior staircase across the back wall. Improbably, on the third floor, where Drim had her apartment, some fresh wash was hanging, frozen solid, from a line strung between two uprights.

The VSP commander keyed his mic, announced his location in a whisper, and waited for each team to respond. He then nodded to those around him. "All set?"

Everyone nodded and the small, silent group picked its way stealthily up the interior staircase, painfully aware of how loud so many boots could be.

It took several minutes to reach the top, by which time everyone was bathed in sweat from the aggressive central heating, the body armor and heavy clothing, and the tension of anticipating what might happen next.

The commander and two of his people positioned themselves to either side of Drim's door and paused there, listening for anything on the other side.

Using his throat mic, with which they were all equipped, the commander asked barely audibly, "All teams in place?"

Over everyone's earpieces the responses were affirmative.

The commander stretched out his hand and prepared to knock.

"We got a runner — out the rear balcony," came over the radio from outside.

"Is it our suspect?"

"Affirmative. But now she's staying put."

"She must've seen the exterior team," he muttered, nodding to two of his men. "Break it down," he ordered.

The battering ram that one of them had slung across his back came into play in one smooth movement, smashed into the door's lock, and blew the door back.

The tac team poured in, shouting and spreading out, leaving Joe and Sam in the hallway. The apartment was small, snug, and now getting cold because of the wide-open door leading onto the rear balcony. Fighting instinct, both VBI officers remained where they were, waiting for the entry team to declare the apartment safe, before they ran to the far door and looked out.

Standing at the far end of the balcony — where the exterior stairs led down to the next level — was Alice Drim, her back against the railing. She'd been staring at the police already climbing toward her, when she whipped around at Joe and Sammie's appearance.

"Alice," Joe ordered. "Do not move."

"Stay away," she shot back, clutching the post beside her. "None of you should be here."

"You don't have any choice, Alice," Joe continued, taking a couple of steps in her direction. Behind him, he heard Sam order the others to stand their ground.

Alice looked around frantically, as if hoping for a set of wings or a fireman's pole to help her out.

"Don't come any closer, Joe."

"Or what?" Joe replied, hoping to make her think rationally. "You're surrounded, Alice, and we know what happened."

Without warning, she suddenly swung up onto the railing behind her, using the post as a fulcrum, but as her feet touched the rail's icy surface, they went out from under her, forcing her to hang on for her life.

Joe started running to help, but she screamed, "I'll let go, Joe. I swear I will. Stop."

He stopped fifteen feet away. "Alice, we know why you did what you did. We know about your brother and how desperate you were to help him. Where's he going to be if you let go? Please don't do this."

"I killed somebody," she said breathlessly, struggling to maintain her grip. "You're not going to make that go away."

"There are mitigating circumstances," he argued. "No one has any idea how this might turn out."

She seemed to consider it, even as her strength was visibly ebbing.

"Alice," he pleaded. "Please, before it's too late. You've been smart up to now. Give yourself time to think. Climb back up." He extended a hand. "Let me help."

She seemed to finally hear him. She swung her leg up and heaved with both arms, as if accepting his offer. But it wasn't enough. Her foot slipped on the ice again, one hand shot out toward the clothesline beside her, breaking it with a loud snap, and — after a half-frozen moment in which her eyes, wide with surprise, locked onto his — she vanished without a sound.

A second later, there was a thud and the balcony vibrated.

Over his earpiece, Joe heard, "Holy Jesus Christ."

He and Sam ran to the end of the balcony and peered over. Alice hadn't reached the bottom. In a freakish twist of chance, she'd become entangled in the falling clothesline, which had looped around her neck and had her swinging twenty feet off the ground.

"Damn," Sam said softly.

ABOUT THE AUTHOR

Archer Mayor, in addition to writing the *New York Times* bestselling Joe Gunther series, is an investigator for the sheriff's department, the state medical examiner, and has twenty-five years of experience as a firefighter/EMT. He lives near Brattleboro, Vermont.

The employees of Thorndike Press hope you have enjoyed this Large Print book. All our Thorndike, Wheeler, and Kennebec Large Print titles are designed for easy reading, and all our books are made to last. Other Thorndike Press Large Print books are available at your library, through selected bookstores, or directly from us.

For information about titles, please call:
 (800) 223-1244

or visit our Web site at:
 http://gale.cengage.com/thorndike

To share your comments, please write:
 Publisher
 Thorndike Press
 10 Water St., Suite 310
 Waterville, ME 04901